OF LOVE

ILLUSION OF LOVE

RECHA G. PEAY

URBAN BOOKS

http://www.urbanbooks.net

This is a work of fiction. Any references or similarities to actual events, real people, living or dead, or to real locales are intended to give the novel a sense of reality. Any similarity in other names, characters, places, and incidents is entirely coincidental.

URBAN SOUL is published by

Urban Books
10 Brennan Place
West Babylon, NY 11704

ISBN-13: 978-1-59983-059-9
ISBN-10: 1-59983-059-0

First Printing: August 2008

10 9 8 7 6 5 4 3 2 1

Printed in the United States of America

Chapter 1

Tatiana

Friday night during the Central Precinct's annual Christmas party, a conversation with my best friend Anyah stopped midsentence when I intuitively felt the heat of a stare. Hoping to confirm the suspicion, I turned my head slowly to the left and at the same time allowed my eyes to scan the large, dimly lit room. Two adjoining ballrooms had been decorated with artificial Christmas trees, garlands, and strings of multicolored lights in honor of the annual employee event. No one among the energetic guests on the dance floor, whose movements seemed robotic against the strobe light, seemed distracted. Head-bobbing onlookers leaned against the far wall while other guests formed small conversation groups. Identifying anyone would be a challenge. Then my eyes stopped. The observer, who happened to be a spitting image of Morris Chestnut, was seated at the bar and winked to identify himself. Determined to remain composed, regardless of his charm and apparent good looks, I glanced away, took a sip of wine, and grooved to the music. Using my peripheral vision, I noticed when he stood up and walked toward our table. His shoulders rose and fell in sync with each step as he moved fluidly through the crowd like a black panther on the prowl. Even though I had resolved to remain calm, watching him glide across the floor made my heart skip a beat. I inhaled slowly.

"Would you look at that," Anyah mumbled below her breath as she fanned back the linen table cloth to pinch my thigh. Her boldness hadn't changed in all the years I'd known her. In college we took a few basic courses together. Our initial interactions were no more than your casual *hellos* and *good-byes* until we pledged the same sorority sophomore year. Because of our acquaintance, she persuaded me to leave campus without our fellow line sisters and attend a step show at another college. All was going well until someone tapped us on the shoulder.

"Enjoying the step show?" our Big Sister Rule Maker asked, wearing a smile so wide she looked like the Joker from Batman.

"Yes, Big Sister Rule Maker," we replied in unison, knowing our evening would be one we would never forget. And it was. Our new line names became Monkey See and Monkey Do. After all the humiliation, we became best friends.

Watching him get closer, I playfully smacked Anyah's hand away, then moved my legs to one side before she could pinch me again. What she didn't know was that I had already made eye contact.

"Good lawd," Anyah said through clenched teeth, sounding as though she was making love but suppressing a climax. "Xavier better be glad I'm married."

She'd been happily married to Xavier for the past

eight years and believed a little eye candy was harmless and good for the longevity of their marriage. When asked if he had the same flirting privileges, she'd quickly respond, "Hell yeah, because, baby, when it's all over, he's coming home to sex mama up."

"Yum, yum. They say the blacker the berry, the sweeter the juice, and he's a black one," she said sensuously, then traced the rim of her wine glass with her index finger.

"Anyah, please don't go there." After her last comment, I began to visualize sweet juices flowing from his black berries, then couldn't help it as my eyes moved downward toward his crotch. His dress slacks were baggy, but even they couldn't conceal the bulge. To hide the mischievous smirk that followed my thought, I lifted my glass and took another sip of wine. For a moment—and only a brief moment— I was ashamed. "You have a husband at home to tame your tiger. All I have is Hercules, a ten-pack of double D batteries, and my imagination."

"Girlfriend, put on your sexy face. His eyes are on you." To keep my attention, she rapidly tapped her fingernails on the table.

"Are you surprised?" I playfully quivered my eyelashes at her.

"I've never seen him around the precinct before, so if he is a cop, remember what I told you in the car," she said, using a serious tone to remind me of an earlier conversation, then nudging me on the elbow. "They're good to look at, but you can't trust 'em."

Hearing how fast she'd transformed from best girlfriend to "overprotective sister," I rolled my eyes to the top of my head. "That's so like you," I said sternly after making direct eye contact. "Lead me to the end of the rainbow, unveil the pot of gold, then forbid me to touch the treasure." Whether she knew it or not, I'd already decided he was worth an introduction before the night was over.

"Well, it's just a warning. Most of them here are married with children." She crossed her legs, placed her elbows on the table, and leaned closer to my ear. "I'm telling you, the majority of them are notorious every year for leaving their wives at the house. Sergeant Clark over there is a prime example." She paused to clear her throat. "He's the middle-aged, gray-headed man sitting to your left."

Not wanting to be obvious, I didn't turn my head but took a glimpse from the corner of my eye while she continued to talk.

"From what I hear, his wife is ten years younger than him and looks better than Halle Berry."

"I don't see anybody," I said, sure it wasn't the chubby, partially bald man whose legs dangled from the bar stool, giving the appearance that he was taller sitting than standing.

"That's him, girlfriend. Some females will do anything to secure a man with a title and a few extra benefits," she said using her sista girl tone of voice to emphasize "man with a title and a few extra benefits."

"You've got to be kidding me." Out of disbelief, I turned my head to take a better look at Romeo. Not only was he short, but he wore a light gray, pinstriped suit with wide legs that looked like a throwback to the sixties. Amazed that anyone closely resembling Halle Berry could stand the sight of him every day or night I shook my head in disgust, then looked toward Anyah.

"Does that woman wearing the black strapless nylon dress sitting beside him look like Halle Berry to you?" She turned up her top lip to touch her nose.

"In her dreams," I spouted, unable to stand the

sight of him or the pencil-thin female with the bad weave any longer.

"I feel you, girlfriend, 'cause I know exactly what you're thinking. She looks like Halle scary. Now pick up your bottom lip, our new friend is getting closer. So do yourself a favor, li'l sister, and check for tan marks on his ring finger," she said quickly as my admirer approached the table.

"Hello, ladies." His deep baritone voice sent a chill down the back of my neck.

"Good evening," Anyah said boldly before I could part my lips to speak.

"Good evening," I responded as he looked toward me, then lifted one eyebrow. Up close, his ebony skin proved to be a perfect canvas for his sensual brown eyes, long eyelashes, and full lips that, once licked, would look like LL Cool J's. He was at least 6'2" with chiseled biceps and pecs that protruded through his dress shirt.

"If my stares appeared rude, please forgive me," he said apologetically.

"Staring? Were you staring? I'm sorry, but we didn't notice." With a sly grin, Anyah looked around the room, letting him know he was only one of many admirers. Anticipating a room full of men and outfit-critiquing women, we'd spent hours in clothing boutiques the day before. Just for the occasion, Anyah had purchased a long red dress, with a side slit and sheer flesh-tone bodice. I'd purchased a knee-length, silver halter dress with a fitted bodice that flared around the hemline. Of course neither of our outfits was complete without matching earrings, purses, and shoes. Anyah was a shop-a-holic who'd spend her last dime on a unique designer outfit and coordinating shoes to avoid being a female look-alike. I, on the other hand, knew if a woman did have on the same outfit, a real man looked at the candy and not the silver wrapper.

"Excuse me?" I asked him over music that had transitioned from a slow jam to a Mary J Blige house mix, making his next comment difficult to hear. Before speaking again, he placed his hands on the table for support and leaned down closer. I inhaled to smell the scent of his cologne.

"What are your names?" he asked again, pointing at me first, then at Anyah.

"I'm Tatiana, and this is my friend Anyah," I said, discreetly inspecting his ring finger. I was relieved not to see tan marks or the impression of a wedding band. Then I only hoped he wasn't a cop.

"It's a pleasure to meet both of you. My name is Courtney Wilkes."

"Hi, Courtney Wilkes," Anyah sang flirtatiously, extending her right hand like a princess awaiting a kiss.

"No disrespect, but are the two of you alone or waiting on your dates?" he asked, looking toward me as if ignoring Anyah's royal gesture.

"None taken," Anyah volunteered, leaned her head to one side, then pulled her hand back slowly. "Tonight is for the girls." Not volunteering too much information either way, she flashed a cover-girl smile. If he became a nuisance, we could use the infamous put-down line "We have husbands waiting at home."

"What are you ladies drinking?" he asked, pointing at each of our empty glasses.

"My girl Tatiana and I are drinking Moet."

That's my girl, I thought to myself as I watched her look him in the eyes and answer without blinking. Both of us were drinking white Zinfandel.

"I'll be right back."

I crossed my legs and leaned forward for a better view once he turned and walked toward the bar. Anyah knew from my body language exactly what I was thinking. Only she was bold enough to stretch out her arm and pretend to grab him. Together we laughed and validated the thought with a wink of the eye. "I didn't see a wedding ring," I sang blissfully into Anyah's ear.

"What if he's a cop?" she asked, reminding me of her earlier warning.

"There wasn't even the hint of a tan line on his ring finger," I added with a "never mind what you said because he's so fine" tone.

"Remember what I said," she reiterated.

"I guess it's hard to believe a man that fine isn't married or in a serious relationship." Desperately hoping neither was true, I had a flashback from a recent experience. Married men with or without children shouldn't play the field until they've learned and mastered all the game rules. Rule number one: never give a woman a business card with your home phone number marked through with a black Sharpie. A little manipulation against bright light makes the number visible. "My bet: he's married," I said sadly, confirming my own thought.

"Shhh . . . here he comes," Anyah whispered, then flashed him a "we really weren't talking about you" smile as he approached the table.

"May I join the two of you?" he asked, maintaining eye contact with me as he placed our wine glasses on the table.

"Sure, have a seat." Anyah made a hand gesture to suggest he sit next to me. No sooner did Courtney sit down than a male who looked like he stepped directly off a muscle and fitness magazine cover approached Anyah for a dance.

"Girlfriend, watch my drink. You know I love me some Mary J." I winked as she took a sip of wine, stood, then swished away from the table, leading him onto the dance floor.

Courtney moved a chair closer to mine, then sat down. "I've worked several shifts and have never seen you around the station."

"Anyah is a 911 dispatcher."

"And you?" he asked quickly, making it obvious she wasn't the one he was interested in.

"I teach elementary art," I answered briefly, then took a sip of wine.

"Oh, so you're a school teacher?"

"I'm an artist teaching until I can open my own art studio," I said, visualizing my opening night, and unable to suppress a smile.

"You'll have to show me some of your paintings one day. Hopefully soon," he said, then moved his chair closer to mine.

"How long have you been an officer?" I asked, inching my chair away while changing the subject to imply that his looks weren't so mesmerizing that he'd be seeing my artwork that night. It had only been nine months since I ended a three-year relationship with Christopher. We'd met at a local art exhibit. Just like me, he was an aspiring artist teaching school until he saved enough money to open a studio. Our initial encounter was surreal and seemed like love at first sight. Our passion for art was obvious and had allowed us to connect on a different level.

"Almost seven years," he said, using his body weight to slide his chair closer to mine yet again. "I just transferred to the north precinct three weeks ago."

"Really?" I responded, keeping my guard up and preparing myself for his big letdown. At that moment, I remembered the brief but heart-wrenching note Christopher had left on my night-stand. I glanced away.

> *My dearest love,*
> *Life is filled with choices. Some are good while others are bad. But remember, they all lead us to the same place in time. You choose to love me and for that I'm grateful. The moment came for me to make a decision and I chose my first love, art. My love for you is real and I will remember you always.*
> *Forever your love,*
> *Christopher*

The initial shock of his moving to New York without notice was inconceivable. But the heartache and pain that followed left me numb to the emotion of love. So I vowed to never lose sight of my dreams as an artist to pursue a relationship.

"I was ready for a change," Courtney said, nodded his head affirmatively, then took a drink.

"Change is good." Unwilling to ruin a good evening with prejudgments, I turned my attention back to Courtney.

"Ever dated an officer before?" He placed his index finger over his top lip, then looked around the room.

"No," I responded curtly, not knowing whether to take offense at his question or body language.

"No?" he asked, then turned his head to make direct eye contact. "You say it like there's something wrong with dating a man of the law."

"Oh, I have my opinions about men of the law. I think ninety-five percent of you are arrogant assholes."

"Whew! Such hostility." He smiled, held up both hands, then leaned away from me. "Well, there's still the other five percent, because all of us aren't arrogant assholes," he said innocently, pointing at himself.

"And I'm not trying to find out, either," I said matter-of-factly, then rolled my neck. By then Anyah had returned to the table with her dance partner. Sweat was dripping from her face and she took no care in the way she sat down. I shook my head as her arms fell to each side of her seat. After taking a few deep breaths, she reached for a napkin and wiped her forehead.

"Before you form an opinion about me, let's dance," Courtney said as he stood, held out his hand, and waited on my response.

"Girl, don't be bothered by me. Go ahead and get your groove on." Anyah waved her hand as a gesture for me to leave the table as her partner sat down.

I looked up and accepted. *Whether he's married or in a relationship, how harmful is a dance?* I thought to myself as we walked side by side onto the dance floor and worked our way through the energetic crowd.

"Whew, dancing has changed since the last time I went out," I said, trying to glance around for the latest dance moves.

"Dancing hasn't changed as much as you think," he said, then extended both hands with the palms up. I smiled and placed my hands inside his. Together we began to move, eventually bouncing our shoulders to the music. It wasn't long before I was lost in the bass beat and making circles around him.

"Thought you couldn't dance," he said into my ear after grabbing my waist from behind, midspin, and pulling me into him.

I gracefully raised my right hand and giggled as he spun me around to face him. "That's not what I said. I said dancing has changed." I smiled, then challenged him with another dance step. Finally, the upbeat tempo slowed, giving me the perfect opportunity to exit the dance floor.

"Excuse me," he said, grabbing my hand. "May I have this dance?"

"Can you?" I asked, turning to look at him. With a humble expression, he extended both hands, making the invitation irresistible.

"Do you attend the Christmas parties every year with your friend?" he asked, making small talk as we closed our embrace and began to sway from side to side.

"Believe it or not, this is my first one. Her husband couldn't make it this year." I leaned my head back to look up at him and smiled.

"Wow, you have a beautiful smile," he said, tightening his fingers around my hand.

"Is that what you tell your girlfriend?" I asked, taking the chance to probe into his personal life.

"I would if my girlfriend had a beautiful smile like yours."

"Thanks for the dance," I said, having known all along it was too good to be true, and loosening my grip on his hand. Disappointed, I was ready to make a straight line across the dance floor back to our table.

"Tatiana, it was a joke." He never let go of my hand. "I don't have a girlfriend."

Whew, I thought to myself, having been ready to abandon him on the dance floor.

"All jokes aside. You do have a beautiful smile."

"Thank you." I leaned into him, allowing myself only to relax a little. His words sounded sincere.

"So tell me, how long have you been painting?" he asked, wrapping his arms around my waist and pulling me even closer.

"As long as I can remember," I said, thinking about my mother's refrigerator art, which included the first turkey we'd painted in preschool using our hand as the template.

"Your beautiful smile makes your love for art obvious." He tickled my ear with his lips as he spoke. "Maybe one day I can make you smile that way."

"Humph, I love to paint," I said and leaned back to look into his eyes.

"You love to paint?"

"More than I love to eat." When the music changed from a love ballad to an upbeat tempo, I twirled to break away from his embrace. Still hand in hand, we continued to dance, using any opportunity to share personal information.

"Think you can use this?" Anyah asked, tapping me on the shoulder. She was holding a glass of water and a napkin.

"What time is it?" The transitions from one mix to another were so smooth that neither of us realized how long we'd been on the dance floor.

"One o'clock," she said, pointing toward the long line of people exiting through the door. "I already have your coat and purse."

"I guess that means it's time for you to go?" he asked, frowning.

"Yes it is, and I had a great time." Careful not to remove what little makeup was left, I patted my face with the napkin Anyah had given me. Together we walked toward the bar and stood as I took a couple of sips of water.

"It doesn't have to end, you know?" His tone became serious.

"Oh yes, it does," I said defensively, letting my smile turn upside down into a frown. Then I sat my half-empty glass on the bar. Although he was used to having his way with women, I immediately let him know with my tone and body language that I wasn't going to go "there."

"Didn't mean to offend you, but that wasn't an invitation to my bedroom," he said, sounding apologetic as he took my coat off Anyah's arm and motioned for me to turn around. I slid my arms in, waited as he pulled it up onto my shoulder, then turned to face him. "I wanted to know if you'd like to go somewhere and have breakfast. You did work up a sweat on the dance floor," he said, wiping a small bead of sweat off the side of my face with his finger.

"Thank you, but I think I will pass on this one." To take a final snapshot of Mr. Fine before leaving, I glanced at him from head to toe.

"May I get a rain check?"

"Sure you can," I said, hopeful that we would see each other again.

"How can I contact you?"

"Give me your cell phone," Anyah volunteered and waited with her hand out as he reached inside his leather phone case. She opened it, pressed a few buttons, then handed it back. "She can be reached at that number."

"Can she?" he asked, closed it, and put it back into the case.

"Can she?" I asked, placing a hand on my hip and looking at Anyah sideways.

"I'm sure of it," Anyah said, locked her arm in mine, and mischievously pulled me away before he could say anything else.

* * *

"Work it, lil' sister. Shake what your mama gave you. I ain't mad 'cause it took her nine months to make ya," Anyah joked, speaking rhythmically, referring to the sway of our hips and the sound of our high heels against the pavement as we strutted out of the hotel and across the parking lot. "You know your friend is watching," she said, then snapped her fingers in a circle formation.

"You're working it enough for the both of us." I laughed but never missed a beat while mentally keeping up the unspoken tempo.

"Bet you ten dollars he's standing in the door right now drooling like a puppy," she said and dropped her keys on the ground. "Oops." She fanned her fingers across her mouth. Then in one motion, she stopped, bent down, and picked them up.

"I don't believe you, sometimes." I only slowed my pace and didn't stop for her theatrics. After the way we connected on the dance floor, I had no doubt Courtney was watching but didn't need her to prove it.

"Humph, men are sooo predictable." She took a couple of steps to catch up with me, then tossed her keys in the air.

"Well, was he standing at the door?" I asked out of curiosity, but not wanting to turn around and look myself.

"You can treat me the next time we go out."

"Whatever." I laughed as she unlocked the doors and we both got inside her car.

"Let's drive to the casino," Anyah said, referring to the Southern interpretation of Las Vegas, once we drove out of the parking lot and turned onto the street. "I'm feeling lucky. Look, my right eye is twitching." She adjusted her rearview mirror to take a look. She looked at me, then pointed at her eye, which, in my opinion, never twitched. "See, there it goes again. Isn't that a sign for good luck? The dollar slots should be good and loose by now. After that we can have the all-you-can-eat breakfast buffet."

"Remember, this is me you're talking to." I pointed toward the clock on her dashboard. "I think your right eye is twitching because it's after one o'clock. So stop pretending like you don't go to bed every night at ten." I turned up the volume on the radio when I heard the last slow jam Courtney and I had danced to. The coincidence made me smile. "Take me home." I pointed in the direction of my condo.

"Home? You ain't acting like someone who is ready to go home."

"I'm exhausted and you're faking like you don't have a husband to check in with," I said, never missing a beat as I swayed from side to side.

"While you were on the dance floor, I eased into a private restroom for a little phone sex. He's good for the night, so never mind me or my husband. I'm going to the casino," she said, then yawned.

"Like I said, take me home." I laughed when I barely completed my sentence before yawning.

"You should be exhausted after squirming against Courtney for hours like a genie in a bottle." She placed both hands on the steering wheel, then gyrated, using her upper body.

"Girl, I hadn't danced like that in months." I closed my eyes and snapped my fingers to the music. "Thanks for the invite. I hate to sound selfish, but I'm glad Xavier had a conference in Atlanta."

"Hah, so was I. This was the first year I got to dance. Xavier is the fire in the bedroom, but on the dance floor he has two left feet."

"Really girl, me too." Just that fast my mind drifted to a moment on the dance floor when the highly charged bass beat had mellowed and the lights had dimmed. After making eye contact Courtney had reached for my hands and placed them on his chest. Slowly, he'd lowered his hands to my waist, then gently moved me closer. Caught up in the moment, I'd closed my eyes as we began to sway from side to side, then relaxed when he leaned down and barely touched the side of my face. The touch was so affectionate that I could only imagine a kiss not being any different.

"Earth to Tatiana. Earth to Tatiana," Anyah said, snapping her fingers across my face. "Did you hear a word that I said?"

"What did you say?" I asked, only having heard her say something about Xavier's feet.

"Never mind. You're in la-la land. Excuse me, I mean Courtneyland, so I'm taking you home."

"What did you think about him?" I asked, temporarily coming out of my trance, and knowing she would give me her honest opinion.

"Physically, he was all that and then some."

"Duh, I could see that with my own two eyes. Now, what did you think?" I asked, referring to her overall impression.

"He was a'ight."

"A'ight?" I folded my arms across my chest and looked at her. "Why did you give him my number?" I asked with an attitude.

"Who said it was your number?" she asked as she looked over her shoulder before merging into the turning lane.

"Honestly, I didn't know if it was my number or not."

"For real. I gave him your cell phone number,"

she said after making a left turn onto the next street but never making eye contact with me.

"Oh you did?" I asked, allowing my arms to unfold, pleased that she had.

"Yes, I did. That guy I was dancing with, Mr. Marvelous, remember him? His name is Lance and he gave me the 411 on Courtney."

"I'm listening," I said, bracing myself for the truth. Just my luck I'd been dirty dancing with a man who had been married fifteen years with three or four children at home.

"He transferred to the central precinct about three weeks ago. Single and stays low key around the station. All the bloodsucking vultures have been hot on his trail. Rumor has it no one has been lucky just yet."

"So, he isn't married?" I asked, sighing from relief.

"If he was, I'd have found you another dance partner hours ago. Girl, after all these years, you know I got your back."

"I don't know what made me think otherwise," I said, remembering numerous times we'd given men we weren't interested in the number for late-night pizza delivery.

"What did you think about Courtney?"

"From first impressions, he seemed nice, easy to communicate with, a very good dancer, and you saw how handsome he was." I held back my true thoughts.

"This ain't the damn Cosby show." She waved her hand for me to say more. "I'm your girl, not Claire Huxtable. Now tell me what you really thought about him."

"Girl, he was sexy as hell," I said, pressing the palms of my hands into my inner thighs. "His voice, his body, not to mention the way he grooved on the dance floor. There should be a law that prohibits a man that fine from leaving his house after dark. You saw him."

"Thank you," she said, briefly letting go of the steering wheel and lifting both hands into the air.

"Anyah, I don't know," I said, quickly leaving fantasy world and snapping back to reality. "Think about it. Thirty-six-year-old male, never been married, and has no children. How odd is that? Most people our age are either married, divorced, or have at least one child. Don't you think he may be too perfect? Something has to be wrong," I said, wanting to close my eyes and erase any skeptical thoughts.

"Hell, what's wrong with your ass?" she asked, almost breaking her neck to look at me. "You're a beautiful thirty-four-year-old, never been married, and you don't have any children."

"I dated Christopher for three years. Close enough."

"Girl, you're special and it will take a helluva man to meet all your needs. God knows it," she said after turning onto my street.

"Yeah, and it suits me just fine," I said, twirling a lock of hair around my finger.

"My point exactly. Now get your special ass the hell out of my car." She turned into my driveway and slammed on the brakes.

"I love you, too," I said ironically, got out of the car, then blew her a kiss before turning to walk up the sidewalk to my front door.

Chapter 2

Courtney

"Yeah, what's up?" I answered with a frown. I knew exactly what Octavious wanted when his number showed on my caller ID display, but his timing couldn't have been worse. I was standing in the hotel lobby entrance watching Tatiana, the woman I'd just met a few hours ago, walk away with her girlfriend. It wasn't my intention for the night to end, but I'm sure her arrogant friend wouldn't have let us leave alone.

"Man, where yo' ass at?" Octavious asked, speaking so fast his words ran together.

"Just leaving the Christmas gig." Right off, Tatiana had stolen my attention. She and her friend were seated at a table to the far right side of the room, but the officer in me decided to have a seat at the bar and observe. See whether she was with someone or indeed alone. I ordered a Heineken and waited. The crowd thickened over the next thirty minutes and no other males sat down at their table. *Straight*, I thought, then finished my beer. I stood, inhaled to tighten my stomach muscles, making them more visible through my fitted silk shirt, then strolled her way. I got within three feet, then almost lost my cool. Dime pieces—slang for the finest females—approached me on a daily basis and not once had I ever gotten nervous. Unwilling to lose any cool points, I paused for half a second to regroup. Judging from her muscular legs, which were crossed at the ankles, she was at least five feet five inches tall. Her caramel skin was smooth and her pointed noise and high cheekbones seemed chiseled like a fine sculpture. I'd never been attracted to a woman with short hair before, but on her it seemed exotic.

"Thought we was on for the night. You go to those damn parties every year and nothin' has changed. No matter what precinct you at, it's always the same big-ass women wearing them little backless tops with all the colors and tight-ass spandex pants." He laughed hysterically.

"Last-minute changes. A brotha is allowed to change his mind sometime." She glowed like an angel and I wasn't the only guy in the room checking her out. Right off the top, she seemed different from the females I normally encountered. Certain females loved men in uniform and would do anything to secure one. Tatiana seemed different. She had her own career and didn't like my line of work one way or the other. Hell, last summer I stopped a lady on the interstate for a broken taillight. When I approached the vehicle she reached underneath her microminiskirt, wiggled out of her thong, and handed it to me.

"I have two first-class strippers from ATL lined up for each of us. Do the math, homeboy. Two plus two equals four fine-ass females. Man, they all goin'," he shouted into the phone.

"Going where?" I asked, then glanced over my shoulder, hoping no one heard his loud and country ass. Disappointed that my evening with Tatiana had ended I stretched my neck to look across the parking lot as she and her friend got into a red two-door Honda Accord. Her girlfriend was driving and I was too far away to see, then memorize, the license plate number. If the girlfriend had given me a wrong telephone number, I could at least use my resources as an officer to look her up and get the right one.

"Wherever you want them to go. That's where," Octavious answered just as loud, to emphasize his point.

"Really?" I asked, still thinking about Tatiana as they drove out of the parking lot and turned onto the street. She came across as wifey material. The kind you would take home to Mom, marry, and have two or three children with. I'd never tell Octavious because he'd curse me out and tell me I had lost my damn mind.

"Don't worry, I'm havin' enough pleasure for the both of us. They freaky as hell," he said even louder.

"Where are you now?" I asked, exiting the building and walking toward my freshly detailed black Corvette with the chrome package and rims. Three women, ranging in clothing size from four to twenty-four, getting into a dark gray Envoy, turned to look my way when I disabled the alarm. I didn't acknowledge their stares and got into my ride. After meeting Tatiana, none of them fit the bill.

"At the Embassy Suites, surrounded by four freaks." He made his words rhyme like a rapper's.

"Wait a minute, lil' mama, I gotta take a breather. I ain't twenty-four no more," he interjected, obviously speaking to his live entertainment in the background. "It ain't too late for you to join us. The night is still young, ain't it sweet thang?" he asked, laughing aloud, and sounding like a damn hyena.

"I'll pass. Man, you know I got to hit the streets in the morning." With a woman like Tatiana, I had to come correct. All of my skeletons definitely had to stay in the closet. She was an independent female with dreams and goals. Not to mention how beautiful she was.

"When has that ever stopped you? Two cups of black coffee and you always good. Hell, I'll even buy the damn coffee." He called my bluff. Just last week we stayed at the club till one AM, then left with a couple of fine females. The fact I had to work the same morning, prepared to protect the good guys from the bad guys, never crossed my mind.

"Hey, I'm taking it to the crib." To convince him I might be tired I faked a yawn. Then I yawned again to convince my damn self. Imagining Octavious alone with not two freaks, but four, sounded tempting as hell.

"Oh shit," he said in a high-pitched voice. "Baby, what is you doing down there?"

"Man, you got it like that?" I asked from curiosity, clutching the steering wheel with my free hand after his voice went up another octave.

"Come and see for yo'self. Baby, damn that feels good," he moaned. "Can you do that again? Hell, man, I gotta go."

"Whoa, wait a minute. What's the room number?" I asked quickly, before he hung up in my face. *Hell, one last fling will not kill a brotha. I ain't committed yet,* I thought to myself and damn near crashed my car rushing to get there.

"Room number 310. You'll hear the moaning from the hallway."

"Room 310," I repeated quickly, making sure I had it right. See ya'll in fifteen." Twelve minutes later, I whirled into the parking lot on two wheels and found a spot near the front door. I jumped out, took long strides into the hotel, through the lobby, and to the elevator. I punched the up button, then counted the beeps as it descended from the twelfth floor. "Ain't this some shit!" I said after smacking my thigh when it stopped on the eighth floor. I blew hard, then punched the button repeatedly. My manhood was throbbing beyond what I could tolerate, so I looked around to find the closest stairwell. I rushed through the door and skipped every other step until I made it to the third floor. With a nervous bounce, I looked up and down the hallway, then followed the arrow that pointed toward his range of room numbers. *That's my boy,* I thought when I twisted the doorknob and let myself into the deluxe suite with a king-sized bed and sitting area. The smell of hot sex met me in the doorway and damn near knocked me off my feet.

"Thought you suddenly grew a conscience and changed your mind." Octavious lifted his head and leaned back on his elbows.

"That's what I'm talking about," I said, unable to believe my eyes. Then I closed the door and locked it. He was lying in the middle of the king-sized bed with a nude female on each side, one stretched across his legs, and another sitting wide-legged in the chair.

"There's room for all us." He pointed to the door that led to an adjoining room.

"I owe you one, playa," I said, then used my hand to cover my erection. All four of the women had different physiques, but each was fine as hell. The one wearing the long platinum blonde wig, who was stretched across his legs, made my mouth water. She had huge breasts, a small waistline, and ass for days.

"You damn skippy."

Just when I turned to take a step, the one sitting in the chair stood and strutted toward me. My lips fell to the floor when she purred like a kitten and began unbuttoning my shirt from the collar with her teeth. "Man, where you find these at, 'cause yo' girl got mad skills." I looked down to enjoy the rest of the show as she moved from one button to the next, staring me square in the eyes.

"Partner, you ain't seen nothin' yet." He chuckled, then fell backward onto the sheets.

Like a dog on a leash, I followed as she grabbed each side of my shirt by the collar and walked backward, leading me into the adjacent room. I damn near exploded when the one lying across Octavious's legs slid off him and gladly followed. "I owe you one, dawg," was all I could say when she used her leg to kick the door open and yanked me across the threshold.

Chapter 3

Courtney

"Oh shit. What time is it?" I asked, startled, not sure when I'd ever fallen asleep. The last thing I remembered was having what felt like an epileptic seizure when the female wearing a long platinum wig used her vaginal muscles to pulsate on the big man after my orgasm. Barely able to move, I forced my eyes open and turned my head stiffly to look at the clock on the nightstand.

"Umm." The female beside me moaned, moved her hand down my chest with her fingers spread, ready to massage me.

"Party is over. Big Daddy gotta go," I said, amazed that sex was so natural she was ready to perform even in her sleep. I lifted the cover to look at her hour-glass figure and regretted having to turn down one last opportunity. "Some of us have real jobs." To get out of bed, I moved her arm, rolled her onto her back, then sat up. I didn't know what home girl had been drinking or smoking the night before because all she did was moan and her eyes never opened. *Must have been a damn good night,* I thought, laughing, then stood to look around the room for my outfit and damn underwear. Soon I found what looked like my jacket, shirt, and pants thrown across a chair on the opposite side of the room. "Hell, I don't have time for this." I balanced my weight on one leg at a time to hop into my pants. The clock was ticking, so I put on my leather jacket without a shirt and zipped it up. Being single, I always keep basic toiletries, my uniform, and a change of clothes in my trunk. You never know when or where your nights will end. I rushed to the car, grabbed my overnight bag, then headed back upstairs to shower and get dressed for work.

Twenty minutes later, with no time to spare, I tossed my overnight bag into the trunk, got into my ride, and turned on the radio before leaving the parking lot. I be damned if a slow jam that Tatiana and I danced to last night wasn't playing. I smiled, turned up the volume, and wondered what she was doing at six-thirty on a Saturday morning. After driving a few more minutes, I couldn't resist the urge to call. Not giving a damn who was behind me, I stopped at the intersection when the light turned yellow, reached into my console, and pulled out my cell phone. I opened it, found her name in my contact list, and pressed "send." Her phone started to ring and I got nervous. *Hell, I can't talk to her after last night. I just got my rocks off with two freaks,* I thought, and closed my phone when the light changed from red to green. *Okay, was that a conscience?* I asked, surprised, then looked at myself in the rearview mirror. *I've never cared about a female's emotions.* Just then I remembered how she felt in my arms on the dance floor. "Damn it," I said, opened my cell phone, and redialed.

"Hello," she answered softly.

"Did I wake you?" Instead of an answer there was dead silence. "This is Courtney." I swore below my breath for not thinking to introduce myself first. "Remember me, your dance-a-thon partner from the Christmas party last night? Please tell me you haven't forgotten me already," I said jokingly, then held my breath, hoping she hadn't left the memories on the dance floor.

"Courtney. Good morning." She sounded more alert. "What time is it?"

"Please accept my apology and promise when I tell you what time it is, you will talk to me again."

"Is it that early?"

"Well, it's ten minutes before seven." Realizing there were only a few minutes left for me to make it to work on time, I sped up.

"I'll forgive you this time." I was relieved to hear the smile in her voice.

"Enjoy the Christmas party last night?" I asked, not knowing why all of a sudden, after hearing her voice, I felt guilty as hell for meeting Octavious. *I should have taken my black ass home,* I thought, remembering how her face glowed when she smiled.

"As a matter of fact, I had a great time. Did you?"

"It was the best one I've attended in seven years."

"Oh really?" she asked, giggling.

"Really. I danced all night with the most beautiful woman in the room." I could only imagine what she looked like first thing in the morning. How sleep filled her big brown eyes. Were her thick black curls all over her head? What did she wear to bed?

"I'll take that as a compliment."

"You should. I hate to end the conversation, but I'm pulling into the precinct's parking lot. Can I

call you back later?" I asked, hopping out of my car
and rushing toward the front door.

"Sure, I'll be at home most of the day. Be safe."

"Thanks," I said, then gazed at my cell phone
before closing it. The words rolled off her tongue
and sounded like music to my ears. *Now that's a good
woman,* I thought to myself, hurrying across the
parking lot.

Tatiana

"What are you doing up this early?" I asked
Anyah, skipping the formalities of a personal greet-
ing when I saw her number on the caller ID display.
I stretched my legs, then used my arms to sit up.
Trying to cover my grogginess, I cleared my throat.

"I dropped you off thinking I would go home,
take a shower, and sleep like a baby." She followed
a deep stretch with a yawn.

"Really?"

"Let me tell you, it was just the opposite. Once I
got into bed, I tossed and turned for at least an
hour. Finally, I decided to get up and turn on the
television. At two-thirty in the morning infomercials
were on every cable channel. Would you believe
after only five minutes I spent two hundred dollars
on some new workout videos? According to the
plan, I should have a beach body in ninety days."

"You spent what?"

"I couldn't rest." She yawned.

"And why not?" I said, unwilling to show empa-
thy toward my best friend, who hadn't slept alone
at night since she'd gotten married.

"Missing Xavier. We've been together over ten

years and have never been apart," she admitted, sounding pitiful.

"Just what I thought, and you were out last night trying to act all grown up."

"His flight arrives tomorrow at noon. I'm going to pick him up at the airport wearing his khaki trench coat with nothing but my bare skin underneath."

"You're crazy," I said, knowing she would find a way to make her fantasy a reality.

"No, I'm horny as hell. Speaking of horny, did Mr. Fine blow up your cell phone last night?"

"Noo," I sang, sat up to fluff my pillows, then leaned back again. Wanting to stay in the moment after Anyah dropped me off, I'd locked my front door, slipped off my heels, and tossed my coat over the couch. Like a prima ballerina, I twirled into the kitchen and poured myself a glass of red wine. I took a sip, leaned against the counter, and closed my eyes to reflect. *Hmm*, I thought, then shook my head from side to side. Everything about Courtney seemed so perfect, almost too good to be true. Good looks. Career. Single with no children. I pondered the thought of his flawless first impression, drank some more wine, then went into my bedroom. I flipped on the light switch, looked toward my queen-sized bed, which was still immaculate, and imagined Courtney nestled beneath the covers. I smiled at the image, walked to the opposite side of my room, and sat on my chaise to undress. With the scent of his cologne fresh in my nostrils, I showered, nestled between the Egyptian cotton sheets, and closed my eyes. Within moments I'd drifted into a deep sleep.

"Noo?" she sang back, imitating me, but using a tone to insinuate there was more.

"He called me this morning. As a matter of fact,

our conversation ended only a few minutes before you called. We didn't talk long because he was on his way to work," I said with a huge smile, closing my eyes to visualize him in his dark blues.

"I'm sure you talked about something."

"Only last night." I reminisced, then tucked the sheet underneath my chin.

"So when is the first date?"

"Slow your roll. What's the rush?" I said, then regretted that I hadn't accepted his breakfast invitation. It would have been the perfect opportunity for us to talk without any distractions.

"No rush. The way he stood in the door last night proves he's not going to waste any time."

"He said he would call later."

"Hold on a sec."

"Sure."

"Girl, gotta go. This is my boo on the other end." She ended the call before I could say "'bye."

Hoping to relax at least an hour before getting up to paint, I slid down into my bed, and turned onto my side.

Courtney

What a damn way to start the morning, I thought, flipped on my siren, then made a U-turn from the far right lane. I'd just driven out of the parking lot and was less than fifty feet away from the station. Calling Tatiana to finish our conversation was the first thing on my agenda, not responding to a domestic violence call. I radioed for backup, zipped in and out of morning traffic, then turned into a lower-income residential area. It was only about four blocks from the station but was the most drug-infested zip code in our jurisdiction. It was no secret that a couple of our most notorious dope dealers called it home. Somewhere within a three-mile radius, you could find a drug to fit every budget. The narrow street, lined with small one- and two-bedroom wood-framed structures, was cluttered by uniquely painted SUVs, Cadillacs, and old Monte Carlos. The ratio of car to house was at least three to one. No eight-hour shift ended without the nuisance of answering several calls. Without reconfirming the address, I slammed on my brakes when I saw a man lying across the driveway. From the street I didn't see blood, so it was safe to assume he wasn't injured. Ready to serve my community as mediator, I confirmed the call with dispatch, then hopped out of the car when my backup turned the corner. *There has to be a better way to earn a paycheck,* I thought while walking down the driveway.

"Would you please tell this fool to get up off the ground before I kill 'em," yelled a female in her early twenties wearing a red V-neck sweater and tight blue jeans with a screaming infant in her arms.

"Ma'am, what seems to be the problem?" I asked calmly, still walking toward her while assessing the situation.

"That's the problem." She pointed at the forty-something-year-old man who was lying with his body against the rear tires of an older model white Chevy Tahoe. "I came to get the rest of me and my baby's clothes out the house and now he won't let me leave." She pointed toward the small wood-frame house, rolled her head around, then popped her hip to readjust the baby.

"You can have your rags, but you're not taking

the truck," the man piped out as Terry, my backup officer walked toward him.

"Sir, is this your vehicle?" Terry asked calmly, never taking his eyes off the irate female.

"Yes, sir, it is," the man responded loudly.

"He bought it for me so I could take his baby to day care. It's mine and I'm not leaving here without it." She made a mad dash toward the door on the driver's side.

"Just one moment, ma'am," said Terry, six feet, two inches and weighing every bit of 210, and standing in front of the car door to stop her. "Not before I check the registration. If this vehicle is indeed his, then you will have to call a cab." To stop her, he stretched out both arms.

"Sir, we do need to check the vehicle registration," I said before walking around to the passenger's side. "Is the vehicle unlocked?" I asked, hoping to expedite the process and resolve their love spat.

"Yes, sir, it is. The paperwork is in the glove compartment." The man's voice echoed from the ground.

What the hell? I thought after opening the door and seeing a brown package peeking from underneath the passenger's seat. *What do we have here?* I thought, unfolding a corner. *Marijuana.* Sure there was more, I lifted my head to keep an eye on Terry and swept the floor with my hand. *Payday.* Terry never turned to look my way. In exchange for Mr. Johnson's freedom, I discreetly eased out the money roll and put it into my pocket. "Shit," I said, almost forgetting to get his registration paperwork. "Mr. Seymour Johnson?" I asked, after glancing at the registration and walking around to the back of the truck with a straight face as though nothing ever happened.

"Yes, sir, that's me, and I mail that five-hundred-dollar check to General Motors every month. Ask her when was the last time she ever worked to pay a bill?"

"I work overtime every night trying to help yo' old ass get a hard-on," she said loud enough to be heard three miles away, then switched her baby from one hip to the other.

"Ma'am, let's try to keep it down," I said, trying to spare what dignity Mr. Johnson had left after her comment. He'd have enough anxiety to deal with once he realized his money was gone.

"Sir, please get up off the ground," I suggested, starting to get impatient. I extended my hand to assist him. By then I was ready to end their charade and find a secluded spot to count my earnings.

"Not until I have the keys to my truck." He crossed his arms in front of him.

"Ma'am, where are the keys?" Terry asked impatiently.

"Come and get them." She challenged us by patting her double D implants, which I had to assume Mr. Johnson had paid for. Judging from his unattractive face and her perfectly proportioned size eight body, she was only using him for additional income.

"Please, we would like to leave without either of you in the backseat of the squad car." I pointed toward my car. It took everything in me to keep a straight face and not bend over laughing. I had gotten paid and didn't give a damn what either of them did.

"You ol' fool," she spat. Terry and I watched as she reached deep inside her bra, pulled out a set of keys and threw them across the street. "And to think you thought this was yo' baby." She turned her lip up at him and swished away. We watched as she walked across two yards, then banged on someone else's front door. A buff young man in his twenties with cornrows wearing a wife beater and slouched jeans opened the door and peeped outside. We shook our heads when she flipped us off before going inside the house.

"You'd think I've learned my lesson by now," Mr. Johnson said as I helped him stand. "Those young girls are too much stress."

"Take your own advice." Before turning to walk away, Terry and I shook his hand and nodded at each other before getting into our cars and driving away.

Chapter 4

Tatiana

I welcomed my gift of life as the morning sun shone perfectly through the half-opened blinds and reflected light off the pale yellow walls. My girl India. Arie was playing softly in the background. Her lyrics sent out positive subliminal messages and created the perfect atmosphere.

I had converted the spare bedroom into my art studio. The 10 x 12 room, in addition to closet space, was barely large enough for my easel and supplies, so I used color to visually enlarge the space. Two walls served as the perfect background for my first four major pieces while another was lined with bookshelves. My favorite painting—of an elderly lady kneeling before an altar holding a cross with her aged fingers—kept me grounded and true to my craft. It served as a reminder that one day my fingers could possibly curl and no longer allow me to grip a paint brush. Pieces of paper and sketches of ideas covered an old wooden draft table that stood against a wall in the left corner. Its legs had gotten weak, moving from one apartment to another, but for me it was a lucky charm of sorts. My father had bought it when I was thirteen, claiming that one day, after I'd achieved fame throughout the world, it would be worth millions. I rubbed the aged wood—like the tree stump at the Apollo Theater in New York—every day.

Relying on divine intervention as a primary source of creativity, I closed my eyes and touched the blank canvas with the tip of my brush. For the past month I had visualized a very romantic piece. Meeting Courtney seemed to heighten the inspiration. A couple, connected with wide pieces of red linen to represent passion, would appear to float in midair as they danced arm in arm. *What is Courtney doing?* I wondered after a few seconds, rolled my head around, then opened my eyes. After hearing Courtney's voice first thing in the morning, my lack of concentration was no surprise. So I put down my brush and took a sip of cappuccino before standing and walking to the window. When I heard the echo of a siren, I peeked through the blinds, then jumped when my telephone started to ring.

"Hello," I answered, smiling at the coincidence when I saw Courtney's name on the display.

"Are you competing with Picasso for a place in history?" Courtney asked, chuckling.

"Not this time." I turned to look at my blank canvas.

"How's your morning?" I asked, trying to mask the concern in my voice for his safety on the streets. As an adult, I had vowed for various reasons never to date a policeman, fireman, or gynecologist. Any time a policeman or fireman left home for work, there was no guarantee he would make it back.

Then I imagined that sexually pleasing a man who examined vaginas all day would be a bit challenging.

"Hilarious." He chuckled.

"Hilarious?" I asked. "That's not the response I expected to hear from a law man. Aren't you guys busy protecting our neighborhoods from the bad guys?" I walked back to the window and opened the blinds, allowing the sunlight to totally saturate the atmosphere.

"Most times it's just the opposite. I work for the central precinct and believe me, it isn't like those cheesy cop shows on television."

"Other than the evening news I—"

"Tatiana?" he interrupted.

"Yes?" I leaned back against the wall. The way my name rolled off his lips sounded so sexy.

"I hate to be so forward, but I can't wait to see your beautiful face again."

"Sure you can." I wanted to express sarcasm instead of revealing my blushing smile.

"You seem so different, and I haven't stopped thinking about you. Please tell me the feeling is mutual?" he asked sincerely.

"I had a great time with you at the party," I responded, not revealing that my earlier thoughts of him had blocked my creativity.

"When can I see you again?"

"I'm on Christmas break another week and a half. Be creative." I arched my shoulders as I made the bold comment, then walked back to my stool.

"Is that a challenge?"

"Are you up to it?" Suddenly feeling a renewed sense of creativity, I sat down in front of my canvas and picked up a brush.

"In other words, I have a week and a half to make a lasting impression."

"Not enough time?" I dipped the tip of my brush into the brown oil-based paint and touched the canvas.

"You tell me. If it's OK with you, I'd like to start when my shift ends this afternoon."

"You're a resourceful man." I watched as my hand started to move back and forth. "Find me."

Courtney

I was cruising down Jackson Avenue thinking how to impress Tatiana on our first date when a blue Maxima with tinted windows sped by on the other side. From a distance, it looked like Big G's car, and he always kept money on him. Big G, who earned the name after damn near killing, with his bare hands, two crackheads who didn't pay up, owned the neighborhood gambling house.

Two collections in one day. After leaving my first call, I'd parked in an alley behind a liquor store and counted my money. With marijuana hidden beneath the seat, who was Mr. Johnson going to report? He's lucky I didn't take that and sell it to my boy J. Just that fast I'd gotten away with six hundred tax-free dollars. That was more than enough to take Tatiana anywhere she wanted to go, pay my utility bill, and buy groceries for the month.

To make the stop legitimate, I clocked the person I presumed to be Big G doing forty-nine in a forty, turned on my siren, and made a U-turn. He immediately turned into a gas station parking lot, stopped, and rolled down his window. I drove up behind him, grabbed my ticket pad, and got out of the car. *Damn, that's not Big G,* I thought after looking inside.

"Young man, do you know why I pulled you over?" I asked the frantic teenager, who didn't look a day over eighteen.

"My Dad just bought me this car last week and he's going to kill me," he said, grabbing the steering wheel with both hands, and then leaning his head down.

"May I see your license and registration?" I extended my hand suddenly, not feeling sympathetic for the spoiled brat wearing an Enyce sweatshirt, starched jeans, and the latest Jordans.

"Yes, sir." He sat up, then lifted his hip to reach into his back pocket for his wallet. With trembling hands, he fumbled to pull out his driver's license, then leaned over to get the registration out of the glove compartment.

"Thanks," I said, using a normal tone when he handed them to me.

"Man, let me hit you back, I'm writing a ticket," I said into my Bluetooth after turning to walk toward my car and getting inside.

"See yo' ass made it to work," Octavious blurted into my ear, disregarding anything I said.

"Barely," I said, hardly feeling the effects of my long night after three cups of black coffee.

"Whatcha think about last night?"

"It was straight." To block a flashback, I shook my head and stepped out of the car.

"Straight?"

"Yeah, straight," I repeated to remind myself it couldn't happen again. As an officer, I'd developed a lot of bad habits, but the wild actions had to end. Tatiana could really be the one.

"What the hell kinda response is that?"

"Young man, I need your signature by the *x*." He extended his right hand out of the car to sign.

"Now slow it down." Feeling no remorse, I handed him his ticket and patted the hood of his car before turning to walk away. "Yeah, man. I'm back." Being single had its perks, but when the fun was over I went home alone. I heard married men complain around the station about their nagging wives and crying children, but after work they beat me to the car. So waking up beside a warm body every day couldn't be that bad.

"Back to last night. You gotta give me credit for that one."

"Umm hmm, it was off the chain." To get him off the phone, I said the first thing that came to mind.

"Damn straight it was. Holla."

Tatiana

"Another day another dollar," Courtney said, then laughed, when I answered the telephone.

"You're singing the chorus to the working-class anthem." Not wanting to miss a stroke, I readjusted my ear piece. Except to use the restroom and refill my mug with cappuccino, I hadn't moved since our last conversation. I refocused my energy and took a step back in time to relive the emotions from a moment on the dance floor. The piece I'd created was everything I had in mind plus more.

"No, I'm crying it after Uncle Sam bites into my paycheck." We both laughed. "What have you eaten today?"

"Hmm . . . do two cups of cappuccino count?" I asked after looking at my empty mug with the permanent brown stain inside. I'd become so engrossed in my work that eating never crossed my mind.

"Tell you what, dinner on me."

"I've been painting all day and I look a mess." Unsure how quickly I could transform the frazzled duckling into a swan, I turned to look at my reflection in the mirror.

"I doubt very seriously you look a mess. Even your worst day couldn't be a bad day, so stop playing. What about it?"

"I'm not in the mood to play dress up," I said, running my fingers through my tousled curls.

"No one asked you to. Just wear your beautiful smile."

"Now that I can do," I said flirtatiously.

"See you in one hour?"

"Let me give you the address and directions."

"Remember the challenge?"

"Oh, so are you going to take it?" I asked, remembering my comment from the previous conversation.

"Yes."

"Well, Mr. Officer, if you get lost, being a man, give me a call," I said mischievously, shook my head, then looked at the clock to check the time. It was four o'clock, meaning he'd arrive by five. I made some final touch-up strokes on my piece, then cleaned the work area.

Chapter 5

Courtney

"That's my girl. You're purring like a kitten," I said, rubbing my dashboard. Anticipating my date with Tatiana, I found the 'vette couldn't get me home fast enough. I hit the expressway driving at breakneck speed and darted in and out of rush-hour traffic until my exit was in view. My tires squealed when I turned into my apartment complex and never stopped until I whipped, rear end first, into my parking space. With my keys in hand, I never lost momentum while jogging down the walkway and up two flights of stairs to my front door. By the time I closed the door and walked through the great room and into my bedroom, I was totally naked. I wanted to meet Tatiana straight from work but decided against it when I lifted my left arm, sniffed, and damn near fainted. My last call ended with my chasing a delinquent sixteen-year-old through a back alley after he stole four cartons of cigarettes. He was lucky we caught him because the Iranian convenience store owners wanted to shoot his ass.

I opened the shower door, turned on the water, and stepped inside. "Dumb ass," I shouted when the cold water hit my testicles. Instead of jumping out, I reached for my soap and wash cloth and took the discomfort like a man until the water reached the right temperature. I stepped out, then rubbed my hand over my face to check for stubble before getting dressed. It was going to be a casual evening, so I put on a pair of freshly starched jeans and a sweater, sprayed on my cologne, and took a look in the mirror. *You clean up well*, I thought to myself, then grabbed my keys.

One phone call to a friend in dispatch and I had the address that matched Tatiana's telephone number, the make and model of her car, and a few other interesting details. I entered the address into my GPS, then followed the automated voice to her apartment complex. To show her who was the man, I dialed her number before getting out of the car.

"I should have followed your advice and gotten the address. I'm so lost," I said when she answered the telephone. "Think you can help me?" I tried not to give myself away by laughing.

"Sure, tell me where you are."

"It's hard to tell." I turned off the ignition, got out of my car, and followed the walkway leading to her condo.

"What street are you on?"

"Let me see." I paused a few seconds, pretending to look around. "I'm so embarrassed." I wanted to stop after hearing so much concern in her voice but couldn't help myself.

"What do you see? Are you near anything familiar?"

"I'm staring at a gray door with the number 110 on it." I laughed when she hung up in my face.

"Oh, so you're a law enforcer by day and comedian by evening?" she asked after snatching the door open and standing with a hand on her hip.

"I like my evening job better." I smiled as she frowned, pretending to be upset.

"Take my advice and keep your day job." She stood to one side so I could enter her condo.

"Good to see you again." I looked and couldn't believe how damn sexy she really was. Within a few seconds, I had checked her out from head to toe. Her dress at the Christmas party didn't tell half the story. She was wearing a pair of jeans that were filled to the max in all the right places and a top that showed just enough cleavage to drive a brotha insane.

"The feeling was mutual until your practical joke." Still pretending to have an attitude, she shut the door.

"Don't be so mean." I rubbed my finger underneath her chin.

"This isn't mean," she said, putting a hand on her hip. "And believe me, you don't want to see it."

"Whatever 'mean' looks like, you're still beautiful. May I have a hug?" I extended my arms for her to embrace me.

"Should you?" she asked, folding her arms in front of her.

"Hey, it was only a joke. Will you forgive me? Please." I walked closer and wrapped my arms around her. *Damn, she feels good,* I thought to myself after rubbing my hand gently up and down her back.

"Maybe I'll forgive you after dinner."

"I can accept that." I left one arm around her waist. "Nice place. I remember the renovation phases but had never been inside."

"Would you like a tour?"

"Yes, I would." I lowered my arm and held her hand.

"This is my great room." She gave me a moment to look around the spacious, two-story room with vaulted ceilings and loft. Judging from the pure white walls and modern decor, there was no doubt she was very artistic. Her black leather couch was simple in design but had an assortment of red and white throw pillows. No two pillows had the same design, but they matched her two oddly shaped red leather chairs that sat at a ninety degree angle to her couch. In the middle of her floor was a fuzzy white rug that had no shape at all. On top of it were two mirrored cubes that served as sofa tables. The room looked like the cover of an interior decorating design magazine I see when I'm in line at the grocery store.

"Wow, are these some of your original paintings?" I asked, pointing to a very unusual painting above her couch. It was a red rose that had shed all but one petal. The other petals were painted swirling around the rose stem as if caught up in a whirlwind.

"Yes, I have only my work displayed." She pointed at other pieces that were arranged on her walls. "The kitchen is to your left and my bedroom and studio are straight ahead." She led the way down a short hallway into her bedroom. We stood in the door as she let me look around the room. The walls were deep gold. Her dark cherry sleigh bed was against one wall. Above it hung another one of her original pieces. It was a female's silhouette from waist up with one hand placed over the opposite shoulder. There was a night stand with a unique light fixture suspended from the ceiling on each side of her bed. To my left was a chaise and three sketch pads on the floor, next to the television.

"Ready for dinner?"

"Let me get my coat," she said as I followed her from the bedroom to a closet by the front door.

"Where are we going?" she asked, handing me her coat and turning for me to assist.

"You'll see when we get there," I said as she put her arms into her coat and turned around. "If I've judged you correctly, you have already been there."

"We'll see how good you really are," she said with a smirk as we exited her apartment and walked to my car.

Tatiana

"Did you get one of your private detective friends to trace my bank card receipts?" Our destination had become more than obvious once Courtney made a right turn onto Main Street. Surprised but not shocked, I leaned to one side and looked at him.

"I'm offended." He looked at me, then put his hand on his chest. "Don't hate me for being observant." Flashing that award-winning smile, he pulled up in front of the venue and parked.

"How you picked my favorite spot to relax and unwind I'll never know." I was positive that being a local cop made him privy to certain information. Pleased with his choice, I watched as he walked around the front of the car to assist me while getting out. Hand in hand, we walked inside.

"Hello, girlfriend," Akilah, the owner and founder of Java and Jazz sang, wearing an angelic smile when we entered the front door. The small café had only been open one year but had quickly become the place where various artists and musicians met to relax, listen to good music, and vibe with poets. From the street, a small wooden sign with hand-painted letters that hung above the door was its only identifier. At a distance it would have been mistaken for any other hole in the wall. But those passing by would be persuaded by one of two things—the sound of good music or the smell of Southern cooking.

"Hello," Courtney and I said in unison as she walked toward us.

"It's always good to see loving faces," she commented, then greeted us individually with a hug.

"This is my friend Courtney."

"We're all family here. A friend of yours is a friend of mine." She took a step back. "You know the routine. Come on in and make yourselves comfortable."

"Sure thing."

"Girlfriend, have you told him about my collard greens?" she asked proudly.

"Not yet," I said with a huge smile.

"You know those collard greens put me on the map, so make sure he tries them. Let one of the girls know when you're ready to order." She waved her hand as we walked away.

"We will," I replied, then led Courtney by the hand to my favorite table in the center of the room. There was no particular theme or color scheme. The dark blue walls served as a backdrop for black art and anything authentic to our African-American community. Framed newspaper articles, inspirational sayings, and photographs filled the empty wall space. The long and narrow stage that extended the length of the front wall supported a set of drums, bongos, and a keyboard. In front of it was a small area reserved for dancing. Tables both round and square, covered in kente cloth, were placed in no particular order around the room. Most times guests would rearrange them to accommodate the size of their party or make more space for dancing.

"Well, what do you think?" He pulled out a chair, then waited for me to be seated.

"I'm impressed," I said once he sat down opposite me.

"Any other challenges?"

"Give me a second. I'm sure I can think of something." I handed Courtney a menu that was printed on yellow copy paper and laminated.

"I've lived in this city all my life. Where have you been hiding?" he asked, putting his menu down on the table.

"I've never hidden." I leaned forward, then crossed my arms in front of me on the table.

"You've been hiding from me." He picked up the menu and glanced at the selections. "I've never been here before. What do you recommend?" He looked at one side, then flipped it over to look at the back side.

"Of course the collard greens."

"What do you usually order?"

"I order the collard greens, chicken, and homemade cornbread."

"That's what I'll try." He placed his menu on the table.

"We're ready." I waved to get the hostess's attention.

"What high school did you graduate from?" he asked once she took our order.

"Jefferson High School." I responded with the well-known Jefferson Bobcat pride.

"No, you didn't." He shook his head from side to side as though I'd made a false statement.

"Why didn't I?"

"What year?" he asked with a quizzical expression.

"1988, the last of the greatest." I pointed at myself.

"This is crazy. I graduated from Jefferson High in 1986. I don't believe we walked the blue and white halls of Jefferson High School at the same time. How in the world did I miss you?" He leaned away from me, then pointed from head to toe. "It's your entire fault. We could have been happily married with a house, a dog, and two children by now."

"I'm sure I wasn't your type." I leaned back, then turned up the corners of my mouth.

"What type do you think was my type?" He leaned back when the hostess placed our food on the table.

"Did you play sports?" I asked, to confirm my thought, unfolding my napkin and placing it across my lap.

"For sure." He pretended to toss a football. "Number 45, baby. My stats proved I was the best running back that ever passed through the doors of Jefferson High." He bounced his shoulders.

"A cocky jock. Like I said, I wasn't your type." I cut into my chicken.

"Describe my type," he said before putting a fork full of collard greens into his mouth.

"You know, the high-spirited cheerleader or the sexy big-leg majorette types. Little Ms. Popularities with big boobs, small waistlines, and huge butts."

"We were young then." He put his fork down and laughed. "Guess what? Most of those butts are a size sixteen now. I saw them at my ten-year reunion. Good lawd," he said after obviously visualizing one. "Plus, you have a perfect butt." With a facetious smile, he leaned back and looked at my hips.

"Yeah, but I never showcased it to get attention in high school."

"I'm sure you were somewhere painting, anyway."

"You're correct."

"I can't really imagine now what you were like back then." He put his fork down and stared into my eyes.

"I was an introvert. I was very quiet and my artistic talents went unnoticed until my senior year when a counselor saw my sketch pad."

"I still don't see how I missed your face and those beautiful eyes." He shook his head from side to side.

"They were hidden behind a pair of glasses."

"You wore glasses?" He pointed, then fell backward against his chair from laughter. "That's why I didn't see you. I didn't kiss girls with glasses," he said, holding his stomach as it bounced up and down. "You didn't have on glasses at the party." He sat up.

"No, I didn't. A pair of contact lenses was my graduation present. I hated those glasses with a passion." I rolled my eyes to the top of my head, thinking how goofy I really did look.

"All jokes aside. Eyeglasses or not, you have the most beautiful brown eyes I've ever seen." He extended his hand across the table.

"Really?" I asked before placing my hand inside his.

"Please forgive me, I was stupid back then. Guess I should count my lucky stars for our timing. Back then you wouldn't have liked me anyway," he said with a frustrated look as though he couldn't complete his thought. "I was an arrogant jerk."

"Don't worry, I will not hold the past against you." I looked toward the stage when the overhead lights dimmed and the band entered.

"Good evening," said a middle-aged man wearing dreadlocks that were pulled back into a neat ponytail. "I love the positive energy in the house tonight." He pointed over the crowd. "Am I right about the vibe in this place tonight? Everybody feeling good?"

"Yeah, we feel good," the crowd responded almost in unison as the female percussionist started a reggae jam on the bongos.

"Do you want to feel better?"

"Yeah," the crowd responded louder than before.

"Well, get on your feet. Let's take it back to my motherland." He motioned with his hand for the other band members to join in. One by one, chair legs grated against the hardwood floors as people stood and made their way to the dance floor.

"Do you like reggae?" I asked, unable to stay seated as the energy became high.

"It's cool." He bobbed his head back and forth as I motioned with my hands for him to stand and follow me.

"Just relax and allow yourself to feel the music," I suggested while gyrating my hips and walking backward onto the dance floor.

"I want to feel you." He grabbed me by the waist and pulled me closer.

Getting lost in the beat, I continued to gyrate, eventually turning my back toward him. Rolling my hips in sync with the beat, I eased back, then wrapped his arms around my waist. Soon I leaned my head back against his chest and allowed our bodies to move as one. He extended my arms, interlocked his fingers in mine then wrapped our arms around my waist holding me tighter and closer than before. Our breathing synced, as did the beat of our hearts. The songs changed, the beats and tempos changed, but we never changed positions.

"Ready?" he finally asked, obviously unable to withstand the intensity of our bodies grinding together any longer.

"Yes." Hand in hand, we inched our way through

the crowd, got our things, and exited the building after paying our ticket.

"Whew, that was intense." Courtney sighed deeply as we drove away.

"The music is always good," I responded, certain he wasn't referring to the music.

"Never been into reggae music, but it was cool. We'll have to go back again."

"I would love to." Just that fast we were turning onto my street. As I did the night of the party, I was enjoying his company and didn't want the evening to end. "Thank you for dinner. I had a great time."

"Let me walk you to your front door." He parked, then turned off the ignition.

"Would you like to come inside for a drink?" After opening the door, I turned around and waited for his response. It was dark outside, but the light from the entryway cast the perfect shadow. He was standing with his legs spread slightly apart and a hand in each pant pocket.

"Why not. I'm off tomorrow." He nodded his head.

"Great. Please come inside and make yourself comfortable." I shut the door and pointed toward the great room.

"OK." Unexpectedly he lifted my chin with his finger and puckered his luscious lips.

"Remember, you don't kiss girls with glasses." I watched his expression become serious as he moved closer.

"Would you be my first?" He kissed me gently on the lips. With a look I couldn't interpret, he leaned back and stared into my eyes.

"I will pay a penny for your thoughts." I wanted to know his exact thoughts. Did he have a good time? Was the physical attraction mutual?

"Your eyes. Your smile. I can't believe how beautiful you are."

"How beautiful am I?" I tried to play it cool, took off my coat, then hung it in the closet.

"Let me tell you." He reached for my hand.

A tender kiss on the lips became passionate as he moved closer to me, placing a hand on my neck and the other in the small of my back. Enjoying the moment, I closed my eyes and allowed my head to rest against the palm of his hand. Starting at the base of my neck and stopping at the top of my hip, he made small circular motions to massage my back. My head fell slightly backward as his wet kisses continued down my neck, across my throat, then up my neck again. After using his hand to ease my top up, he reached inside my bra and fondled my nipple with his fingertips. I squirmed when the tender touches on my breast were followed by a wet kiss.

"Would you like something to drink?" I asked, speaking slowly, trying to cover the nervous tremor in my voice. Then I slid my top down and pulled out of his embrace.

"What do you have?"

"I have red wine, Crown Royal, or Rémy Martin." I pointed toward the couch for him to have a seat. Pretending to be calm, I turned to walk away but couldn't stop my heart from palpitating.

"Rémy and coke sounds good." He followed me into the kitchen instead.

"Sure," I said, fixed his drink, then poured myself a glass of wine. Hoping the wine would ease my tension, I took a huge sip. He took one drink, then placed his glass on the counter. "Is everything OK?" I asked, assuming he wasn't pleased.

"It's better than great." He took the glass out of my hand and placed it on the bar.

"Better than great?" I asked, unable to imagine what could ever be better than great as he walked around and stood in front of me. The intensity in his eyes was alarming as he raised my shirt and placed both hands underneath my bra. I reached behind me to grab the countertop for balance when he exposed my breasts and put them both into his mouth. My heart raced when he held one breast at a time and flicked my nipples with his tongue. Caught up in the moment, I arched my back to allow more of myself in his mouth. I wanted to resist when he eased his hand down my stomach and rubbed between my legs. With both hands I pushed his head away and fought silently to regain my composure.

"Excuse me for a second." I looked into his eyes to avoid staring at his erection. I went into the bedroom, then shut my bathroom door after going inside. *Damn,* I thought, placing my face in my hands and leaning back against the door. My panties were saturated. *What are you thinking about? Never ever make love on a first date,* I thought. I inhaled to compose myself, got a fresh pair of panties and a clean face cloth. I unzipped my jeans, tucked my fingers inside the waistband of my panties, then wiggled to pull them off together. Trying to ignore the tingle between my thighs, I turned on the water, lathered my cloth, and washed. I re-dressed, checked my face in the mirror, and went back into the kitchen.

"Would you like me to pour you another drink?" I asked after looking at his watered-down Rémy.

"That would be good."

"I haven't bought any movies lately." I refreshed his drink, then walked around the counter and into the great room. He stood and followed so close I could feel his breath on the back of my neck.

"That's not a problem," he answered, held up the television remote, and handed it to me before sitting down on the couch.

"Maybe there's something good on television." I turned on the television, sat down beside him, then looked away when a man and woman tore each other's clothes off. The coincidence was almost embarrassing.

"Football?"

"ESPN it is." I changed the channel as we looked at each other and laughed.

"Relax, I promise I will not bite." Slowly he wrapped his arm around my shoulder.

"Anything with teeth has the capability to bite." I took a sip of wine, then leaned onto his chest.

Chapter 6

Tatiana

"How long have you been awake?" My eyes opened when I felt Courtney rubbing my arm. Somewhere between his football game and my second glass of wine, I'd fallen asleep.

"At least an hour." He kissed my forehead. "Don't worry, I've been watching football highlights and player interviews. Where are you going?"

"Why didn't you wake me? I'm going to take a shower and freshen up." I was so embarrassed. I sat up and turned my head away from him to hide any first-morning offenses. I wiped the corners of my eyes and rubbed my fingers through my hair.

"You were resting so peacefully last night, I didn't have the heart to wake you." He never let me leave his embrace. "I looked in your hallway closet and found a blanket."

"Are you always so thoughtful?" I leaned against his chest to find another comfortable position.

"All I can say is that you bring the best out of me." He leaned his head down to touch the top of mine. "What do you usually eat for breakfast in the morning?"

"Fruit smoothies. I'm normally running late so I have to drink my breakfast while driving to work. And you?"

"Can't you tell I'm a big eater?" He smiled and rubbed his stomach.

"No, not at all." I rubbed my hand over his perfectly defined six-pack. "It feels like you hardly eat at all."

"I love to eat. I inherited this athletic physique from my father. He doesn't have an ounce of fat on his body and has never spent an hour in the gym. Unfair, isn't it?" He laughed and patted his stomach again.

"Very unfair. If I look at a doughnut, I gain two pounds. There are people who work themselves to death for your definition."

"Guess what I'm thinking about right now?" He placed his index finger on his temple and looked toward the ceiling.

"I can't imagine."

"I'm visualizing three buttermilk pancakes, three slices of bacon, and scrambled eggs."

"Is that a breakfast invitation?"

"Yes it is, but we're going to eat here."

"Are we? Let me warn you, the kitchen is closed because I'm on vacation." I turned to look at him.

"So that's how you stay so fine. You can't cook." He gently tickled the inside of my arm pits.

"Remember, I deal with children every day so the mind tricks will not work either."

"Come on, beautiful. Let me show you how it's really done." He took me by the hand and led me from the couch into the kitchen. "What do you want for breakfast?" He pulled out a stool for me to have a seat at the bar.

"What are my options?" I smiled and placed my hands below my chin.

"The sky is the limit. Speak it, and watch me make it appear." Like a magician, he spread his fingers apart.

"Omelets are my favorite."

"An omelet? Is that it?" He rubbed his hands together.

"That it? I've never seen you cook before."

"Baby girl, there's a lot you haven't seen." He pretended to wipe dust off of his shoulder. "Two Courtney omelets coming up." I watched as he opened the fridge, took a quick inventory, then gathered his ingredients. One by one, he placed them on the counter.

"Let's see. I need a skillet, utensils, and your beautiful smile." He turned on the water, dispensed the soap into the palms of his hands, and washed them.

"Let me show you." I stood to show him where everything was.

"No, you sit down. Just tell me and I can find it myself." He looked around the kitchen.

"The skillets are in the bottom cabinet and all the utensils are in the drawer beside the sink." I pointed toward each one.

"I got it from here." He dried his hands and then bent slightly at the waist to open a lower cabinet. *Damn, he's fine and likes to cook,* I thought to myself as he stood.

"What do you think about a cooking law man?" He diced his onions, tomatoes, and bell peppers, then moved them to one side. In a bowl he cracked four eggs, added milk, and used a whisk to beat the mixture.

"What woman wouldn't love to have one?" I asked, watching as he moved around and prepared our meal effortlessly. During the night he'd taken off his shirt, and he was wearing only an undershirt and jeans. In awe, I watched his muscles flex with every move.

"Voilà, omelet extraordinaire," he said several minutes later, then placed a perfectly prepared omelet, napkin, and fork on the countertop. "What would you have to drink?"

"OJ please."

"One OJ coming up." He picked up a cup and tossed it into the air.

"I don't know what's sexier, a man wearing a tool belt or an apron," I said, then cut into my omelet.

"Next time I'll wear my tool belt." He walked around the counter and stood behind me. Dropping my fork was a natural reflex when he grabbed my waist and started to kiss the nape of my neck. Naturally wanting more, I closed my eyes and leaned my head forward. For a second the kisses stopped, and I could feel him back away. "That feels good." I rolled my neck around when he started to deep massage my shoulders.

"Relax."

"Hmm," I responded as the tension in my neck and shoulders began to ease. With one hand he leaned my head to the side and nibbled the side of my neck. "Oh my goodness, that feels so good." The nibble became an aggressive kiss down the side of my neck. I didn't resist but never turned to face him when he lifted my arms to remove my shirt. I shivered when the tip of his tongue glided across my shoulder blades, down the small of my back, then up again. Affirming the natural effect he had on my body, he unzipped my pants and felt inside my panties. Satisfied with the outcome, he lifted me off the bar stool, lowered my pants, and leaned my body forward. Still with my back toward him, he felt with his fingertips, positioned my body, then entered. "Oh my God." My inner muscles relaxed when his manhood reached its full potential and filled every aspect of me. Wanting maximum pleasure, he pressed into the small of my back with his hand to maintain the arch. My vagina throbbed as he used short but strong strokes to gyrate inside me.

"Do you like that?" He grabbed my waist then moved back and forth. "Do you like that?" His penetration was so deep I swore I could taste him.

"Yes." Lost in a state of ecstasy and barely able to maintain the position as his strokes became stronger, I could feel my legs start to tremble. No man, Christopher included, ever made me feel that way.

"Then tell me."

"Courtney." Barely able to breathe, I lowered my head and grabbed each corner of the stool. "I like the way you're making me feel." I panted after my sweet release but maintained the arch in my back for his enjoyment.

"Like it! I want you to love it." He thrust himself back and forth, each time harder than before, then shook uncontrollably.

Courtney

Whew, I thought while still shaking from my orgasm. The room was spinning, so I closed my eyes and gripped Tatiana's waist. A few seconds later I shook my head from side to side, stood erect, and took a step back. "That was amazing." I gave her props as she stood, pulled up her jeans and panties, then put on her shirt. She didn't respond verbally but looked over her shoulder and smiled. Interpreting silence as a good thing, I pulled my pants up and watched her walk across the floor into the bedroom. Like a pendulum, her hips rocked from side to side. *What the hell*, I thought, and followed her like a dog in heat. She didn't hear me enter her room, so I stood in the doorway and watched as she turned on the shower and began to undress. Finding pleasure in the moment, I looked down, then pressed my hands against my jeans to cover another erection.

"Are you trying to give me a heart attack?" She snatched her drying towel off the rack, covered her body, and laughed.

"A heart attack is the last thing I want to give you." Not wanting my animal magnetism toward her to be so obvious, I inhaled and eased my hands into my pockets.

"The remote is on the nightstand if you want to watch television." She smiled and pointed toward her television. What she didn't know was I wanted more. "I'll be out of the shower in a few minutes." She opened the shower door, let the towel fall from her body, then stepped inside.

"Can I watch you instead?" I wanted to finish what I started in the kitchen. I'd been with several females, but no one like Tatiana. Her innocent looks and subtle mannerisms had me completely fooled. She definitely knew how to please a man.

"Don't you think there's something more interesting on HBO?" She stuck her head out of the shower and pointed toward the television.

"Like what?" I looked at the television and hunched my shoulders.

"Sports?" She laughed and closed her shower door.

"This is better than any sporting event I've ever seen." I walked to the shower, opened the door, and watched as she stood beneath the water, allowing it to wet her body. Her movements seemed choreographed as she leaned her head back to expose more of her neck, then turned around. Never taking my eyes off her, I took off my clothes and stepped inside.

"This shower isn't large enough for the both of us." Her eyes widened as she spoke.

"It is now." I closed the door, leaned against the back shower wall, and pulled her body against mine. I'd never been the romantic type, so I reached for her sponge and filled it with gel. Starting on her chest, I made circular motions, moving from one body part to another, eventually cleansing every inch. I turned her around, lathered her back with gel, then used my body to massage her instead of the sponge. When I felt that she was totally relaxed we exchanged positions underneath the water flow. In awe, I watched her return the simple pleasure of bathing me from head to toe. We took turns rinsing and stepped out of the shower to dry off. I reached for the large towel, wrapped it around our bodies, and kissed her passionately. Making love had been my intent, but the intimacy seemed better than anything I'd ever seen on HBO.

Tatiana

"Hey girl. Whatcha doing?" Anyah asked when I answered the telephone.

"I'm lying down on the couch watching a movie." Still experiencing an emotional high, I leaned back against Courtney's chest, pulled the blanket up, and tucked it underneath my chin. *Phenomenal* was the only word I could think of to describe our morning.

"You're doing what?" she asked, knowing I never took time to watch television, let alone a two-hour movie.

"Lying down on the couch . . ." Ready to repeat my last statement, I squirmed when Courtney kissed the side of my neck.

"I heard what you said the first time but didn't believe it. What are you watching?" Her tone was condescending.

"Something New," I sang, then closed my eyes for a moment of reflection.

"Hell, I invited you to go see the movie with me on opening weekend."

"Oh yeah," I said when Courtney's kiss moved from my neck to my ear lobe.

"But you were too busy painting, which brings up my next question. Is Mr. Fine at your apartment?"

"Yes," I said promptly because Anyah knew me all too well.

"I knew it 'cause yo' ass don't stay out of your studio long enough to watch anything. So what's really going on?" she asked loudly.

"Yeah, it's been a good day," I sang to avoid answering her question.

"Please don't tell me you gave it up already," she yelled into the phone. "But who am I to criticize you? His ass was fine."

"OK." Ignoring her comment, I moved the phone to my other ear, hoping Courtney hadn't heard her outburst. "I will talk to you later." By then I was ready to hang up in her face. She knew from the tone of my voice that he was sitting beside me. I didn't know why she insisted on asking so many questions.

"You damn right you will and I want all of the details." She spoke louder than before.

"Bye," I said sharply, then nestled against Courtney's chest.

Chapter 7

Tatiana

"Good morning," I answered energetically, feeling as though I'd slept an entire eight hours. The night before Courtney had worked from seven PM until seven AM. We'd talked on the telephone almost half of his shift.

Between us there were so many questions. What are your plans for the future? Where do you see yourself five years from now, ten years from now? Are there any plans for marriage? Would you like to have children, if so, how many? Then there was the deeper side of the conversation, past relationships. Even though discussing the topic seemed taboo, we shared the good and the bad. He, like many of our men, had been heartbroken in the past, and for that reason avoided monogamous relationships. Sharing my experience about Christopher seemed easier only because he could relate. He said, "Christopher was a damn fool for leaving you to chase a dream. I'm a man of my word and promise never to break your heart." Hearing his confirmation only validated my personal opinion about our breakup and aided in another aspect of my inner healing.

Like teenagers, we continued to talk on the telephone about no one thing in particular until I could barely keep my eyes open. Even then our *good-byes* were followed by seconds of silence. As a compromise for ending the conversation, we agreed to see each other when his shift ended at seven AM.

"Good morning, sunshine. I've waited all night to see your beautiful face. I'm parking right now."

"Great." Excited to see him, I tossed the covers back, hopped out of bed, and went to open the front door.

"I couldn't stop thinking about you once we got off the telephone last night."

"Tell me anything," I said, not ending the call until I opened the door. I placed a hand on my hip and flexed my right foot. Just as he requested the night before, I was only wearing a T-shirt and panties.

"You look great. Now go get back into bed." He kissed me on the lips, then smacked me on the bottom when I turned around. Thinking we were going to finish our conversation over a cup of coffee, I went into the bedroom with a puzzled look and he went into the kitchen. Before I'd gotten back into bed, I could hear cabinets open and close. Next I heard eggs crack, then the clatter of utensils against a glass mixing bowl. Soon the smell of breakfast permeated the air from the kitchen into the bedroom. *How can only a week and a half with Courtney feel like a year?* With a smile, I leaned my head against the pillow and closed my eyes. Even though I'd broken every rule in the "Ten Things Not to Do on Your First Date" handbook, I didn't regret a single moment.

"A Courtney omelet prepared the way you like it." He stood in the door holding a breakfast tray. His uniform shirt was pulled out of his pants and unbuttoned. His white cotton undershirt clung to his perfectly defined chest muscles, making him a sight for sore eyes. *Thank you, God, for sending Mr. Perfect to me,* I thought with a smile as he walked toward me.

"You're absolutely amazing. It looks wonderful." I sat up and smoothed my covers so he could place the tray over my lap. "Are you going to join me?" I patted the other side of my bed.

"Sure, I'll be right back." He went into the kitchen, then returned with another tray.

"I wasn't expecting breakfast." On my plate he'd neatly arranged an omelet, two slices of toast, and a spoonful of grape jelly. "Thank you," I said, picking up my fork and cutting into my omelet.

"Did I surprise you?" He sat down beside me, adjusted his tray, and placed it over his lap.

"Most definitely."

"I couldn't stop thinking about you last night and wanted the last day of your Christmas vacation to be special. Today is your day."

"How thoughtful. I've never had a special day before."

"Whatever you want to do, just say the word and it shall be done."

"Whatever I'd like to do? Is there a price limit?" I said playfully, then put my hand underneath my chin. "I'd like to go to the art gallery."

"The art gallery," he repeated, then nodded his head up and down. "Whew! You were starting to make me nervous."

"There's an awesome exhibit on display and today is the last day."

"Sure thing. When you finish eating and get dressed, we can go to my place so that I can shower and change clothes."

"I can't wait."

Together we finished eating breakfast; Courtney took his tray into the kitchen, then returned to get mine. Soon I heard water running and the clatter of dishes as they were being put into the sink. Impressed by his thoughtfulness, I got out of bed, put on my robe, and went into the bathroom to shower. Pondering whether I should wear my black knit turtleneck or red V-neck sweater, I turned on the water, let my robe fall to the floor, and stepped inside. Using a floral scent Courtney would love, I filled my loofah sponge, showered, and then patted myself dry before getting out. I could still hear water running in the kitchen, so I walked to the closet and decided to wear my red V-neck sweater, blue jeans, and red leather ankle boots. No sooner than I put on my sweater and slipped into my jeans, Courtney was standing at the bedroom door. He watched as I sat on the edge of my bed and put on my boots. We exchanged smiles as I stood and walked by him into the other room.

"Wow, you smell good." He turned on one heel and followed me.

"Thank you." Looking forward to the day ahead of me, I got my coat and purse. With our arms interlocked, we exited my condo, got into his car, and drove to his apartment.

"Welcome to the place I call home," he said thirty minutes later when we turned into the parking lot of his apartment complex. We made a few short turns through the maze of three-story dark red brick buildings, then parked in a covered space clearly marked with his apartment number. I waited as he opened my door. We walked up six steps and followed the narrow walkway landscaped with ever-green shrubbery and variegated grass to his front door. He opened it and moved to one side.

"It's a nice home," I said once I had stepped inside the door of a typical bachelor pad. Almost every-thing was black except the color of his dark tan walls. Black leather sofa and love seat, black linen curtains, and zebra print rug. Except for a large black art print of a male figure wearing a tribal costume, hold-ing a sword, which hung over the couch, his walls were bare.

"There's no need for a tour because you can see everything from here," he said jokingly, referring to the one-bedroom open floor plan with a com-bined kitchen and eating area that flowed into a larger living space. "Make yourself comfortable." He pointed at his fifty-two-inch plasma screen tele-vision and stereo equipment that dominated an entire wall.

"What am I supposed to do with this?" I asked when he handed me a remote control large enough to fly a toy airplane.

"You know boys like toys." He laughed. "Come into the bedroom while I shower. Everything in there is simple and less complicated."

"Sounds like a plan." I carefully placed the remote on his glass-top table and followed him into the moderate-sized bedroom.

"Better?" he asked, turned on the thirty-two-inch television that sat on a black stand with a DVD player on the lower shelf, and handed me a remote that seemed familiar.

"Much better."

"Sit on my bed, take off your shoes, and relax while I take a shower."

I sat on the edge of his king-sized water bed, took off my shoes, and leaned back against the black leather headboard. *It should be a law,* I thought to myself as he stood in front of me, unbuttoned and removed his shirt, then unzipped his pants.

"I'll be done in a few minutes."

"According to you, we have all day. So take your time." After undressing down to his undershorts, he turned and walked into the bathroom. I tried to focus on the television but was distracted by his firm buttocks and hamstrings. I was certain he left the bathroom door wide open for my viewing pleasure. Trying not to be obvious, I used my peripheral vision to watch as he turned on the shower, pulled off his boxers, and stepped inside. The vision of him naked with beads of water falling on, then rolling off, his firm body made me moist. I crossed my legs at the ankle to control the tingling sensation and closed my eyes to resist the urge to undress and join him. To mask the sound of flowing water, which had started to contribute to my wetness, I turned up the television volume.

"What are you watching?" he asked from the shower.

"Nothing yet." I pressed the button to display the cable guide. He dried himself, wrapped the towel around his waist, and stood in front of the sink to brush his teeth. *He's making me wet again,* I thought with clenched teeth when he leaned against the sink and used one arm for support. Again, every muscle in his back and arms flexed. I looked away to regroup, then asked myself whether he was trying to entice me with his seductive poses.

"What time do we need to leave?"

"It's Sunday, so the museum will not open until one o'clock."

"What time is it now?"

"Eleven."

"Hmm." He tapped his toothbrush on the sink before placing it in the plastic holder, wiped his mouth with a face towel, then looked at me. He walked to the bed, placed an arm on either side of me and kissed me. Wanting him just as much as he wanted me, I welcomed the kisses that started at my neck and ended at the top of my waistband. I wanted to stop him but couldn't when he unfastened my pants and wiggled them below my hips. He eased his hands underneath my top and massaged my nipples while using his tongue to kiss the inside of my navel. As he began to move downward from my navel, the tingling sensation alone made me squirm. My body became limp and fell backward onto the bed when his head disappeared between my legs. The act was unselfish; he serenaded my clitoris with wet kisses. My legs started to tremble and I used my hands to push his head away.

"No, Tatiana," he said passionately, making me want more; he clenched my wrists, and moved my hands away from his head.

"Please, Courtney, stop." I gripped the comforter with one hand and tried to push his head away with the other. Ignoring my pleas, he continued until the moment of ultimate satisfaction had been reached. Never saying a word, he went into the bathroom and returned with a wet towel lathered with soap. Unable to respond, I stood to wash, pulled up my pants, and sat, feeling weightless, on the edge of the bed.

"Lie down," he said softly, then sat down and held me as we leaned back together. He turned me onto my side, pulled me into him, and hugged me from behind. Still basking in the moment of ultimate satisfaction, I closed my eyes.

"That was great." Still feeling the heat between my legs, I pulled his arms tighter around my body.

"The pleasure was mine," he commented softly, then kissed the back of my neck.

His desire to satisfy me left me dumbfounded. That was the first time anyone gave of themselves without expecting to receive in return. From the moment we met, it all still seemed too good to be true.

"We still have time for a short nap." He rested my head on his arm, then gently rubbed his hand down the small of my back.

"What time is it?" Almost simultaneously our eyes opened and we stretched together. We'd only been asleep about thirty minutes, but I felt well rested and relaxed.

"Almost twelve thirty." Courtney kissed me on the back of the neck before getting out of bed.

"May I have another clean face towel? I'd like to freshen up a little before we leave." Still in a daze, I sat up slowly.

"Let me get one for you."

"Thanks." I stood and followed him into the bathroom. He opened a small closet and handed me a face towel.

"Did you enjoy the rest of my surprise?" He gazed into my eyes, reached for my hand, and held it.

"I'm speechless." Still amazed that he had made me climax without penetrating, I stared into his eyes. With my fingertips, I rubbed his hands and imagined the experience only becoming better with time.

"That's what I wanted to hear." He smiled and let go of my hand.

"It was only the truth." While Courtney dressed in the bathroom, I washed my face and reapplied my lipstick and eyeliner.

"Ready for our museum adventure?" he asked as we walked toward his front door.

"Yes, I'm ready." He held up my coat and waited as I slipped my arms into the sleeves.

"After you." He opened the front door and suddenly our eyes met.

"No way," we said together after obviously entertaining sexual thoughts, then exited his apartment and walked to the car. Once we left the parking lot and turned onto the street, he placed his hand on my thigh and gently rubbed it.

"I haven't been to a museum since elementary school." Courtney chuckled as he opened the door of the museum's front entrance. "My mother made me go."

"Are you sure about this?" I turned around and asked. I watched as he held on to the door handle a few seconds before letting go. "Why didn't you say anything when I made the suggestion?"

"I'm fine. Like I said, this is your day and I'm a man of my word." He playfully rolled his eyes to the top of his head when we walked into the lobby of the museum.

"I'm sure you'll enjoy the experience. Believe me, it's nothing weird or eccentric. It's actually an exhibit of photographs taken by a local artist depicting the African-American religious experience from slavery until the present day."

"It sounds interesting." He paid the desk attendant for our admittance, then purchased two brochures.

"I heard it was an awesome display." We reviewed the guide, then began our tour. The small one-story building was an old warehouse that had been left vacant for at least five years. A group of local artists had purchased the facility and successfully converted it into a multicultural museum and art school. The gray concrete floors were cracked from daily abuse. The exposed air-conditioning and heating duct work weren't refurbished, to honor the building's original characteristics. The building itself was no more than 2,500 square feet but hosted the most talked-about exhibits and art shows.

"That was very interesting," Courtney said two hours later when we exited the museum.

"Not too bad, huh?"

"I never realized how many amenities we've taken for granted." He turned to a picture with a caption in our brochure. "My great-grandparents probably walked in their bare feet on dirt roads to a small wooden church with no air-conditioning."

"Amazing, isn't it?"

"Guess I should have talked to my grandparents more. It's amazing how they managed to make a lot out of nothing at all. You know, like their Sunday dinners."

"By the way, what is your favorite meal?" I asked once we got into his car and drove out of the parking lot. His comment also reminded me how home-cooked meals were used to show love and express feelings of gratitude.

"I'm a meat and potatoes man."

"Just for you, I'll declare myself off vacation a day early and cook dinner."

"You can't cook."

"Are you brave enough to try if I do?"

"I'll try anything once."

"OK," I responded, pondering several mouth-watering meal combinations as he drove.

Ready to prepare a heart-winning meal, I opened the front door, hung up my coat and purse, and went into the kitchen. Mother always said the way to a man's heart was through his stomach. For Courtney's affection, I was willing to put the old wives' tale to the test.

"Let me know if you need some help in there," he said, sounding arrogant, then pointed around my kitchen.

"I'm sure I can manage." Laughing at his comment, I opened the freezer and removed two packages, one with steak and the other with chicken. Courtney pointed at the steak, so I put the chicken back. "In the meantime, would you like a drink?"

"Rémy and coke would be good."

Anticipating his response, I'd already gotten a glass and the Rémy out of the cabinet. I fixed his drink, then sat it on the counter in front of him. He took a sip, sat down at the bar, and placed his hand beneath his chin.

"You can't harass the chef." I reached into my wire basket for an onion and bell pepper and placed them, along with my cutting board, on the countertop.

"And why not? You don't want me to see you open everything and heat it up in the microwave."

"Now you're banned from the kitchen." I turned

around sharply, then pointed toward the great room.

"OK, I'll leave you alone."

"We can watch a movie once I get everything started." He went into the great room while I stayed in the kitchen. It was my first time cooking for him, so I wanted everything to look and taste perfect. I looked at my raw vegetables, then took a deep breath. Forty minutes later, our meal had been started, so I set the timer and joined him on the sofa to watch television.

"What do you know about football?" When I sat down, he rested his head on my lap.

"When the team scores, it's called a touchdown." I rubbed my fingertips through his hair and laughed.

"That's better than nothing. At least you didn't think it was a home run."

"No, that's basketball," I said playfully, then waited on his reaction.

"Basketball?" he asked, sitting straight up.

"Rest your nerves, I was only kidding. I know you get home runs in baseball."

"Whew, you did make me nervous." He exhaled, then lowered his head onto my lap. I leaned my head back on the couch to relax while he watched ESPN.

"That's my timer." I used my hands to lift his head when it buzzed and went into the kitchen to check dinner. He stood and followed me.

"You got it smelling good up in here." He inhaled.

"Everything will be done in about ten minutes," I said after opening the oven and checking the temperature of the meat.

"I can't wait to taste it."

"Ten minutes." I smacked his hand when he

reached for my fork, then closed the oven door. He jerked his hand back and leaned against the kitchen door.

"I could really get used to this." He nodded his head up and down.

"Get used to what?" I asked, wanting to know exactly what he was referring to.

"I could get used to you and all of this." With a serious expression, he pointed at me, then looked around the room.

"Go ahead and sit down." I waved my hand at him.

"Tatiana, I'm serious. I'm really feeling this . . . beautiful woman who has it all." With an expression I couldn't interpret, he looked at me a few seconds longer, then sat down at the table. I took the meat out of the oven and stirred my side dishes before fixing our plates.

"Your dinner is served." Before placing the plate with steak, green beans, and scalloped potatoes on the table, I waved it beneath his nose.

"Umm, this smells good and looks even better." He used his index finger to scoop a bite out of the potatoes and put it into his mouth.

"No, I can't cook. Remember?" I turned to walk away, but he grabbed me around my waist and pulled me to him.

"Who said that? I know it wasn't me." He looked around the room as if someone else was standing there.

"Oh yeah, it was you." I pulled away and went to get my plate.

"Is that all you're going to eat?" he asked when I sat down in front of him.

"Cooking always makes me lose my appetite." I

looked down at my serving of green beans and spoonful of potatoes.

"Don't worry. I'll eat enough for the two of us." He cut into a piece of steak and put it into his mouth. "Who taught you how to cook like this? This is too much. You're beautiful and can cook too."

"My mother taught me. She's a very good cook."

"Where is she?" he asked, then looked around me into the kitchen. "Tell her she can come out of the kitchen now."

"You're crazy."

"Look at how tender this meat is." He used his fork to cut his steak. "Normally I smother my meat with steak sauce, but this is awesome."

"Enjoy." I watched him finish his meal, one forkful at a time.

"Come here and let me kiss the chef. I owe you an apology. You're a damn good cook. Oh, please excuse my language. I mean you're a really good cook."

I walked to his side of the table and he pulled me down onto his lap. Pleased that he had enjoyed the meal, I picked up our empty plates and went into the kitchen. We cleaned up the kitchen, then cuddled on the couch and decided to watch a movie.

"Do you hear that?" I asked, then lifted my head off his chest to listen.

"Yeah, it sounds like rain." We stood and walked toward the door.

"Where did this storm come from?" I asked when I pulled back the blinds and saw the tree limbs in my front yard bending to the ground. My vision became limited as the heavy winds started to blow the rain against the window pane. "Oh my." I jumped back from the window when I saw a streak of lightning flash across the sky.

"Let me leave before it gets worse. I had a great day and dinner was fantastic."

"You don't have to hurry home. I'd feel a lot better if you'd wait until it stops raining." I was concerned, so I stood in front of him and folded my arms.

"Remember, I work in this stuff. It's nothing but a little rain."

"OK, it's just a little rain," I said after hearing a loud clap of thunder.

"Well, it's more than a little rain, but it's nothing I've never driven in before. I have to protect, whether it's rain, shine, sleet, or snow."

"You're more than welcome to stay."

"You look concerned."

"I am. Plus there's plenty of room for you on my full-sized couch."

"Correction: there's plenty of room for me in your bed. Just for the record, if I stay, I'm sleeping with my clothes on."

"Judging from this morning, I'm the one that should be worried." I put my hands on my hips before walking to the sofa table for the remote and turning off the television.

"Oh yeah."

"You heard me." As though I was light as a feather, he picked me up, carried me into the bedroom, and put me down beside the bed. Pretending to be strangers, we turned our backs to each other, undressed down to our undergarments, and got underneath the covers.

"Sweet dreams."

"I'm certain they will be," I said, referring to the early-morning orgasm, then reached over to turn off the lamp light.

Chapter 8

Tatiana

"Baby, where are you going?" Courtney moaned, still half-asleep, then tightened his embrace when he felt me move.

"Remember, today is my first day back to work," I said, rolling my body forward to turn off the alarm clock. "It's time for me to wake up and get ready."

"What if I don't want you to go? Holding you all night felt so good." To restrain my movement, he put his leg on top of mine and kissed the back of my neck.

"I've not sold that $50,000 dollar piece yet. Until then I have to teach." I moved my body back against his until there was no space between us. Sleeping in his arms all night did feel good. His body was warm and just his being there made me feel secure.

"I guess you have a point. May I have a kiss?" He rubbed my back, then turned my body over.

"Sure." Really wanting to stay in his embrace, I kissed him, rolled out of bed, and felt my way into the bathroom. Still half-asleep, I turned on the light, then closed my eyes from its brightness. I felt with my hands to turn on the water and wasn't surprised when he walked up behind me.

"Give me ten minutes," he whispered into my ear, then rolled his tongue around inside my ear lobe.

"Courtney, it's my first day back, and I don't want to be late," I whined, knowing I'd give in if he asked me again.

"Seven minutes. I promise I'll be quick," he said, then pulled me closer to him, allowing me to feel his early-morning erection.

"Seven minutes. That's it," I said, unable to find the strength to resist, then turned off the water. He held my hands and led me back into the bedroom. Before I could get back into bed he was pulling down my panties. Once they were around my ankles, I stepped out of them and lay back on the bed.

"Oh my goodness, you're beautiful even in the morning." He rubbed his fingers through my hair. With one arm, he supported his body weight, then used his other hand to massage that sweet spot between my legs. His body was close enough for me to feel him swell. Within seconds, my sweet juices started to flow, so I parted my legs and allowed him to enter. Forgetting about the time, I rotated my hips beneath him to feel his fullness. He lowered his head onto my shoulder, then thrust back and forth.

"Ohh," he moaned as his body started to shiver. "Please come with me."

"Baby, are you ready?" I asked, then elevated my hips, allowing him to feel more of me.

"I'm ready."

"Yesss," I sang, digging my fingernails deep into his back.

"Oh, that was great," he said, rolling over so I could get out of bed.

Disoriented, I stood, then walked at an angle toward the bathroom. Compared with before, the time was shorter, but the orgasm I experienced was by far more intense.

"Zzzz."

I turned to look over my shoulder when I heard a soft snore. Confident that he was pleased, I showered, applied my makeup, and dressed without disturbing his power nap.

"Courtney, it's time for me to leave." To wake him, I rubbed him gently on the shoulder, then rocked his body back and forth.

"It's that time, huh?" He sat up, wrapped his arms around my waist, and leaned his head against my stomach.

"Yes, if I leave now I'll make it to work on time." I rubbed my hand over his head.

"OK." He stood slowly, put on his pants, and slipped his arms into his shirt. He stretched, then followed me into the great room to get our coats out of the closet.

"When can I see you again?" he asked after helping me into my coat, then placing his hands on my shoulder to turn me around.

"When would you like to see me again?" I asked, giving him a quick glance. I opened and shut the front door and headed to my car.

"I'd like to see you as soon as possible. I'm already missing you." He rested his arm on the door and leaned down.

"I get off at four-thirty." I put the key into the ignition and turned it.

"Four-thirty. That's too many hours from now." He frowned. "Can you make calls on your break?"

"Sure."

"Call me as soon as you can. I'll be waiting." He closed the door and stepped back when I put the car into reverse.

Courtney

Before Tatiana backed out of her driveway and turned onto the street, my cell phone started to vibrate. I reached into my pocket and cussed when I saw Octavious's name on the display.

"'Bout time you answered yo' cell."

"Hmmph," I said, not admitting how many times I hadn't answered the past few days. I shook my head and got into my car.

"Where yo ass at?"

"Headed to the house." I put my car into reverse, backed out of her driveway, and turned onto the street.

"Headed to the house? Thought I was gone have to put out an APB on yo' ass when you didn't show up at da club last night."

"You know, something else came up."

"The past week a lot of something else been comin' up. We've been meeting at the club every Sunday night for how many years?"

"Hell, I don't know."

"Seven. Man, in seven years ain't nothing ever came up before. What's up witcha? I need to know what's really goin' on."

"Ain't nothing going on," I said, not ready to justify why I spent my night with a beautiful woman instead of chasing gold diggers. "Hey, let me hit you back."

"Awww hell . . . must be a female. Is it a female you met at the Christmas party?"

"Later." I said, closed my flip phone, turned on the radio, and drove in the direction of my apartment.

Tatiana

"Good morning, Cathy Sue," I said to a fellow teacher with a smile and a wave of the hand. My morning with Courtney had left me floating on cloud nine. Not even Mrs. Houston, the teacher next door, with all her griping and complaining about cheating men and bad relationships, could ruin my day.

"Excuse me," Cathy Sue said, stepping away from her door and into the hallway to stop me. "From the smile on your face, it looks like someone had an especially good winter break."

"It was interesting," I said, waving at returning students as they swarmed like bees in the hallway.

"How long have we worked together? Plus, I'm ten years your senior." She followed her comment with a roll of the neck. Cathy Sue was correct. I had done most of my internships in a private school setting and had assumed that was where I wanted to start my teaching career. Initially there were no availabilities in the private school system, so I accepted a job at an inner city public school called Norwood Park Elementary. My initial plan was to teach there while applying elsewhere.

Cathy Sue had been the first teacher to introduce herself and welcome me onto the campus. Soon casual *hellos* turned into lunch and lengthier conversations. Before long we were friends and talked during summer vacations. That was ten years ago. Several new teachers had come and gone, but the two of us were still there.

"Ma'am?" I asked to irritate her. She hated it when anyone called her *ma'am*. Even on her worst day, Cathy Sue looked like a Vogue Cover Girl. She was a forty-four-year-old Caucasian female, married with two teenaged sons, but had the figure of a twenty-five-year-old. The natural blonde, blue-eyed bombshell was slim, with a small waistline and long, lean legs. All the teachers were jealous of her.

"Don't 'ma'am' me," she said, standing close enough to rub shoulders with me. "I wasn't born yesterday, and you weren't walking like that before break." She pinched me on the hip.

"Walking like what?" I asked, knowing she was referring to the additional sway of my hips.

"I know that 'good sex walk' all too well, and you didn't have it before break." She leaned closer to my ear. "Who's the new man?" she asked, placing a hand on her hip and looking at me from head to toe.

"New man? Why couldn't it be the new pair of shoes I'm wearing?" I asked, pointing my right toe to model my shoes.

"Oprah Winfrey doesn't own a pair of shoes that will make a woman strut like that." She nudged me on the shoulder.

"We'll talk later," I said with a mischievous smile, then swished away when the tardy bell rang. "Later, Cathy Sue," I said again, knowing she was still in the hallway watching me walk away.

"Good morning, class," I sang, once my first period students had settled into their seats.

"Good morning Ms. Anderson," they sang in unison.

"Did everyone enjoy their Christmas break?" I had missed them all. Watching their expressions and body language always made me smile. Some eyes would sparkle, while others would be half-closed, accompanied by an occasional yawn. There was always the faithful fifteen percent that came in with pencil and paper in hand, prepared to work. Then there was the eighty-five percent whose mental capacity for learning varied on a daily basis.

"Yes ma'am," a few of them sang. "Yeah," others piped out.

"Since this is our first day back to class, the assignment will be a review."

"Assignment?" someone shouted from the back of the room. "Can this be another free day?"

"We're reviewing what we learned before break, so it is a free day."

"Awww."

"We love art, don't we, class?"

"Yeah, when are we going to draw some real things like a bowl of fruit?" Joshua yelled from the back of the room.

"Oh yeah, Ms. Anderson. I know what we can draw," added Mitchell, Joshua's No. 1 partner in crime.

"Oh really?" I asked, sorry I'd opened the door for any lewd comments.

"Yes, ma'am. We can draw Lakeisha," they said, pointing to Lakeisha Jenkins, who rolled her eyes and lashed out with a finger sign. She'd been retained in the sixth grade two years in a row, which made her more physically mature than your average sixth grader.

"Mitchell." I placed a hand on each hip.

"Ma'am?" he said, then sniggled.

"You owe Lakeisha an apology."

"Sorry, Lakeisha." The class roared with laughter when he looked at her and sounded out every syllable.

"Now it's your turn, Lakeisha."

"Sorry, Ms. Anderson." She looked at Mitchell and rolled her eyes again.

"Would each of you like a zero for the day?" I threatened, trying to hold back laughter myself.

"No ma'am," someone's voice echoed from the back of the room. "No ma'am. My mama would kill me. I just got a new X-box for Christmas," another student added.

"Calm down, class and let's get started."

"Yes ma'am. We'll be quiet," Mitchell volunteered, then sshh'd his other classmates.

"Keeping in mind the following terms, I want you to draw a picture showing a special moment during your Christmas break." I turned on the very used overhead projector, then held it with both hands to stop the table with loose legs from rocking. "The terms are color, texture, line, and space. Before we start, let's take a moment to review the terms. Who can define 'line'?" I asked, then waited on a show of hands.

"Marques, would you define it for the class?" I smiled when Marques responded with the correct definition. "Thank you, Marques. You have until the end of class to work on your assignment. If it isn't complete, take it home and bring it back tomorrow." My cell phone started to vibrate so I reached into my pocket. Hoping it wasn't an emergency, I turned my back to the class and pulled it out. It was a text message from Courtney:

Missing U.

Miss U2, I responded, hoping no one noticed, then wiped the smile off my face before turning back around.

"How's it going?" I asked, stepping away from my desk and walking around the classroom.

"I still want to draw Lakeisha," Mitchell said underneath his breath.

"Mitchell," I said sharply.

"Yes, ma'am."

"Finishing the drawing is your homework assignment," I said when the bell rang for dismissal. Papers rustled as they scurried to pack up and move to their next class.

"Did you think I would forget?" Cathy Sue asked after tapping on my door and peeping inside the room.

"Nothing gets by you, does it?" My morning had gone well, but I'd decided to stay in my room for lunch and catch up on some lesson plans.

"Not eating lunch in the break room. Now that's a first." As if someone was listening she looked over her shoulder, then closed the door. "Guess what?" she asked, holding up her lunch bag. "I'm going to join you." She wet a paper towel at the small sink by the door, wiped off a student's desk, and sat down in front of me. "We only have twenty-five minutes left, so I'm listening." She crossed her legs, took an apple out of her bag, and took a huge bite.

"Where do you want me to start?" All I could do was laugh at her antics. Ready to give her my attention, I closed my calendar and moved it to one side.

"I want you to start from the beginning." She dabbed each corner of her mouth with a napkin.

"You know, the usual information, like his name, his mother's name, where you met him. You know the drill."

"His name is Courtney, and I met him at a Christmas party," I said dryly, without smiling.

"Umm hmm. So you think I'm supposed to believe that ole Courtney from a Christmas party made you strut like that? Try again," she said, then leaned her head to one side.

"Whew . . . ," I said, then crossed my legs at the ankles thinking about the effect he had on me earlier. "His name really is Courtney and I met him at a Christmas party Anyah invited me to."

Cathy Sue fanned her fingers for more information. "He's single, never married, and no children. Works as a police officer and is very kind to the eyes."

"He's been kind to more than your eyes." She turned up one corner of her mouth.

"Excuse me," I said when I felt my cell phone vibrate in my pocket. "Hello."

"Is now a bad time?" Courtney asked.

"Actually it's not. I was having lunch." I pointed at my cell phone and lip-synched to Cathy Sue. "This is Courtney."

"Oh, I see," he said slowly, as if he wanted to say more. "I was on my way to the gym. I hadn't heard from you and was calling to leave a message."

"Talk to you later," Cathy Sue whispered, repacked her lunch bag, then tapped on my desk. "We're not done yet." As if to say, "Yes, we were done," I waved at her, then nodded my head up and down.

"Sorry to disappoint you by answering the phone. Now I guess you'll have to tell me personally."

"Here it goes." He cleared his throat. "Roses are

red, violets are blue, calling to say you're beautiful and I was thinking about you. What do you think?"

"Very original." I turned my chair to one side and looked out the window. I had been thinking about him too. He wasn't poetic, but his corny antics still made me blush.

"Glad you like it."

"I'll give you an *A* for effort. It was either that or you repeating the words of a song to me."

"Seriously, though. I'm glad I went to another one of those boring Christmas parties."

"Boring? Would you say the last one was boring?"

"It was far from boring. I met you and have enjoyed every single moment."

"I'm sorry, but the bell just rang. I need to get ready for my next class."

"Will I hear from you when you get off from work?"

"Definitely." Wearing a smile, I repacked my half-eaten lunch and put it away.

Chapter 9

Courtney

"Hey, Courtney," Juanna, a bartender from a local gentlemen's club, sang once I walked by the section of treadmills situated in the center of the gym.

"Hello," I said and didn't turn my head to acknowledge her presence. Not thinking about bumping into her, my goal had been to work out early so I could see Tatiana when she got off. Hoping Juanna wouldn't say anything else, I took longer steps toward the locker room.

"Hello?" she said loudly, hit the stop button, then hopped off her treadmill. "At the club you were my best friend. Now you don't know me. What's up with that?" she asked with an attitude after walking up behind me.

Not in the mood for drama, I turned around, then tried not to stare at her bulging double Ds. She was wearing a black bra top and matching Lycra biking shorts. I had to admit the girl was fine as hell. "I really don't have much time," I said, not wanting to put my business out on Front Street,

and regretting I'd ever had sex with her. One night
at the club and three beers too many, her big ass
and store-bought boobs started to look exceptionally good. I liked what I saw, had some extra cash,
and decided to take her out dancing after hours. A
slow dance led to a kiss, then another kiss led to
rubbing and grinding. Before long, we'd left the
club and I was paying for a hotel room. The sex was
the bomb, and after that night, all my drinks at the
club were on the house. A few telephone conversations and hotel visits later, she thought we were es-
tablishing a relationship of some sort and joined
my gym. For me it was only good sex—nothing
more and nothing less. The first time I saw her
there, I played it off, changed my workout time
from mornings to late evenings, and patronized another gentlemen's club.

"Ummph." She jerked her head back so hard
the clip on her ponytail almost flew off. Then she
looked me up and down.

"Please, Juanna, enjoy your workout." I'd been
going to the same gym for six years, and everyone
knew me. If they didn't know me from the gym,
they knew me from the streets. Even though the
other guests continued to work out, I knew they
were watching and listening. I was embarrassed as
hell and wanted to turn around and walk out the
front door.

"Oh, and tell your boy Octavious I said the pleasure was all mine." She flung her ponytail back,
stuck out her butt, and swished away.

"Yeah." I held my shoulders back like nothing
had happened and went into the locker room.
Frustrated that she'd taken up at least five of my
minutes, I found an empty locker and took off my
sweats. To plan my workout just right, I looked at

the time on my cell phone, got my towel, gloves, and bottled water out of my gym bag, and stuffed it inside the locker. To avoid another confrontation, I turned on my i-pod, adjusted the volume as high as it would go, and hit the incline bench first. It was the closest bench to the locker room door and the farthest away from Juanna.

Tatiana should be off by now, I thought at the end of my workout an hour later, lifting the weight bar until it was secure on the rack. *Good, it's twenty minutes before five.* I took a sip of water, removed my gloves, and wiped off my face with a towel. Hoping she'd at least be in her car, I hurried to dress and get my things out of the locker room, then left. As soon as I got into the car, I dialed her number.

"Hello, Courtney."

"How was your first day back at work?" I asked when she answered, put the key into the ignition, and turned it.

"It was good. You know, the students couldn't wait to see each other and brag about their gifts."

"Yeah, I remember the first day back to school after Christmas break. Everyone couldn't wait to show off their new outfits and shoes." I put the car into reverse, looked over my shoulder, then put it back into park. For some odd reason, I wanted her to have all my attention.

"So you can imagine how high-spirited they were today."

"Oh yeah, I can imagine. Are you tired?" I asked, thinking it would be the perfect opportunity for me to do something considerate, if she was.

"Not really. Why do you ask?"

"If you haven't already made plans, I'd like to eat dinner with you. That's if you're in the mood for take-out."

"What did you have in mind?"

"Chinese."

"I would love to have Chinese for dinner."

"Let me guess. Sweet and sour chicken, extra sauce, and egg rolls."

"You're very close," she laughed. "I'd like sweet and sour chicken with extra sauce and two egg rolls. I love Chinese food."

"I'll call the order in and pick it up. Since I was off today, that's the least I could do."

"You're great. I can't wait to see you again."

"See you in a couple of hours." "Can't wait to see you again," I repeated to myself. *Sounds like she missed me,* I thought as I drove out of the parking lot.

Tatiana

"Will I ever get any grandchildren from you one day?"

"A simple 'Hello and how are you doing' would be nice," I answered, gasping for breath after getting out of the shower wet and rushing to answer the telephone. If it was Courtney calling, I didn't want my answering machine to pick up. I looked over my shoulder and laughed at the trail of wet footprints I'd left on the floor. "Where did that comment come from?" I asked with a confused look, pressed the button to engage my speaker phone, and followed the wet pattern of footprints back into the bathroom.

"What did you say?" she asked loudly.

"Where did that comment come from?" I repeated loud enough for her to hear me, grabbed my large towel off the hook on the door, and patted myself dry.

"Do you have me on that darn speaker phone again?" she asked, sounding frustrated.

"Yes, Mother, but that's not the issue right now. Please explain your comment."

"I was just sitting here watching television and got all emotional during an AT&T commercial." I stopped moving when I heard a few sniffles in the background. It sounded like she was crying. "The grandchildren were calling their grandmother long distance to say 'Happy Holidays.' It was adorable." She blew her nose loudly into the telephone. "Excuse me. That commercial really got to me."

"Hmm . . . sounds like a very heartwarming commercial," I said, thinking I'd never seen a long-distance telephone commercial that made me want to cry.

"I told James when you were three years old we should have another child. You needed someone to play with, plus it would have increased my odds of becoming a grandmother. Did he listen to me? No, he didn't," she spat into the phone, suddenly sounding temperamental.

"Did you take your hormone pills today?" I asked, regretting the day she started experiencing menopausal symptoms. In less than one minute, her emotions had gone from one extreme to the other.

"Hmm, let's see. Now that you ask, I don't remember," she said calmly, then chuckled at herself. "Anyway, I'm thinking about going natural. These hormone pills could give me breast cancer. Plus, I don't remember from one day to the next if I took them or not."

"That's why I bought you a pill box with enough

compartments for one week. You know how your mode swings when you don't take your medicine," I said calmly, not wanting to contribute to the present emotional imbalance.

"Whether I took them or not, a couple of grandchildren would be nice."

"Don't I need a husband first?" I looked at the clock on my nightstand.

"That was my next question. When are you coming back to church?"

"I don't know," I answered vaguely. I had had no intention of ever going back after my father's funeral. He had been a tithe-paying usher and Mother sang in the choir every Sunday and never missed a rehearsal. When he was diagnosed with lung cancer, Mother solicited help from the church and all she got was, "Sister, we'll keep you in our prayers." Hurt by their response—or lack of one—I attended the funeral but vowed never to go back.

"Well, you need to come back and rededicate your life to the Lord. You grew up there. Plus, church is the perfect place for you to meet the father of my grandchildren. Every woman needs a God-fearing man in her life."

"Umm hmm." I rolled my eyes to the top of my head. Mother knew how I felt about returning to church but said like Jesus I needed to forgive.

"Don't ignore me, because you're not getting any younger," she said, using that tone of voice that made me feel like an adolescent.

"Yes, Mother." Like a child, I flopped down on the side of my bed to apply my scented lotion.

"Listen," she said, sharply demanding my attention. "Two weeks ago, a nice young man joined our congregation. He's thirty-six, an electrical engineer working on his master's degree, good credit because he drives a new Mercedes, never been married, and has only one son," she said all in one breath. "At least I could have one grandchild to spoil," she said under her breath but loud enough for me to hear.

"I don't believe you," I said after she quoted his statistics. "Did you memorize his license plate number?" I asked ironically.

"No, because I didn't have on my good glasses."

"Mother," I sang into the telephone.

"Don't play with me. This is serious business," she said, then laughed in spite of herself.

"You know my career goals. Getting married and having children isn't a perfect fit right now." I looked at my reflection in the mirror and visualized a relationship with Courtney instead.

"Why don't you go with me to Bible study tonight? Last week he was in the new members' orientation class. Oh, did I tell you he's tall and a sight for sore eyes?" Like any mother would, she ignored my comment and continued to talk.

"Mother, that's great. I'm sure he'll make someone a fantastic husband," I said, then imagined what he really looked like. A sight for sore eyes to a mother and daughter could be two different things. Painting a mental picture of a partially bald man with a bulging midsection, I went into my closet and got out a clingy two-piece cotton jogging suit. Half-listening to mother's plan for my future, I got dressed.

"My point exactly. Bertha Jennings has already claimed him for her daughter. She was telling another choir member about him at rehearsal last night. I wouldn't be surprised if that demon hadn't already invited him over for homemade apple pie. So we don't have time to waste. Honey, your biological clock is ticking."

"No, I'm not getting younger, but didn't you

teach me to wait on the good Lord to send me a husband? So that means I don't have to go to church to find him," I said, knowing that would irritate her to the point of ending the conversation.

"Oh Lord, look at the time. I'm running late. I'll talk to you later. Love you." She blew a kiss into the telephone.

"Love you, too, Mother," I sang with a smile, then ended our call. Our agendas were totally different. She was thinking husband and grandchildren and I was thinking career first, husband maybe. For that very reason alone, I hadn't told her about Courtney. She'd invite him to church on Sunday morning and dinner afterward to ask one hundred and one questions. *Perfect timing,* I thought when I heard the doorbell ring. Before opening the door, I checked my outfit in the mirror and rubbed my fingers through my hair.

"Hello, beautiful." He was holding a greasy-bottomed brown paper sack in each arm and wearing faded blue jeans with a navy blue sweatshirt.

"It smells delicious." I took a bag out of his arm, shut the door, and admired his physique as I followed him into the kitchen. We placed the bags on the counter, then greeted each other with a hug and kiss.

"Yummy," he said, then smacked his lips. As if it had been days since we'd seen each other, he leaned down and kissed me again.

"You're acting like you missed me." I pulled out of his embrace.

"Can't you tell?"

"Missed you, too," I said with a smile, unable to count how many times I'd actually thought about him that day. "Like your kisses, dinner is hot." I got clean plates and glasses out of the cabinet while

Courtney unpacked the bags and placed the food on the table. He took off his jacket and draped it over the back of the chair.

"I brought two movies from home for us to watch. One is a comedy, and the other is a bang bang shoot 'em up." He held them both up for me to see. "Which one would you like to watch first?"

"I want to laugh tonight." Wanting limited sexual content, I pointed at the comedy. During dinner I didn't want any unnecessary distractions.

"We can watch this one another time." He placed the other movie on the counter.

"Great, let's fix our plates and eat in front of the television."

"Sounds like a plan." He started to open the white cartons while I got sodas out of the refrigerator and poured them. We each made mounds on our plate, then went into the great room. Courtney became comfortable on the floor while I started the movie.

"Can we watch this and eat?"

"Of course we can." He patted the floor beside him for me to sit down. I sat down, then stretched my legs out.

"I should have saved the second egg roll for later," I said after my final bite, leaning my head back on the couch and rubbing my stomach.

"Don't worry. It will be gone in less than two hours. You know how Chinese food does you. It's in one way and out the other."

"You're crazy," I said, laughing at his bluntness.

"See, listen. What did I tell you?" He rubbed his stomach when it started to churn.

"Oh my goodness, what did you swallow?" I asked playfully, rubbing his stomach.

"This is what I swallowed." He grabbed my other

hand and placed it on his stomach. I laughed as he pulled my body closer, then leaned me back onto his chest. A playful moment became serious when I began to rub his stomach with one hand and massage a nipple with the other. "This is what I really swallowed." He leaned over for a kiss. One at a time, we eased our legs from beneath the table. Soon our bodies were outstretched on the carpeted floor and he was positioning me on top of him. In the heat of the moment, I pressed my torso against him and began to rotate my hips. He lowered my head, then whispered into my ear, "I want you."

"No more than I want you." I held his sweatshirt by the waist and pulled it over his head. Soon the moment became intense, as we took no care in how our clothes came off and where they were thrown. He sat up, wrapped my legs around his waist, then stood. With ease, he carried me into the bedroom and placed me in the center of the bed. "Don't move," he said, holding up his hand and stepping back. Turned on by his sensual tone of voice, I inhaled and didn't move a muscle. "Your body is perfect." As though interpreting a fine piece of art, he leaned back and placed a finger over his mouth.

"Thank you." I repositioned my legs into a more seductive pose.

"Right there. Keep it right there." He started to walk toward me.

Chapter 10

Tatiana

At what I thought to be the first indication of daylight, my eyes opened. Tucked tightly beside Courtney, I stared at the ceiling, then turned my head suddenly in a panic to look at the clock. What started out as dinner and a movie had turned into a lovemaking marathon. Like a WWE wrestler, he tossed me effortlessly from one position to another, barely giving me time to recover between orgasms. The sex was wild and untamed. Neither of us could seem to get enough of each other. "Courtney," I called softly, then rubbed his arm before sitting up in bed and turning back the covers. At some point during the night we'd exhausted ourselves and finally fallen asleep. "Courtney," I said again when he didn't respond, and rocked his shoulder back and forth.

"Yes, baby." He turned onto his side with an arm lifted to embrace me.

"Are you off again today?" I asked after looking

Recha G. Peay

at the clock and realizing I'd fallen asleep before setting the alarm.

"I go back Tuesday morning." He moaned, turned onto his back, and pulled the cover over his chest.

"It *is* Tuesday morning." I leaned to one side, unsure how he would respond to being late.

"Dammit." Like a jack-in-the-box, he popped straight up. "What time is it?" he asked, looking around the room with wild eyes.

"It's fifteen minutes after six."

"Hell, I hate being late for work." With wide eyes, he turned and looked at me. "Where are my clothes?" He patted around the bed, then threw the covers back.

"They're in the other room where we undressed." Naked, he hopped out of bed and rushed into the great room. I got out of bed, grabbed my robe, and put it on as I followed him.

"I can still make it on time from here." He snatched his pants off the back of the couch and hopped on one leg to put them on. Still anxious, he got his shirt, pulled it on over his head, and stuck his feet into his tennis shoes. "I have an extra uniform in the car." He hurried to the door and fumbled with the lock.

"Let me get it." I unlocked it with one smooth turn and opened the door. He brushed past me, almost stepping on my foot, went to his car, and returned with a large, black duffel bag. "Please accept my apology. I didn't know you were scheduled to work." I followed behind as he took long, heavy steps into the bedroom, dropped his bag on the floor, and opened it. He yanked out his uniform, gave it a few hard shakes, and went into the bathroom. "Let me get you some soap and a clean washcloth." When I turned around, he'd already shed his clothes and gotten into the shower. "I have your washcloth." He opened the shower door and stuck out his hand with wide spread fingers to get it.

"Coffee?" I asked over the running water.

"Black," he said, splashing water with his washcloth over the top of the shower, hurrying to finish.

Feeling somewhat responsible, I went into the kitchen and started a pot of coffee. *Next time I'll remember to ask,* I thought to myself before realizing there was no reason for me to assume total blame for the oversight. *Not once during the entire evening did we discuss his work schedule,* I rationalized, pouring Courtney a cup of coffee, then turning to take it to him.

"Talk to you later." Courtney snatched the cup of coffee out of my hand and left. Expecting a good-bye kiss, I stood in the middle of the floor and listened as his engine roared and his tires squealed when he backed out of the driveway. Ignoring his abruptness, and blaming it on anxiety, I locked the door and went into the bedroom to shower and get dressed for work.

"Remember me?" Anyah asked, skipping formalities, as usual, when I answered the telephone.

"Good morning, girlfriend," I responded, happy to hear her voice, then gave Courtney's bad attitude another thought. We had hit it off so well the night of the party that everything between us had moved unusually fast. With Courney, I'm blissfully happy. Although his sensitive and romantic sides were the only traits I encountered. Then I realized that, being caught up in the highs of a new romance, it was only natural for a person to put on his best face at all times.

"Damn, is it that good, you've forgotten my name and number already?"

"Girl, shut up." Just that fast my thoughts reverted to a position from the night before. Courtney was standing up and had my legs wrapped around his body. He used his arms and with no effort at all moved me back and forth. *Hmmph he is good*, I thought, then blamed his abruptness on his being late. With lovemaking that good, some things, like a bad morning, could be overlooked.

"Well, is it?" she asked again when I didn't answer. "We haven't talked since last week."

"You know you're my girl," I said, wanting to avoid the sex conversation, then walked into my closet to find an outfit for work. "I was going to call you—" Grasping for an excuse, I looked into the air.

"Umm hmm . . ." she said before I completed my sentence. "Is he there now?"

"Noo," I sang, looking toward my bed and smiling at another unusual position we tried after turning onto our sides and interlocking our legs. Together we gyrated like serpentines on a pole.

"Oh, see, there. So that means he just left. You can't hide nothing from me. I can hear it in the tone of your voice."

All I could do was laugh.

"Anyway, I know you're getting ready for work, but you can spare five minutes. We haven't had the girlfriend talk yet."

"For you, yes, I can spare five minutes." We were girls, but some things, like toe-curling, breathtaking sex, weren't meant to be shared. I didn't mind telling her about the guys that were OK in bed, but Courtney was an exception to the "girlfriend" rule. The secret things she shared about Xavier were done so on a volunteer basis. I never asked.

"Hell, I know you can. For lack of time, let's skip the boring details. He's had you tied up since the party. All I want to know is, is the sex as good as he looks?"

"It's better than good," I said omitting any specific details. "But good sex isn't everything." Not believing myself, I rolled my eyes to the top of my head.

"What?" she screamed into my ear. "I beg to differ. Good sex is everything. Any expert that says communication is the key to a successful relationship ain't getting any. Yeah, communication is the key all right. After a good orgasm or two, any problem in my house can be solved," she said, laughing.

"You are insane."

"No, girlfriend, I'm real."

"Bye. I'm going to be late for work," I said, looking at the clock. "I promise we'll talk later."

Courtney

Damn, I snatched the cup out of Tatiana's hand and didn't kiss her before leaving. That was messed up, I thought after hurling out of her driveway on two wheels. If I wanted to deal with Tatiana, my emotions had to stay in check. After the night we had, I couldn't afford to screw it up. Never in a million years did I think she would be that damn good in bed. Yeah, we'd made love since we met, but last night she unleashed the dragon on my ass. At the party I looked at her and saw conservative, but with the flick of the right switch she's outperformed anybody I'd ever been with. "Shit." I swore, then looked down at my cell phone. For me, she would be the ideal combination. A lady in the streets and a freak in the sheets. Wanting to make things right before clocking in, I dialed her number.

"Tatiana?" I asked slowly when she answered, to get a feel for her attitude. Trying to get to know one female was all new to me. In my world I had huge assets: good looks, a job with benefits—which the females loved—and my own place. But there was something about Tatiana that was starting to drive me insane.

"Yes?" Then there was silence. "Good morning, Courtney," she said in a dry tone I'd never heard before. It was the first time I didn't hear the smile in her voice. "Did you make it to work on time?"

"Yes, I'm turning into the parking lot right now." *Jackass*, I thought. *This could be your last conversation with her.* I had to apologize, and quick.

"Good."

"Tatiana?" I parked, grabbed my bag, and got out of the car.

"Yes."

"I'd like to apologize for being rude this morning." I took a deep breath. "Being late for work is a huge pet peeve of mine. Hope you understand." I exhaled.

"Oh yeah, I understand. Have a good day at work and be careful."

"You do the same." I felt a little more at ease. I closed my cell phone, then took long steps across the parking lot and into the precinct for roll call. Some things only happened once in a lifetime. If she dumped me, I would regret it the rest of my life.

Chapter 11

Courtney

"Dammit, Octavious," I said when I saw his name on my caller ID. Already frustrated from running late, I rolled my eyes at the cell phone and didn't answer. To impress Tatiana for our "three-month milestone," I'd purchased tickets to see the Alvin Ailey dancers. Not that I knew a damn thing about the dance troupe, but I overheard two female officers raving about them last week in the break room. I stood by the door until I got enough details to make arrangements without involving them. Letting a female on the job see my romantic side was a negative.

"I don't have time, dawg," I said, not answering when my cell phone started to ring again. Looking like a dumb-ass, I'd been standing in the middle of my closet for fifteen minutes with a wet towel wrapped around my waist. The show was scheduled to start in less than two hours and I wasn't close to being ready. "To hell with it. The women I'd dated before her didn't do dance theatre. Hell, they barely did the movie theatre," I said, yanking a pair of black slacks off a hanger and finding a coordinating silk shirt and wool-blend sports jacket. *Tonight my charm will have to do,* I thought, grabbing my newest pair of black leather dress shoes and going into my bedroom to get dressed.

"Let me hit you back later, dawg," I answered after yanking my home phone off the base, realizing he was going to bug the hell outta me.

"'fore you hang up, got us VIP passes for your favorite gentlemen's club. As always, you can thank me later." Like a hyena, he laughed loudly into my ear.

"You'll have to find someone else tonight. My girl and I are going on a date," I said, thinking another lie would have been better. Since our rendezvous at the Embassy, I'd met him for drinks but came up with an outlandish lie to leave before things with the females ever got out of control. Leaving with one or two of them for a wild night of sex at the nearest but cheapest hotel wasn't uncommon.

After meeting Tatiana, I didn't want that lifestyle anymore. The routine of casually meeting, quickly impressing with any lie necessary, then sleeping with different females on a weekly—sometimes daily—basis had gotten old. Yes, there were a million and one fine females to date, but I wanted more than just casual sex.

"A date? That's what boyfriend and girlfriend do, not people that are jus' kickin' it."

"Hey, I'm already late. Hit you back later." I stepped into my pants and walked to my chest to find a pair of dress socks. That was the issue: I didn't want to just kick it with Tatiana anymore. I wanted to secure our relationship, make a commitment.

"Where in the hell yo' primitive ass taking a female?" he asked, ignoring my attempt to end the call.

"Out, man," I said, thinking that was the very reason I'd kept Tatiana on the low for three months.

"Like out to eat?"

"That's part of the plan," I said, not ready to get into a question and answer session with him.

"Hey, butthead, remember to eat with your utensils."

"Man, go to hell." I slipped my undershirt over my head, adjusted it, then put on my silk shirt.

"After dinner, then what?"

"Man, look, I gotta go."

"Oh, so you don't wanna to share? We been dawgs for how long now?"

"Alvin Ailey dancers," I said, allowing my voice to fade.

"Alley what?" he asked. "Never heard of that restaurant before."

"Fool, it's not a restaurant. We're going to see the Alvin Ailey dancers."

"Aww, hell, naw, you ain't. I'm on my way over right now to save your ass. So that's what you been doin' all this time. I'm thinking it was overtime, but now I see it was a female. You done let a female get to you. Don't you remember the first rule in the player's handbook? Never ever fall in love. Man, I'm officially taking away your player's card."

"Holla." I tossed the handset on the bed. I stood in the mirror and put on my sports coat, grabbed my keys off the nightstand, and left.

Tatiana

"Hello," I answered sensually when I saw his name on the caller ID. We'd been dating for three months and decided mutually to celebrate the milestone in our relationship. Courtney said our destination was a surprise, but he did tell me to wear my finest little black dress.

"You sound so sexy."

"You're such a charmer," I responded because sounding sexy was my intention all along.

I wanted everything from head to toe to be perfect, so I spent most of the evening preparing for our date. On my way home, I stopped by a full-service hair salon for a haircut and wash, French manicure, and pedicure. Shopping for a new dress wasn't necessary because there was a black halter minidress with plunging neckline hanging in my closet with the tags still attached. Anticipating our evening together, I put on my favorite India.Arie CD and imagined what was in store while driving home. Preserving my pedicure, I got out of the car still wearing lime green disposable flip-flops and tiptoed to my front door.

With two hours to spare, I showered in my most seductive Victoria's Secret scented body wash. *Three months,* I thought, patted myself dry, then sat down on my vanity stool to apply the scented lotion. I stood, readjusted the towel around my upper body, and took a few short steps to my closet. *Lovely,* I thought after getting my dress, shoes, and matching evening bag. Carefully I spread the dress on my bed, put the evening bag beside it, and placed my shoes on the floor.

"I'll be there in twenty minutes."

"I'll be waiting," I answered, sure to maintain the mellow tone he'd already complimented me on, then sat down in front of the mirror to apply my foundation.

"Tatiana."

"Yes?" I answered, tilting the small bottle just enough to wet my foam wedge with the brown liquid. Requiring minimal coverage, I blotted my nose with the sponge, then moved on to my right cheekbone, eventually covering my entire face.

"What are you wearing?"

"A dress." I turned to look over my shoulder at the little dress I'd laid so perfectly on my bed. Again I looked at my reflection, picked up an eye shadow brush and covered its tiny bristles in an earth-tone color with glittery highlights. One eye at a time, I closed them and applied my shadow.

"A dress? What type of dress?" he asked, sounding surprised.

"A black dress." With a large brush, I set my foundation with a mineral powder, lined my lips with a chestnut lip pencil, then filled them in with a light gold gloss that glittered as well.

"I want more details."

"Guess you'll have to see when you get here." Enjoying every second of the telephone play, I stood, walked to the bed, and picked up my dress. Like a princess before a ball, I placed it ever so gently against my body.

"What if I can't wait?"

"I promise it's worth the wait." I smiled when I heard the loud roar of his engine as he accelerated. "See you in a few minutes." Gracefully I turned to look at myself in the mirror. Pleased with the dramatic look I'd created, I removed my towel and carefully slipped the dress on over my head. I pulled it down over my hips, then tied a double knot behind my neck. Making sure everything was perfect before stepping into my black peep-toe pumps with the rhinestone accents, I modeled in the mirror. *Perfect*, I thought when the doorbell rang. I got my evening bag, which I'd laid out earlier, then glided to the door.

"Hello, handsome," I said after opening it.

"That is a no-no. Never open the door before asking who it is and looking through the peep-hole," Courtney said, waving his index finger.

"I knew it was you." I gestured with my hand for him to step inside while I got my wrap out of the closet.

"Never assume." He shut the door, then stopped me for a kiss on the lips.

"I forget you're a man of the law." Pretending to have an attitude, I placed a hand on my hip but checked him out from head to toe. Wearing black dress pants and a coordinating sports coat, he looked like a million dollars.

"You look absolutely beautiful. Turn around and let me look at you."

I stood in front of him and turned around slowly, making sure he got a glimpse of my dress from every angle. He pulled me to him, lifted my chin with his finger, and leaned down for another kiss. Unconcerned with my makeup, I didn't resist as he put a hand on either side of my face, and leaned my head to one side. "Umm," I said as he rolled his tongue down the side of my neck.

"Whew, let's go before we're late," he said, stop-ping suddenly and embracing me.

"I could never agree more." I opened my purse to remove a compact, checked my lipstick, then re-touched my makeup with a powder sponge.

"You're still beautiful."

"I'm sure your opinion is biased." I closed my purse and handed him my wrap.

"Are you ready for a night on the town?" I turned around and waited as he opened the wrap and draped it over my shoulders.

"Ready," I said, anticipating every moment of his

surprise date as we walked out the door and to his car. Before driving away, he lifted my hand and kissed it gently. With both hands, I grasped his, placed it over my heart, then rested it on my lap. For the next ten minutes we reminisced about the first night we met.

"The Alvin Ailey American Dance Theater," I said, once we drove by the downtown performing arts center and turned into the parking lot.

"Surprised?"

"Am I!" I knew they were in town but never imagined asking Courtney to purchase tickets.

"Hold on to your seat, pretty lady, this is only the beginning," he said before getting out of the car and walking around to assist me. Hand in hand, we walked across the almost filled parking lot, then waited in the short line to gain entrance to the theatre.

"We still have a few minutes before the show starts," Courtney said after looking at the time on his cell phone. "Would you like a glass of wine?"

"A glass of wine sounds good." Still holding hands, we walked toward the cash bar located in the lobby and purchased drinks. We each took a few sips, then found an entrance and waited to be seated by a hostess. "This is perfect," I said, referring to our seats, which were in the center aisle and only six rows away from the stage.

"Nothing but the best for you," he said, reaching over to rub my leg as the lights dimmed and music started to play. The curtain lifted as darkness slowly revealed itself, then transformed before us in the blink of an eye. Panels of sheer white material served as a backdrop, giving the impression of wind as they whisked to and fro. I panted when a male and female dancer, both dressed in white, appeared to float effortlessly from the ceiling, like two doves being born into a world of nothingness. Their romantic interpretation of life and death left me amazed.

My hormone level soared during another scene when a male dancer, lying flat on his back, used his stomach muscles to move like a centipede across the stage. When Courtney rubbed my thigh, the sudden wetness made me want to grab my purse and hurry home to make mad, passionate love to him. "Umph," I said below my breath, crossing my legs to ease the tingling sensation that pulsated from my vagina to the tip of my big toe.

"Enjoy the show?" Courtney asked two hours later once the curtain fell and the lights came on.

Instead of giving a verbal response, I leaned over and kissed him on the lips.

"I'll take that as a 'yes,'" he said as we stood and moved out into the aisle.

"A definite 'yes,'" I said as he reached for my hand and wrapped his arm around my shoulder.

Courtney

"How may I help you this evening?" asked the middle-aged maître'd, who was wearing a black tux with tails, stiff white shirt, and white gloves, and who spoke from behind the large mahogany podium as we entered the lobby.

"I have a nine o'clock reservation for two," I said proudly because it had taken me two weeks to make a decision. I wanted to take her somewhere she'd never been before. So I made reservations at Joseph's, an exclusive downtown restaurant. It was on the rooftop of a five-star hotel. Other than the city's elite, very few people ate there.

"Last name, please, sir?" he asked, using a gloved finger to check a list in front of him.

"Wilkes," I said, watching Tatiana's response closely while he verified our reservations.

"Mr. Wilkes, please follow me." Like a church usher, he put one hand behind his back and gave directives with the other one.

"Thank you." I stepped to one side so Tatiana could walk in front of me.

"Will this table be OK for you tonight, sir?" he asked after leading us to a small, square table in front of a huge picture window facing the outdoor garden area.

"Yes, this is fine," I said after Tatiana smiled, nodding her head up and down.

"Great." He pulled out her chair, and with one shake spread a white linen table napkin that was folded like a triangle in the middle of her place setting and placed it on her lap. I sat down and leaned back as he did the same for me. "Juan will be your server tonight." He waved his arm at the young man wearing a white tuxedo shirt, black cummerbund, and pants already walking toward our table with a smile. "Please enjoy your meals," the gentleman said with a slight nod before walking away.

"What do you think?"

"I think it's wonderful." She smiled, looking around. The fluorescent accent lights were dimmed, creating a romantic ambience. Each table, covered with a burgundy tablecloth, had a small, white candle burning in the center.

"Good evening. My name is Juan and I will be your server for the evening," the tall, slender young man said, then displayed a bottle of wine. "Merlot is our house wine for the day. Would you like a sample?" he asked, placing a wine glass in front of each of us.

"Yes, please." We waited as he poured a small amount into each of our glasses before placing a menu in front of us.

"The entrée for the day is Englewood Farms Chicken Breast, wonderfully prepared and covered with a saffron broth. It is to die for," he said, blowing a kiss into the air. "May I take your drink order while you take a few moments to look over the menu?"

"Tatiana, what would you like to drink?" I asked.

"I'd like a glass of Merlot."

"And for you, sir?"

"Rémy VSOP with coke," I said, opening my menu.

"Please take your time and I'll be back with your drinks."

Tatiana opened her menu, closed it, then leaned forward. "Courtney, this is really nice for a three-month celebration."

"Maybe, but for me it's been a great three months. So please enjoy your meal," I said as the waiter returned with our drinks.

"Merlot for you and a Rémy VSOP and coke for the gentleman. Would you like to start off your meal with an appetizer?" he asked, looking at Tatiana.

"No thank you," she responded, looking up.

"Would you like some more time to peruse the menu?"

"Yes, please give us a few more minutes," I said, unable to pronounce half of the items on the menu.

"Let me know when you're ready." He smiled, nodded his head, and walked away. We looked over our menus for a few minutes, then waved when we were ready to order. Wearing that same "I love my job" smile, he walked toward our table and took our orders. Tatiana ordered wild salmon and I chose the featured entrée.

"The show was spectacular. I'd heard rave reviews about them but never had an opportunity to see a live performance. But I have a confession to make." Tatiana leaned forward as though she was getting ready to tell me a secret.

"What is it?" I asked, leaning toward her.

"I knew they were in town for performances, but dared not ask you to take me."

"And why not?"

"Please. I never imagined you watching men in leotards leaping across a stage." She chuckled. "But for a man I guess there was an upside. The females did have bodies to die for."

"Ahh, you have a point. So there was something for both of us to enjoy." Our conversation continued until our meals arrived. Even then we talked. There was something I wanted to discuss with her but didn't know the right time. In the middle of our meal, I put down my fork and reached across the table for her hand.

"Is everything OK?" She put her fork down and patted each corner of her mouth with her napkin.

"Yes. Tatiana, we've dated for a solid three months now. I don't know why, but it seems like I've known you forever."

"I hope that's a good thing." With a confused expression, she smiled slightly. She had no idea where the conversation was going.

"In a way it is, but I don't know." I couldn't help but frown. "I want to be with you every day."

"You are with me every day."

"No, that's not what I mean. I want to fall asleep with you in my arms at night and wake up with you in the morning."

"Oh," she said, then took a sip of wine.

"I'd like for us to move in together and make our relationship official."

"Really?" she asked, taking another sip of wine. "What do you mean by 'official'?" she asked, leaning her head to one side.

"I'm ready for us to take our relationship to another level."

"Hmm."

"What are you thinking?" I asked, wanting to know what was going through her mind.

"I'm totally caught off guard by your suggestion. I never thought it would be a man's idea to move in with his girlfriend. Most men I know would run and hide at the first indication of their girlfriends wanting to move in together." She looked at me, then took another sip of wine.

"I'm not expecting an answer this second, but just think about it." Sharing my thoughts made me nervous as hell, but her response made me more nervous. Talking about everything except moving in together, we finished our meals. I waved my hand to get the waiter's attention for the bill. He unfolded a leather case, stood it up on the table facing me, then waited as I slipped my bank card into the clear vinyl pocket. He nodded his head and walked away. A few minutes later, he returned with my receipt. We finished our drinks and left. In silence we rode to her condo.

Tatiana

"Thank you for a fantastic evening," I said after opening the door and stepping inside. "Everything from the theater to dinner was well thought out. I really appreciate it." I looked into his eyes and gently rubbed the side of his face with the back of my hand. I couldn't interpret his expression, but imagined he was anxious to know how I felt about his proposition at dinner to move in with me. Yes, we'd dated for three months, and I had to admit it was the best three months of my life. But moving in together was a huge step. In so many words, he would reap the benefits of a marriage but without the legalities. In terms of career goals, I had several, but becoming a permanent friend with benefits wasn't one of them.

"You're more than welcome," he said, then moved stiffly to one side while I closed and locked the door.

"It's gotten late. Are you scheduled to work in the morning?" I remembered to ask, never wanting to repeat the first time I saw him upset.

"Yes, I have to work." He eased his cell phone out of his pocket to check the time.

"I'm sure it's after midnight. You're more than welcome to stay."

"Thanks," he said, but didn't move away from the front door.

"Would you like another drink?" I asked, wanting to ease the apparent tension so we could at least finish our conversation.

"Please," he said with a slight tremor in his voice, then folded his hands in front of him.

"Let me get comfortable." I went into the bedroom to undress and change into something more comfortable. I was shocked when he didn't follow me but sat on the couch instead. Unsure how the evening would resolve itself, I stepped out of my shoes and placed my purse on the dresser. Looking at my reflection in the mirror, I untied my dress, then held it as I allowed it to fall around my ankles. I stepped out of it, tossed it over my arm, and went into the closet to hang it. Since it was late, I slipped on a pair of dark blue cotton pajama pants and matching lace spaghetti strap camisole.

"This feels so much better," I said after going back into the room with him. Sitting with a hand on either side of his body, he didn't move but followed me with his eyes. I walked into the kitchen, poured a glass of cranberry juice for myself and fixed him a Rémy with coke. "This one is for you." I handed him his drink and sat down on the couch beside him.

He took one swallow. "Tatiana, have I screwed up?" He took another swallow, then placed his glass on the table.

"No, you haven't screwed up."

"Why didn't you respond at dinner?"

"Moving in together?" I placed my glass on the table and turned to look at him. "That is a huge decision to make. I've got to be honest with you. I'm not used to a man making the suggestion. Like I said earlier, most men would run never to be heard from again, when a girlfriend wants to take the relationship to another level," I said, making quotation marks in the air to emphasize *another level*.

"Yeah, I had to ask myself that same question. What bachelor wants to give up his freedom?" Courtney asked, his eyebrows meeting as he frowned.

"My point exactly. We've dated three months and I've had a great time, but there's a lot of territory we haven't covered."

"Let's cover it," he said, turning to face me.

"Marriage. Children. Future career plans. Retirement plans. Savings. You know, the list goes on and on. Other than the great sex we've been having, have you seriously thought about any of those things?" I asked sternly. He rolled his neck around, then leaned his head back on the couch. "My point exactly. You haven't."

"Yes, I've thought about them, but not in great detail. All I know is that when I go to bed at night and wake up the next morning, I want you in my arms. I don't believe I'm saying this, but I'm falling in love, and I want to see where this emotion is going to lead me."

At a loss for words, I looked into his eyes and yes, it was there. For the first time, he allowed me to see into the deepest part of his soul. "You're not alone. I'm falling in love with you, too," I said, then leaned his head over, allowing it to rest on my shoulder. He kissed me gently on the neck, then stood and extended his arms. I rose and followed his lead into the bedroom.

"I want tonight to be different." He went into my bathroom and returned holding three red candles that were on my bathtub. I watched as he lit them and placed one on each nightstand and the other one on my dresser. "Come here." He motioned with his hands until I was standing in front of him. He tucked his hands inside the elastic waistband of my pants, then eased them down around my ankles. All I could do was place my hands on his shoulders and step out. He started at my ankle, then rolled his tongue up my leg and inner thigh.

"Courtney," I said as he eased his hand underneath my shirt, unfastened my bra, and lifted my arms to remove my top. As if one piece, both articles of clothing fell to the floor.

"No, don't move." I watched as he unfastened his shirt, tossed it to one side, and unfastened his pants. "I want you to take them off," he said, then looked down. "You're so beautiful," he said when I'd lowered them until they rested around his ankles. Then he looked up. He stepped out of his pants and extended his arms for me to stand. "This is what I want every day for the rest of my life." He looked into my eyes as he got down onto one knee and began to orally massage my clitoris. My head fell backward and my knees got weak. With a firm grasp on my hips, he allowed me to take baby steps and move backward until the backs of my legs were against the bed. Gently, he lowered me onto the bed and leaned my body back as the forbidden kisses continued.

"I want you now," I said as my breathing became shallower. Rapidly he flicked his tongue back and forth, then tugged my pearl gently. He stood, placed a knee on either side of me, then lowered his body, almost touching me. He reached for my hand and allowed me to feel his fullness. With that same hand, I ushered him inside me. Gently but passionately we moved as one to complete the chorus of a sweet song. "The answer is yes. I want you to move in with me," I sang into his ear as my muscles contracted uncontrollably and sweet juices flowed.

Chapter 12

Tatiana

It was a beautiful Saturday morning. The sun was shining and the temperature was mild, with a slight eastern breeze. Courtney called from his cell phone to let me know he was only a minute away. I walked to the front door and watched as he turned the corner and backed the small moving van into the driveway. Feeling both excited and apprehensive, I knew our decision to live together would develop or destroy what we thought was the beginning of a good relationship. So many times I'd heard that people changed when they either moved in together or got married. Hoping neither would be the case with Courtney, I was willing to put all my chips on the table. Worst-case scenario, it didn't work out and we'd both go our separate ways. Best-case scenario, our love would grow, we'd get married, and live happily ever after.

"Whatcha doing, girlfriend?" Anyah asked when I finally answered the telephone.

"Nothing, really." I folded my arm across my

chest and leaned back against the door. Over the past month, our conversations had become somewhat limited. I was embarking on new territory with Courtney and didn't want my decisions to be influenced by her strong opinions.

"What's 'nothing, really'?"

"I was standing in the door enjoying this fresh breeze." The moving van coughed, letting off a small, gray puff of smoke, then jerked when Courtney stopped and put it into park. The door on the driver's side opened and he jumped out wearing a huge smile. I acknowledged him with a wave of the hand and pointed at the handset. He nodded and waved back.

"It's Saturday morning and I was hoping we could go out clearance shopping."

"Today isn't a good day because I've already made plans." I watched as Courtney lifted the back door, extended the silver ramp, and walked up its center, momentarily disappearing inside the truck. One at a time, he unloaded variously sized brown cardboard boxes and placed them in the driveway. All I could do was cross my legs at the ankles. He was wearing baggy blue jeans and a long-sleeved thermal shirt. It was fitted in all the right places and allowed me to see the perfect V shape that formed where his broad shoulders tapered into his small waistline.

"What plan of yours is more important than a day chasing sales? Never mind. It must involve Courtney. What was I thinking? I ain't mad at you, though. Things must be going pretty good between you and Fabio."

"Courtney's moving in," I interjected, knowing if I didn't tell her, she would eventually figure it out. Sooner or later, he would be answering the telephone.

"What in the hell did you just say?"

"I said Courtney's moving in."

"We've talked and you never said nothing about him moving in with you. Damn, is the sex that good? When did all of this take place?"

"We made the decision about a week ago."

"You've only know him . . . three months."

"I know how long it's been. You were with me the night we met."

"You know you're my girl. Hell, you're like a little sister to me. Has he met your mother yet?"

"Not yet," I said, preparing myself for a million and one questions.

"He moves in, then what? Where are we going with this plush arrangement?"

"Anyah."

"Do I hear wedding bells in the near future?"

"Anyah," I said, gritting my teeth.

"Who came up with the bright idea?"

"He did. Last week we celebrated our three-month milestone together. He surprised me with tickets to see Alvin Ailey and a romantic dinner afterward."

"That ain't all he surprised you with, is it? I'm listening."

"During dinner he shared his feelings and told me he wanted to take our relationship to another level."

"Ummph, moving kinda fast, don't you think little sister?"

I took a deep breath because I hated it when she referred to me as her little sister. It meant she was getting ready to go from girlfriend mode into big sister slash mother mode.

"Where did he live?"

"He lived in a one-bedroom apartment on the east side of town," I answered, starting to become impatient as she continued to fire questions at me.

"An apartment? Huh. So you had the larger and much nicer place?"

"Yes. I mean no. It was easier for him to move in with me. The setup for my studio is perfect here and I didn't want to move it."

"That's another thing. When was the last time you picked up a paint brush?"

"I'm still painting," I said, then leaned my head to one side because it had been two weeks since I'd painted. For the past month, all I'd been able to do was keep up with my daily lesson plans. Courtney in one way or another managed to monopolize my free time and I enjoyed every second.

"All I want to know is are you sure about the decision you've made? I hope you ain't letting Satan himself move into your condo. He's fine as hell. Now that I have to admit, but watch his ass. He is a cop. I don't mean no harm, and I know you don't want to hear what I got to say, but I'm going to say it anyway," she said so fast that all of her sentences ran together. "He's moving in a little bit too fast for me," she said, smacking her lips together. "Hell, Xavier and I dated almost two years before we decided to take it to another level and live together as he so kindly put it. Then, a year later, I had his last name."

"Yes, I'm sure. Girl, let me get off the telephone so I can help him get his things," I said, knowing she was on a roll and would go nonstop for another thirty minutes.

"Lil' sis, you know I love you, and I'm here if you need me."

"As always, I appreciate you," I said, opening the

front door as Courtney approached, holding a medium-sized box in his arms.

"Daddy's home," he said, easing by me as I held the door open.

"Welcome home." I looked at him and used the back of my hand to wipe the beads of sweat off his forehead. Hearing him say "home" was music to my ears.

Courtney

"What is the woman of my dreams doing?" I called from my cell phone only five minutes after leaving our condo. Last night was the first night we'd spent together officially as a couple. Maybe it was my imagination, but the sex was ten times better than the night I took her to the theater. We made out on top of a cardboard box, the kitchen table, and the bedroom floor. Go figure that shit out. We exhausted ourselves, showered together, then went to bed. Waking up with her in my arms was much better than I thought.

"The same thing I was doing when you left here five minutes ago," she said, sighing as though she was stretching.

"Let me guess. You're looking more beautiful than ever wearing your black bikinis and white T." It was amazing how something as simple as a T-shirt and panties suddenly turned me on. I'd been around professionals who couldn't arouse me like her.

"If that wasn't what I was wearing when you left, I'd think you were clairvoyant."

"Baby, you looked so good lying in bed this morning when I left," I said, painting a mental picture and fighting back an erection with everything in me. She'd been lying on her stomach, her back slightly arched and her hips in the air. It looked so perfect, I'd sworn she'd done it intentionally to drive me crazy.

"Did I really?"

"Good enough to eat for breakfast, lunch, and dinner. Can you handle it?"

"I'll die trying."

"I'm going to wreck my 'vette just thinking about last night. I should turn around right now, come back, and pick up where I left off."

"Oh, so you think you have it like that?"

"You tell me."

"Humph, I need to reevaluate before making a conclusion."

"Tell you what, I'll provide you with all of the evidence you need to fully evaluate me."

"You're too bold."

"Bold enough to try again when I get off at three. Ready for the challenge?" I asked, then whirled into the parking lot ready to get my eight hours over with.

"More than you'd ever imagine."

"I can't wait."

"By the way, we're having dinner at my mother's house at four. I thought it would be the perfect opportunity for you to officially meet the family."

"Talk to you later." I grabbed my bag and went inside the precinct.

Tatiana

"Good morning, Mother," I answered, standing in the middle of my closet trying to visually rearrange my clothes and shoes to accommodate Courtney's things.

We'd taken the moving van back, gotten his car, and stopped for take-out. After eating, we looked at the mess we'd created in the great room, decided we'd done enough unpacking for one day, took a shower, and tried to relax on the sofa. But it turned into another night of breathtaking lovemaking and I didn't get out of bed until ten o'clock. The house was torn to pieces and I wanted to use my time alone to at least get the closet organized before he made it home from work.

"Good morning. You're sounding exceptionally perky this morning."

"Let's just say I rested well last night," I said, held up the silk shirt he'd worn to dinner last week and placed it against my face to smell his cologne.

"That's good to hear. You know Sunday dinner's at my house this afternoon."

"Yes ma'am, I remembered. What do you want me to bring?" I asked, placing the shirt on a hanger, then starting to arrange his other clothes in the closet.

"Please fix the potato salad. Aunt Helen volunteered to make it again, but I told her you'd already made it."

"Mother," I said, laughing. "How could you tell a fib on the Sabbath?"

"I didn't, because I talked to her yesterday. Honey, it was just a little white lie. Now you know yourself her potato salad is too soggy."

"Mother, she makes it every month, and I thought you liked it," I said, smiling when I unpacked the shirt and slacks Courtney had on the night of the Christmas party.

"Have you ever seen me eat it?"

"Hmm, I never paid attention and assumed you'd eaten it like everyone else."

"Baby, you know what they say about assuming."

"What, mother?"

"Oh no, you're not going to make me go there this Sunday morning. Plus, I'm getting ready to go to church."

"Mother, I'm disappointed."

"What are you doing today? And please don't tell me you're going to spend the day painting."

"OK I will not," I said, then thought how Courtney could be introduced at dinner. "Mother, this is my live-in boyfriend Courtney." Or "Mother, this is Courtney. I've known him for three months and he moved in with me yesterday." I sighed, then rolled my eyes to the top of my head.

"You still have time to slip into something nice and meet me at church." She cleared her throat. "Preferably that cream suit with the A-line skirt that stops right above your knees. You remember—the one I bought you for Christmas last year that still has the tags hanging on it. You have legs like those Williams sisters that play tennis. You know the ones I'm talking about. Most men love nice, muscular legs."

"Mother, please don't start. It's too early in the morning."

"I haven't given up on my grandchildren yet. That young man I was telling you about? His name is Eugene Jordan."

"Eugene?" I screeched into the telephone. "Mother, what kind of name is Eugene for someone our age?"

"Say what you want. He's a prime catch, plus Bertha hasn't totally gotten her hooks into him just yet. So I still have time. Plus, you're so much prettier than that daughter of hers. I know if he ever lays eyes on you, it will be love at first sight."

"Mother, you never cease to amaze me." I looked around the closet and decided to reorganize my shoes next.

"I know. That's what mothers do, and if you don't hurry up, you'll never find out, either. Service starts at eleven."

"Love you, Mother," I said, allowing the words to fall off the end of my tongue.

"Love you, too."

"Hey, babe," I answered, pleased to hear his voice, then transferred the potato salad into a plastic container. It would be our first family dinner together. His personality was pleasant and he was kind to the eyes. I had no doubt that, after the initial shock of us living together, Mother would forget about the guy from church and fall in love with Courtney.

"Sorry, but you'll have to go to dinner without me today."

"I've already gotten an outfit out for you to wear so I can wait if you're running late," I said, turning to look at the time on the microwave. Knowing he would be pressed for time, I'd selected a pair of freshly starched jeans, a beige linen shirt, and casual brown leather shoes. So we'd look more like a couple, I put on a pair of blue jeans, beige blouse, and pumps to coordinate with his outfit. "It's only a family dinner, not morning roll call. There's no penalty if we're late."

"No, go ahead. We've made an arrest, and it will be at least two more hours before I'm able to leave the station."

"I was looking forward to your meeting the

family," I said, trying not to whine. Then I frowned. For three months, I'd avoided my mother's intuition and I'd promised myself I would not go another day without telling her. My preference was telling her with him by my side.

"Maybe next time. Enjoy dinner, and I'll see you when you get home."

"Be careful." Disappointed, I ended the call and looked at the handset. "Duty calls," I said with a slight attitude. Thinking that might be the first of many missed engagements, I got the bowl, along with my purse and keys, and left.

After pulling into Mother's driveway, I turned off the ignition and used both hands to massage my temples. During the twenty-minute drive I'd mumbled to myself and dealt with several emotions. Yes, Courtney was an officer, but in three months it was the first time he'd been delayed by an arrest. Like clockwork, thirty minutes after his shift he was calling me or ringing my doorbell.

Not once during our conversation had he apologized for missing our family dinner. Now that bothered me more than anything else. *Tatiana, calm down. You're overreacting*, I thought, then massaged my temples in the opposite direction. I couldn't sit in the car all evening, so I put on a happy face and got out and followed the brick path to the front door.

"Hello, Mother," I said, once she opened the front door, and I gave her a kiss on her smooth, brown cheek. Mother was fifty-six and didn't look a day over forty-five. Her big, dreamy brown eyes were framed by a pair of glasses that mostly hung by a chain around her neck. She kept her naturally curly, jet-black hair short. We were the same height and had the same body build. So I was pleased to know that, in twenty years, my size six would get no larger than a well-developed ten.

"I'm glad you're the first one to get here." She closed the door, slipped a floral apron over her head to cover the dress she'd worn to church and tied it behind her back. I followed the scent of her home cooking down the hallway and into the kitchen. "I finished cooking this morning before church. All I have to do is reheat everything and set the table," she said, turning to take the bowl out of my hand. "I missed you at church today. Service was so good."

"Was it really, Mother?" I asked looking around the kitchen for something to do. I didn't want to hear about Eugene Jordan or Bertha Jenkins and her daughter again.

"You missed a really good sermon. He preached about the blessings of Abraham and took his text from the book of Genesis."

"What do you want me to get out of here first?" I asked, opening the refrigerator door and looking inside as a distraction. I knew immediately where her conversation was going. Marrying a man of God and having children.

"Umm hmm," she said, rolling her eyes.

"Mother, there's something I need to talk to you about." I interrupted before she got overly religious, removed the huge roast pan, and set it on top of the stove. There was no perfect time before or after dinner to tell her about Courtney.

"What is it, baby?" she asked, then turned on the oven while I continued to remove items from the refrigerator.

"During the Christmas holidays, Anyah invited me to their annual party."

"That was nice. Did you have a good time?" she

asked, not really paying attention as she lifted an edge of the foil on the roast pan for ventilation.

"Yes, I had a great time. While I was there I met a very nice gentleman named Courtney. He's a police officer, never been married, and has no children."

"Hmm . . . so he has potential," she said, opening the oven door and placing the roast pan inside.

"We exchanged numbers, went out on several dates, and he moved in yesterday," I said, rushing my sentence to an end.

"You did what?" she asked, letting the oven door slam shut and finally turning around to look at me. "Did you say what I thought you just said?" she asked with a hand on her hip.

"Yes ma'am," I said, knowing there was no good way or perfect time to tell her. She was a Christian and believed some rules were never meant to be broken. Not living together before marriage was one of them. Sure I'd never hear the end of it, I leaned against the counter. Yes, I was an adult and capable of making sound decisions, but she was still Mother.

"Lawd have mercy. You know how I feel about people living in sin. It's an abomination in the sight of the Lord. I wanted you to get married and have children, not have children, then get married. Let me sit down before I pass out in the middle of the floor. If you met him at Christmas . . ." she said, counting on her fingers, ". . . that was only three months ago." She plopped down in the kitchen chair and rested her arm on the back. "You never mentioned a Courtney to me or no one else for that matter. We talk about all of your boyfriends. He could be a serial killer or a con artist for all you know. Times have changed," she said, then rested her head in the palm of her hand. "Why was he such a big secret?" she asked, then glanced up at me with a look of disappointment.

"He wasn't a secret. We met at the party and hit it off really well. I never said anything because it all seemed too good to be true and I was expecting the fairy-tale romance to end any day."

"Who is that at the door?" she snapped when the door bell rang. "We'll finish this conversation later." With one arm she pushed herself up and hurried to put the food in the oven.

"I'll get the door," I said, feeling responsible for her sudden bad mood. All I could do was hope she'd taken her hormone pills. If not, everyone would have to pay for my shocking news. "Hello, Aunt Helen and Uncle Henry," I said loud enough for her to hear, then hugged them.

"It's so good to see you," Aunt Helen said, holding a huge Tupperware bowl.

"Aunt Helen, let me take your bowl," I said, then grunted when she placed the heavy bowl in my hands.

"Your mother told me you were making the potato salad, but I made some anyway. You can never have too much potato salad," she said, shook her finger, then readjusted her auburn-colored wig. As if to say "don't ask me," Uncle Henry hunched his shoulders behind her back.

"You're right," I said as they followed me into the kitchen. Then, like clockwork, over the next thirty minutes, more family members arrived. The tradition continued as the children played games and the adults gathered around the kitchen table for gossip and small talk.

Mother was distant toward me but managed, as always, to be an outstanding hostess. Everyone was stuffed. They fixed to-go plates, then bid each other farewell until the first Sunday of the next month. When mother started to clean up, the tension in the air was thick enough to cut with a knife. With her head down, she moved around the dining room as though I was invisible, then finally spoke.

"Mothers always want what's best for their children, no matter how old or young they are. Parenting doesn't come with a handbook, and from day one I've always tried to do what was right in front of you. If your father was living, I'm sure he'd agree." She leaned back, looked at me, and wiped her hands on her apron. "Remember, I'll always have your best interests at heart. I'm disappointed in your arrangement but more disappointed that you didn't tell me. But when it's all said and done, you're an adult and that I have to respect," Mother said, removing an empty dish from the table.

"Thank you," I said, feeling somewhat relieved, then gathered the remaining dishes before we went into the kitchen together.

"Your Aunt Helen is something else, isn't she? She made that potato salad anyway," she said laughing.

"Yes, ma'am, she is," I said, glad to hear the humor in her voice. The tradition continued as she washed the soiled dishes and I dried. An hour later, the dishes were washed and all the leftover food was put away. The evening ended with sweet good-byes and kisses on the cheek.

"Honey, I'm home," I said after walking into the great room and seeing the back of Courtney's head. He was slouched down on the sofa watching television. I was disheartened that he'd missed dinner, but I still couldn't wait to see his face. "I fixed you a plate," I said, holding it up for him to see.

"I'm not hungry right now. You can put it in the fridge," he said, never looking up.

"Sure." I placed my empty container in the sink and put his food in the refrigerator.

"Can I get a kiss?" he asked when I entered the room, lifting both arms over his head.

"Of course you can." I walked around the couch to face him. "My, you did have an awful day," I commented after kissing him on the lips and looking at his dingy sock feet, propped up on the table. His uniform shirt was unbuttoned and his hand was tucked inside his waistband. *OK,* I thought to myself, because seeing him like that was by no means romantic.

"And a hug?" he asked, pulling me down onto his lap.

"What time did you make it home?" I asked, looking over at his work shoes, which were toppled on each other beside the couch.

"I guess it was four-thirtyish or so."

"Hmm," I said and frowned, thinking there had been time for him to call me and join us for dinner. "Sooo, you wrapped the arrest up sooner than you thought." I looked at him out of the corners of my eyes. During our last conversation, he'd said it would take at least two hours. Four-thirtyish was only an hour after we talked.

"Yeah," he said, picking up the remote and starting to surf the channels.

"Yeah," I said slowly, thinking he would elaborate. He didn't, so I sat up and turned to look at him.

"How was dinner?" he asked, overlooking my obvious attitude. Then he used his hand to lean my body back against him.

"You missed a delicious meal. Mother fixed roast beef, collard greens, yams, black-eyed peas, and chocolate cake. Look—I ate enough for the both of us," I said, rubbing my distended stomach.

"Sounds good."

"It was, and that's why I fixed your plate before everyone had eaten. If nothing comes up, maybe you'll make it next month."

"Maybe," he said, leaning his body to one side and resting on his elbow to get a better view of the television.

"I told Mother that you moved in yesterday. I want the two of you to meet soon. I think you're really going to like her. I have a three-day weekend coming up and maybe I can cook and we can invite her over for dinner."

"Baby, that's an entire week from now. Tonight all I want to do is relax, make love to my woman, then fall asleep. I had a very rough day today. Would you like to do me a huge favor?"

"It depends."

"I would like to take a long, hot bath with you tonight. That's if it isn't too much trouble."

"For you nothing is too much trouble." He kissed me on the forehead, placed his hands beneath my hips and lifted me off his lap. He gave me a hard pat on the behind as I walked away.

That was weird. Why isn't he interested in meeting my mother? I thought to myself when I leaned over the tub and turned on the water. Then I tried internally to resolve his lack of interest, poured a cap full of bubble bath into the running water, and lit some candles. "Courtney," I called when the tub was full.

"Now that's what I'm talking about," he said, already standing in the bathroom door. He took a few long steps until he was standing in front of me. Then he undressed himself and undressed me. "Who wouldn't love to come home to this after a long day's work?" he said, stepping back to look at me.

Tomorrow is a new day, I thought, already forgetting any anxiety I'd experienced as I looked down at his thickness. We submerged ourselves into the hot water filled with bubbles. I sat between his legs and leaned back onto his chest.

Chapter 13

Courtney

"Whatz up, dawg?" Octavious said when he answered his cell phone. Moving in with Tatiana was cool but came with conditions I'd never considered, like meeting the family. Next I guess she'll want me to have dinner with her girlfriend from the Christmas party.

My circle of influence has always been small. I was the older of two children and my parents and younger sister live in LA, where I was born. Both of my parents were in constant search of wealth, had an estranged relationship with each other, and never spent much time at home. Except for an occasional good night kiss from my mother, the nanny did everything for me and my sister. She cooked, cleaned, took us to school every morning, and even went to our PTA meetings.

After high school I moved as far away as I could and promised—except for my sister's wedding or a funeral—never to go back. So doing the "family dinner thing" sounded uncomfortable, and there was no way to tell Tatiana without hurting her feelings. "Ain't heard from ya lately. Guess you been all up on O'girl. Ain't mad at you, though."

"No need, 'cause you get more action than P. Diddy," I said and looked over my shoulder to back into a secluded drive that faced a busy intersection. It was the end of the month and I hadn't met my ticket quota. I enjoyed patrolling the streets and thought hiding in the cut waiting for someone to go four miles over the speed limit was boring as hell. But that, too, was all part of the job.

"Yeah . . . yeah. I do, don't I?"

"I need to get out tonight," I said, then leaned my head back.

"What? O'girl gonna give you a free pass for the night? Hell, I thought you'd be going to cooking class."

"Go to hell," I said, really unsure how she would react now that we'd officially moved in together.

"Let my Pops tell it, I'm already there. Didn't you hear I keep the fire burning?"

"You're crazy as hell," I said, laughing to myself at the preacher's son. They always said they were the worst children and in Octavious's case, it was the truth.

His father was the Bible-toting, hell, fire, and brimstone-preaching pastor of a church with over five hundred members. I met Octavious at a strip club and never in a million years pictured him as a minister's son. One night after too many drinks he got all emotional and ruined my high with his childhood stories.

His family damn near lived in the church. He grew up attending Sunday school, morning, evening, and night services. Any time the church doors were open, he was there. Octavious had a BS in theology and was

being properly groomed to follow in his father's foot-
steps. Until . . . he walked in on the church secretary
underneath his father's desk giving him a blow job.
Octavious never told his mother, but he lost respect
for his father and cursed the day he was ever born.

"What's on your mind? Anywhere you wanna go?"

"Anywhere they're serving alcohol. I just got out
of a meeting with the big dawgs downtown. They
took all of one hour to tell us the city was in trouble,
and that overtime, along with a few other perks,
would be taken away within the next year. You know
the majority of my income comes from overtime."

"That's why you need to come work wit' me."

"Hell man, you ain't got no real job," I said,
laughing at the countless get-rich-quick schemes
he'd confronted me with.

"Whatever, and I ain't the one complainin'
either. But I hear you talkin'. Don't worry, we gone
take care of all of that tonight. I already know
where we need to go. Appolonia should be dancing
at our old spot tonight. What time you gettin' off?"

"I'll probably stretch it out until five today, man.
My plan is to get as many hours as I can before they
tighten up."

"We gettin' out around our usual time, then?"

"Yeah, man, that's cool. It'll give me time to shower
and rest up before we get started. I'll call you when
I'm on my way to your place."

"Hey man, tonight everything including the trans-
portation is on me."

"I'm cool. I don't mind driving," I responded
in a hurry. He didn't know that I'd moved in with
Tatiana.

"Man, take a break tonight."

"Call me before you leave so I can give you directions." I agreed because letting him drive

would give me the opportunity to drink without thinking.

"Directions? You moved since the last time we talked?"

"Sort of."

"Aww, hell, naw. Have you moved in with O'girl?"

"Yeah."

"I'm really taking yo' player's card tonight. First she got you looking at half-naked dudes jumping across a stage and now you done moved in. That's deep." He let out a heavy sigh into the phone. "I'll call you when I'm headed your way. The drive-through window at Mickey D's is open twenty-four hours. I can take you there for a Happy Meal and small orange soda."

"Later." I shook my head, then pointed my radar gun toward a red sports car flying down the hill. *That looks like Big G's main girl. She always keeps at least five hundred dollars on her. Hell, I need another payday.*

"Baby, I'm gone," I said when my cell phone started to ring and I went into Tatiana's studio for a kiss. On my way home I'd called Octavious to give him directions, then called her to share my plans. I told her it was a bad day but didn't want to go into any details only another man would understand. She seemed OK with the idea and told me dinner along with dessert would be ready when I got home. I'd dated enough females to get the hint. Even though I was tired and frustrated as hell when I got off, I ate dinner, took a shower, then made love to her. Most females seem to think if they take care of the man, he will not stray, and in some cases it's true.

"Have a good time," she said, then kissed me on the lips. I hugged her, then smacked her on the butt before turning and walking out of her studio.

"Octavious, I'm on way my outside," I said, opening the front door.

"Whatz up?" Octavious said in a high-pitched voice, imitating Martin Lawrence's radio introduction.

"What the hell?" I asked, closing my cell phone and looking behind me to make sure Tatiana wasn't in the room.

"You do know I've gotta meet any female that has you watchin' men jumping across a stage in tights," he said, stretching his neck to look inside the condo.

"She's in her studio and gets very upset when anyone disturbs her," I said, using my hand to push him backward to prevent him from stepping inside. "You can meet her another day," I said hurriedly. "Plus, I don't want your ugly ass to scare her away." I looked down at his baggy blue jeans that were cuffed at the bottom and his yellow-striped collar shirt that was three sizes too big. To impress the cheap dates, he was wearing a diamond knuckle ring that spelled his nickname and a long, gold chain with a pit bull. For the club, his gangsta look was OK, but not for Tatiana. I could only imagine what she would think.

"Scare her away? What the hell is that supposed to mean?" he said, pressing against my hand and using his body weight to enter her apartment. "I wasn't so damn scary at the Embassy," he said, still looking around. "Nice place. She got class, huh?" he asked, then pushed by me.

"Thought I heard voices," Tatiana said, stepping into the great room.

"Yeah, Octavious and I were just leaving." I

leaned my head toward the door as his cue not to say another word and get the hell out.

"Who's in a hurry?" he asked, then walked toward Tatiana with his right hand extended. "Excuse my best friend. He forgets his manners sometimes," he said properly, then looked at me with a sly grin. "My name is Octavious. I'm sure you've heard a lot about me."

"I'm sorry Octavious, but he's never mentioned you. Either way, it's a pleasure to meet you." She wiped both hands on her smock and returned the gesture. "Guys, I've got to get back to work. Courtney, behave yourself," she said with a half smile, stared at Octavious, then kissed me on the lips. "Octavious, it was a pleasure meeting you."

"See you later, babe," I said when she turned to walk back into her studio.

"Man, she pretty as hell." Octavious said before I completely closed her door.

"What was that all about?" I asked Octavious, upset that he had forced an introduction. He was my boy, but I never knew what bag he was going to come out of and when. Around Tatiana, his loose lips could sink a lot of damn ships. We'd shared some wild times together and Tatiana was the last one I wanted to hear about them.

"I'm yo boy, right?" He said, extending his fist. "Aww, so it's like that, huh?" he asked when I didn't give him some dap. "I'd go see male dancers for her, too," he said as we walked down the sidewalk toward his black Range Rover. "Does she have any sisters?" he asked, then popped his collar.

"Hell, naw," I said, getting into his ride and slamming the door.

"Damage my girl if you want to. I'm suing yo' ass."

"Go right ahead because you will get nothing. I

work for the city, remember?" We laughed as he backed out of the driveway and turned onto the street.

"Damn, it's on and popping tonight," Octavious said when we entered the smoke-filled gentlemen's club. It had been a few months since I'd been there. I stopped, waved my hand in front of my face to clear the air, and looked around the room. Fine topless females wearing black leather microminis and G-strings and three-inch-high stilettos were swishing through the crowd.

For a weeknight, "Hell's Den," as I casually referred to it, was packed. Guess I wasn't the only one who needed a breather. We excused our way through a group of men huddled around a topless waitress to the huge U-shaped bar in the center of the club. We found two empty seats that faced the main stage, which was painted all black and shaped like the capital letter *T*. In the middle of it was a silver pole that went from the floor to the ceiling.

"Good evening, Octavious." Juanna said, smiling at him, then rolling her eyes at me. I placed my elbows on the bar and stared her in the face. She for damn sure wasn't going to punk me out in front of my boy. "The usual?" she asked him with a smile, then leaned across the bar almost close enough for him to touch her double Ds.

"Yeah."

"What can I get for you?" she snapped at me.

"Rémy and coke. Strong." She stood, then went to the other side of the bar to fix our drinks.

Octavious looked at me. "Player, what was that all about?"

"Something stupid," I said, not wanting to go

into any details. "She fronted me at the gym about a month ago."

"Aww, hell. Was your new girl with you?"

"Man, no. I was alone."

"That's what I told you about having sex and tryin' to talk afterward. Females like that you've got to get the goods and keep a steppin'," he said, then flashed the fake smile I'd ever seen when she came back with our drinks. "Thank you with yo sexy self," he said and blew her a kiss. "Now that's what I'm talking about," he said, when Appolonia's theme music started to play. The black curtains separated, conversations and the clatter of glasses against the tables suddenly stopped, making the room totally quiet for one second. I turned to face the main stage. Appolonia was standing in the middle wearing a crotchless Catwoman suit and holding a whip between her teeth. All of a sudden the crowd went wild. "O'girl got skills," Octavious said when she started to walk the runway and swirled her head to pop the floor with her whip.

I watched as she started to slither out of her clothes, then thought about Tatiana. *What is she doing right now?* I wondered looking up at the dancer, who was on her back, spreading her legs apart in my face. *How would I feel if some sweaty dude was dangling his goods in her face?* I asked myself as she turned over onto her stomach and began to roll her hips. I looked at her, suddenly disgusted with what I saw. All I wanted to see, smell, or feel was Tatiana. *Damn, I really have fallen in love.*

"Look at that shit," Octavious said, taking a roll of one-dollar bills out of his pocket and unfolding them. "I said tonight was on me." He handed me half. "Slide closer to Daddy, baby," Octavious said, starting to fan his money back and forth. "Would you look at that."

"Yeah, look at it," I said, turning up my Rémy and coke and tapping the bar for a refill.

Tatiana

I turned on my side and looked at the clock when I heard the locks tumble and the door creak open, then close. It was two o'clock in the morning and both of us had to work. I couldn't sleep and had been staring at the ceiling all night long. In the dark, he felt his way through the great room and into the bathroom. Obviously intoxicated, he turned on the light switch and left the door open while taking his shower. "Baby, I'm home," Courtney said after getting into bed and snuggling his damp, naked body behind me. *Getting home at two o'clock, now that's something to get used to*, I thought, then moved my body away from his.

"Where are you going?" he asked, pulling my body back against his and wrapping his arms around my waist. "You feel so good," he said, then started to rub my hips. "Baby, are you awake?"

"Have a good time?" I asked with clenched teeth, snatching the sheet and tucking it tightly underneath my chin. Even though he'd taken a shower, his pores reeked of smoke.

"Yeah, I had my usual Rémy and a few beers." He turned me onto my back.

"So where did you go?" I asked, imagining where he went with his friend who looked like a retired rapper.

"We hung out downtown."

"Any place in particular?" I asked, not expecting the truth.

"No, not really. Can we talk about this later? Right now I want to make love to you."

"Who's Octavious?" I said, crossing my legs at the ankles. I found it odd that his name had never come up in a conversation. "We've talked a lot and you never mentioned him to me."

"He's just my boy. Now uncross your legs and let me feel you," he said, easing his hand between my thighs and attempting to spread my legs apart.

"He doesn't look like your type, if you ask me. He looks like he'd do anything with anybody or to anybody. We're working professionals and too old to be playing thug."

"Dang, Tatiana, why would you want to ruin a good moment talking about someone who means nothing to me. We've been boys for a while and his looks are deceiving," he said, snatching his hand away.

"They always say birds of a feather flock together."

"What is that supposed to mean?"

"You know what it means." I turned onto my side and tucked the sheet underneath my hips to create a barrier between the two of us. Within minutes, I heard a soft snore coming from his side of the bed.

"Dang," I said, hitting the snooze button with my hand. It seemed like I had just fallen asleep. Precisely nine minutes later, it buzzed again. Groggy from my restless night, I turned off the clock, moaned, and sat up on the side of the bed. With a hand on either side of me, I leaned my head down, then stretched my legs, attempting to stand up.

Courtney felt me move, so he reached over and grabbed my hand.

"Octavious is harmless." His voice was raspy, so he cleared his throat and continued to talk. "He's just someone I used to kick it with so I never felt the need to mention him. I'm willing to bet a hundred dollars right now that you haven't told me about everyone you know," he said, rubbing the top of my hand. "You went to sleep upset with me, so don't go to work upset with me. That's not how two people who love each other act." He moved closer to me, then eased his hand between my thighs. "I want us to make up before you go to work. Please make love to me."

Two people who love each other, I repeated to myself, thought about his comments, then rolled my neck around. With a finger he started to massage that secret spot between my legs, then felt inside to confirm my wetness. Like a puppet on a string, I leaned back onto the bed and spread my legs apart to welcome his early-morning caress.

Chapter 14

Tatiana

"Let's get married."

"Where did that come from?" I asked when Courtney tugged my hand slightly as a gesture to stop in front of the jewelry store. We'd been living together almost four months, and except for an occasional lovers' quarrel, things were progressing well. He'd finally met my mother, and I was spending more time in the studio.

"I want you to become Mrs. Courtney DeShaun Wilkes. No big, expensive wedding that will take a year to plan with hundreds of guests. Let's just do it. Get married, then go on a cruise to Mexico." He turned my body to face him and reached for my other hand.

"Courtney, we've stood here long enough." His expression seemed sincere, but that was the first time he'd ever mentioned marriage. We'd confessed our love months ago, but making a lifetime commitment had never been a topic of discussion. "I need to get Sonja's gift. The shower starts in less than two hours," I said, turning to walk toward the department store. Ignoring my comments, Courtney led me into the store and walked toward a salesperson who wasn't assisting another customer.

"Welcome to Harwell's Fine Jewelry Store. How may I help you?" said the tall, thin, fair-skinned lady wearing a two-piece black suit and crisp white blouse, walking toward us.

"I'd like to look at your engagement rings," he said, never letting go of my hand.

"Oh my." Gracefully, she covered her heart with her hand. "Congratulations. The two of you make a lovely couple."

I wanted to say "thank you," but shock and disbelief forbade me from being as excited as she was.

"Is there any particular cut or designer in mind for the beautiful bride-to-be?" she asked, walking behind a showcase and pulling a key attached to a string from her waistband.

"Tocari has always been my favorite," Courtney answered without hesitation. Surprised by his knowledge, I turned to look at him again.

"Well, well. Sir, you have exquisite taste." She looked at me, then nodded her head. "We have several designs. But this one . . ." she said—unlocking the sliding door and removing a solitaire that appeared flawless without a magnifying glass—" . . . just arrived three days ago. It's one of Tocari's latest designs."

"Tatiana, what do you think?" I stood speechless as Courtney gently removed it from her hand and held it toward the light to examine it.

"It's beautiful," I said, temporarily mesmerized by the dazzling center stone.

"As you can see, it is platinum with a one-carat emerald-cut center stone. The total weight is two carats," she said, after looking at the tiny white tag tucked inside the ring. "Please allow your beautiful fiancée to try it on. It looks like the perfect fit."

"What do you think?" he asked me as he turned the stone to look at it from a different angle.

"It's absolutely gorgeous." Without warning, Courtney bowed on one knee and lifted my hand.

"Courtney, what are you doing?" I asked, looking at the small group of employees as they formed a semicircle behind me.

"Tatiana, I never believed in love at first sight until the first moment our eyes met. It was then I decided I wanted to spend the rest of my life with you. Tatiana, will you marry me?"

My lips fell apart. "Yes, Courtney I will marry you," I said, then covered my mouth with both hands.

Without standing, he wrapped both arms around my waist. Time stood still as I embraced the moment and allowed the essence of our love to saturate the atmosphere. He stood, kissed me passionately on the lips, then walked to the counter to complete the transaction. Still awestruck, I stood alone for a few seconds to admire the beautiful ring before joining him. Basking in the moment, I wrapped my arm around his waist and leaned my head against his shoulder. He leaned down and kissed me gently on the forehead.

"Congratulations," the saleslady said with a warm smile. She placed a white satin ring box inside a gold bag with black lettering and handed it to me.

"Thank you," I said. My head still against Courtney's shoulder, he wrapped his arms around my waist to embrace me as we exited the store.

No longer in the mood to shop for a shower gift, I purchased a fifty-dollar gift card from a department store. With it, Sonja could purchase whatever she needed most. Hand in hand, we exited the mall and walked to Courtney's car. Feeling like I'd won a million-dollar lottery, I fastened my seat belt, turned sideways to face him, and crossed one leg beneath me. All the way home, Courtney and I chatted nervously while jumping from one topic to another about our future plans together as husband and wife.

"Hey, girlfriend," I said, lifting my left hand off the steering wheel and holding it in front of me. I wanted to spend the rest of my evening with Courtney but had promised my co-workers I'd attend the shower. So Courtney and I agreed that I'd show my face and we'd celebrate later. "If you and Xavier are busy, I can call you back," I said, laughing when she sounded short of breath. It was nothing for the two of them to have a quickie in the middle of the day.

"Honey, I wish we were, but it's not what you think. Xavier's at the office and I was exercising."

"You were *what*?"

"Whew," she whistled into the telephone. "Let me press pause on the DVD player. I'm glad you called because these skinny helfas are starting to piss me off. I needed a water break."

"OK," I said, still anxious to tell her my good news after she put the telephone down. If I wasn't already late for the shower, I would have driven by her house.

"Honey, yeah. I picked up a few pounds during the holidays. It must have been all those cocktail parties I was attending with Xavier after his promotion. Girlfriend, I went into the closet thinking I was going to put on my skinny jeans with the rhinestones on the legs and the damn things wouldn't fasten. So I found my scale, blew the dust off, and weighed myself. When the numbers stopped bouncing back and forth, I damn near had a heart attack.

I got off the scale, took off my watch and anything else I thought might add an ounce, and got back on again. Hell, it was worse, so I kicked the damn thing back into the closet. Since Christmas I've gained ten pounds. You know I ain't gonna eat solid food for three weeks."

"All right, Anyah, you know the last time you did that, we had to rush you to the emergency room."

"Whatever. If I get any bigger I'm going to look like the damn emergency room," she said, laughing at herself. "So tell me what's going on in your world. We're long overdue for a shopping spree."

"Are you sitting down?" I asked.

"I am now. What's up?"

"Courtney proposed to me today in the mall. My engagement ring is Tocari with an emerald-cut center stone. It is to die for. I can't wait for you to see it." There was complete silence. I looked at my cell phone to make sure the call hadn't been dropped. My signal was excellent. "Anyah? Are you there?"

"Yes, I heard you, girlfriend."

"Aren't you excited?" I asked after she'd almost blown my natural high with her silence. Then I waited on her rebuttal.

"He proposed in the mall? Why is he in such a big damn hurry? You haven't known him a year yet."

"Anyah, he proposed. It's not like we're getting married tomorrow. The proposal only solidifies our commitment to each other." Again there was silence.

"Is your mother excited?" she asked, using a condescending tone because she already knew the answer.

"I wanted to tell you first. I'm going to call her after I leave Sonja's baby shower."

"You're my girl and I love you like a sister. If you're happy, then I'm happy."

"Thanks a million," I said, glanced at the directions, then turned into the parking lot.

"But still watch his ass. That's all I got to say."

Highly disappointed in her reaction, I parked and turned off the ignition. If nothing else, I expected her, of all people, to be happy for me. Remembering how excited I was when he proposed, I looked at my ring, reached for Sonja's gift and got out of the car.

Courtney

"Mrs. Tatiana Wilkes," I said, then repeated it to myself, once I drove into the gym's parking lot and parked. Never in a million years did I think one woman could possibly make me happy. I'd dated one female almost two years and never thought about giving her my last name. She was fine as hell, made my toes curl in bed, but I never woke up thinking about spending the rest of my life with her. Matter of fact, when we broke up, I hooked up with another female that same night and never had second thoughts about it.

Tatiana had me. When she was not around I was constantly asking myself what she was doing. Sometimes I closed my eyes and could smell the scented lotion she wore to bed at night. I hadn't even known her a year. But she was everything I thought I wanted in a woman, plus more.

"I did it, dawg," I said, still in shock when Octavious answered his cell. I hadn't planned to propose, but the moment seemed perfect.

"You did what, playa?"

"Proposed to Tatiana," I said, then remembered

the look on her face. It was a Kodak moment that couldn't be recaptured.

"What da hell did you just say?" he shouted into my ear.

"You heard me. I said I proposed to Tatiana."

"Baby, you got to hold up a minute."

"Man, if this is a bad time I'll hit you back later."

"Naw, dude, this is an emergency. I can pick up with her right where we left off. Ain't that right, sugar," he said speaking to whomever he was with.

"I love her."

"Aww, hell, naw. You done shot off. Do we need to go kick it at the club tonight? This ain't the Courtney I know. Are you sure 'bout this?"

"Yeah, man. I'm sure."

"You my dawg and I'm happy for you. Know what this means, right?"

"What?"

"Bachelor party, dawg," he sang into my ear.

"Later," I said, grabbing my gym bag and getting out of the car. I strolled into the gym and no one but Juanna was on the treadmill closest to the front entrance. She was wearing a red bra top and short Lycra biking shorts with a thong on top. It was a helluva combination. Like any man, I glanced, then looked straight ahead, focusing on the neon sign above the men's locker room. I'd just proposed to the woman of my dreams and wouldn't be distracted by shattered pieces of my past.

Tatiana

"Hello, Mother," I said, excited to hear her voice when she answered the telephone. I'd waited until

Sonja opened her last gift, then used Mother as an excuse to leave early.

"How are you?"

"Doing well," I said, then started to drive in the direction of her house.

"That's good to hear. I just took three cakes out of the oven. Tomorrow is Annual Choir Day at the church, and I promised them I would bring two of my homemade chocolate cakes."

"Did you make an extra one for the house?"

"Honey, you know I did. Only two of them are for the church. You should come and get some while it's hot. That's if you're not too busy."

"Actually I'm not. I was headed that way anyway. I should be there in about two minutes."

"Good, I'll unlock the front door so all you have to do is come on in."

"See you in a few," I said, ended the call, and called Courtney.

"Hey babe," he answered. "I just finished working out."

"I was calling to let you know I was going to stop by Mother's before going home, so take your time."

"OK, but I was getting ready to leave anyway."

"I'm not going to stay long. Just wanted to tell her the good news and show her my ring."

"No problem. See you at the house later."

"I love you," I said, not at all surprised when the words flowed so smoothly from my lips. Then I turned into her driveway and parked.

"Love you, too."

"Hello, Mother," I called once I entered the house and started to walk down the hallway. She was expecting me, but I didn't want to startle her.

"I'm in the kitchen." Her voice echoed through the narrow hallway.

Before entering the kitchen, I stopped to reflect on a picture she'd taken of Daddy and me after church one Easter Sunday. He was holding me, along with a huge Easter basket filled with stuffed toys and goodies in his arms. My long legs dangled at his side. "*Wish you were here.*" I kissed the tips of my fingers, then touched the picture. A lonely tear fell, and I hurried to wipe it before another one followed.

I stood in the doorway to inhale the smell of Mother's homemade creations. She was standing by the kitchen table icing one of the three cakes, so I walked over and kissed her on the cheek.

"Mmm . . . mmm," I said, putting down my purse and washing my hands in the sink.

"Here, let me cut you a piece while it's hot," she said, rinsing a knife beneath the flowing water and then drying it off.

I dried off my hands and wiped the edge of the bowl with my fingers to get leftover chocolate icing. "This is so good." I licked my fingers when she handed me a piece of cake. "Thanks," I said with a huge smile, then flicked my wrist downward so she could see my ring.

"Oh my." She held up my hand to get a closer look. "Is that what I think it is?"

"Yes ma'am, it is. He proposed to me in the mall earlier today."

"In the mall? Now that's different," she said, then stepped back.

"He went with me to get a shower gift for my coworker. We passed a jewelry store and he stopped me in front of the display window. Out of the clear blue, he said, 'Let's get married.' We'd never talked about it, so I ignored him until he started to pull me inside the store. He basically picked out the ring. I tried it on and, believe it or not, it was a perfect fit. In the middle of the store, he got down on one knee and proposed."

"Wow." She made a final swirl with the icing in the middle of her cake, put down the spatula, and wiped her hands on the front of her apron. As if she wanted to hear more, she leaned against the counter and folded her arms across her chest.

"I wanted to show you my ring and tell you the good news face-to-face. No more surprises."

"It does seem kind of soon, but I'd rather for you to make it right in the sight of the good Lord," she said, lifting her hands toward the sky. "Have you talked about a date?"

"Not yet. This was unexpected, so we're going out to celebrate tonight. I promise to keep you posted this time."

"Well, he seemed like a pretty nice fellow. But no one knows that better than you," she said, then rubbed her index finger underneath my chin.

I pondered her words as she stepped forward, moved the first cake to the side, and placed another one on the table. As in times past, I pulled out a chair and sat down in front of her with my hands underneath my chin. She picked up the spatula, then stirred the icing as words of wisdom about marriage flowed from her mouth. I listened intently.

Chapter 15

Courtney . . . two months later

"Baby, I'm gone," I said, then gave my bride-to-be a long kiss.

"Don't forget, tomorrow we'll be husband and wife," she said, then shocked me when she rubbed my crotch.

"I hear you loud and clear, but don't worry, these are all yours. In less than twenty-four hours it will be official." I pulled her body closer to mine and kissed her on the neck.

"You better go, plus Anyah should be here in about thirty minutes."

"Octavious is so country," I said, embarrassed when he started to blow his car horn loud enough to be heard three blocks away. "Behave," I said, giving her a final kiss on the lips. She giggled, shut the door, and I rushed to his car.

"Have you lost your damn mind?" I asked Octavious, who was showing nothing but teeth once I got into his car. "This is a residential area, not the hood," I said, slamming his door shut.

"Jeez, you already actin' married. Loosen up and if you tear my whip up, you payin' for it." He put his car into reverse, then sped out of the driveway and into the street.

"I *am* loose. Now where are we going?" I asked, rubbing the palms of my hands together, anticipating a long evening of drinking and no thinking.

"Here, take this and chill out." He reached into a cooler behind my seat and handed me a Heineken. "Just thinkin' ahead, Mr. Married Man."

"You're my boy," I said, ready to forget how he'd already pissed me off, acting like an idiot.

"Now let me handle this." He turned onto the interstate and headed in a direction that was all too familiar. Twenty minutes later we drove into a parking lot only half-filled with cars. He parked, we got out, and I laughed because the music was so loud the pavement beneath my feet seemed to vibrate.

"Yeeaah boy," Octavious said after pushing the doors apart and entering the facility he'd reserved for my bachelor party. "How ya like me now?" he asked, nodding his head up and down once I entered.

"Courtney. Courtney. Courtney." The all-male guests started into a deep-throat chant while clapping louder and louder.

"What the hell?" I asked, first looking around the smoke-filled room that reeked of testosterone. "Octavious, is this all you?" I asked, knowing he hadn't planned a party alone. First of all, the live DJ was elevated on a stage centered against the wall to the right and had the music bumping. The lights were dim, but the area around the dance floor was well lit and a crystal ball hung from the middle of the ceiling. There were four podiums, one by each corner of the dance floor, with a female wearing nothing but tassels on her breasts and a sequined thong.

"You know Octavious don't play. As always you can . . ." he said, holding out his hands with the palms up.

". . . thank you later," I said, finishing his statement, then giving three of my co-workers a high five.

"Man, this party is straight up Las Vegas style," said my nerdy co-worker who wore glasses an inch thick, then damn near broke his neck when a dancer grabbed her ankle and lifted her leg to touch the side of her face. "Aww shit," he yelped, then pushed his goggles up on his nose. "See you boys later. Man, thanks for the invite."

"My pleasure," I said, taking full credit for his experience. Then I took a beer off a waitress's tray when she passed by wearing only a black lace teddy and a thong.

"Let's party, boys," Octavious said, stopping two dancers by wrapping his arms around their waists when they walked by. "This is my boy's last night as a free man. Girls, let's make it one he'll never forget," he said with a huge smile as they started to gyrate against his body. "Enough for me." He chuckled. "Tonight is Courtney's night."

"Tonight is my night," I repeated, finishing my beer and reaching for another one as the two of them led me by the arm to the middle of the dance floor.

"Girls, excuse my boy for a minute," Octavious said before the song ended, pulling me away.

"Man, what you do that for?" I asked, looking over my shoulder at the pair, who started dirty dancing with each other.

"Hey, you know I got you. Got something for ya to see." He led me through the crowd on the dance floor to a door at the back of the room. "Are you ready, my man?"

"I'm afraid to ask," I said, watching him put his hand on the door knob.

"This ain't for the little boys." He opened the door slowly.

What I saw made my mouth fall to the floor.

"What you waitin' on? Take yo ass inside." He pressed his hand in the middle of my back to push me inside the room and shut the door before anyone else noticed.

"You ain't got no real job," I said, looking at the gigantic purple chair with three of the most exotic girls I'd ever seen seated on the arms.

"I may not have a real job, but I got mad connections." He gestured with his hand for me to take a seat in the chair.

"Here man, have another beer. Naw, have two."

I took a beer out of his hand, walked toward the chair, then climbed up.

"Are you the lucky man?" one of the females purred as she helped me up and onto the chair.

"Yes, I'm the lucky man," I said, looking at the stripper but seeing Tatiana's smile. "Tomorrow I'll be marrying the most beautiful girl in the world," I said as a stripper spread her legs across my lap.

"What are you drinking, handsome?" the one on my left asked, motioning for Octavious to give me another beer.

"What's your flavor?" Octavious asked, pointing toward a small fridge in the corner of the room. "I got Heinekens, Coronas, and Bud Lights chilled and ready to go."

"I'm the guest of honor, so you pick."

"Corona with a slice of lime coming up," Octavious

said, turning his back momentarily, then walking toward me with a fresh brew.

"Relax, baby," the stripper wearing the gold tassels whispered into my ear as she rubbed her hand across my head, down the back of my neck, and into my shirt.

"Yeah," I said nervously, still thinking of Tatiana, then took a gulp of beer. A man like me, with such a scandalous past, didn't deserve her, but I was going to do my best to make it work.

"I'm outta here," Octavious said. "Girls, take care of my boy. This is his last time partying as a single man." He flashed me a peace sign and backed out of the room.

"Don't worry. This will be a night sweet daddy will never forget," the stripper wearing the red tassel said, giggling uncontrollably.

Tatiana

"What's up, girlfriend?" Anyah asked once I opened the door. "Do you have everything?" She picked up my overnight bag and placed it on her shoulder. Before closing the door, I looked around the great room, thinking I would return as Mrs. Courtney Wilkes.

The past two months seemed to have flown by as Courtney and I spent hours discussing our future plans together as husband and wife. Finally we decided to exchange our wedding vows at a small chapel downtown and take an extended vacation the next year. We were both in our thirties and the money we'd spend on a ceremony and reception could be used as a down payment on a new home.

"Whew, I guess so." I draped my garment bag over my arm, grabbed my purse, and pulled the door shut. Following tradition, Courtney and I had agreed not to stay with each other the night before the wedding. As silly as it seemed, he would spend the night at home and I would stay at the hotel where we planned to honeymoon over the weekend. The next time I saw his face would be at the altar.

"Starting to get a little nervous?" she asked, wrapping her arm around my shoulder as we walked to her car.

"Why do you ask?" I said, then heard the tremor in my own voice.

"I can see it in your eyes."

"I think so. We've been living together for a while. How is it that I get butterflies the night before we say our vows?" I asked, starting to wonder if things between us had really gone too fast. *We've only known each other nine months. Anyah has always been apprehensive. Maybe her concerns about the length of our relationship were right,* I thought as she unlocked the trunk and put my bag inside. I wanted to discuss my apprehension with her but didn't want to hear the infamous "Girl, I told you so." So I looked at her, smiled, and laid my garment bag flat in her trunk. *Everyone gets nervous,* I thought, got inside her car, and fastened my seat belt.

"It's natural. But damn that. You can be nervous tomorrow. We're having fun tonight. Look out downtown. Here we come." She turned on the radio, and we bobbed our heads back and forth to Jill Scott's latest release. "This is it," she said ten minutes later when we turned into the parking garage, got out, and walked toward a popular night spot. "Come on, girlfriend." She grabbed my hand and worked her way through the crowd of anxious people to the front of the line. The burly bald-headed man standing at the front door nodded his head and we went inside the club.

A live band with six members was already performing a rhythm and blues medley on stage. Ready to dance I started to walk toward the dance floor. "No, no, girlfriend," she said, locking her arm in mine.

"I thought we were here to party," I said, looking over my shoulder as we walked by the band, through a door and up some narrow wooden steps.

"We are."

"Surprise!" everyone in attendance jumped up and screamed once she opened the door.

In awe, I looked around the room. "Oh my God. Mother, what are you doing here?" I asked, unsure how Anyah ever got my mother into a night club. She was already standing by the door.

"I wouldn't have missed this shower for nothing in the world," Mother said, hugging me. "Honey, I hadn't always been saved. How do you think you got here?" she asked, putting her hands on her hips.

"Too much information," I said, then kissed her on the cheek. Cathy Sue and several teachers from the school were there. Even my Aunt Helen was there.

The private room was decorated tastefully in purple, silver, and white. Round tables were randomly placed around the dance floor, and tall ficus trees adorned with clear lights lit up each corner. On the far right side was a long table filled from end to end with refreshments. From where I stood, I could see shrimp cocktail, meatballs, an assortment of cheeses, and a vegetable tray. If I had to guess, that was Mother's doing. She was a caterer at heart.

"Girlfriend, no, you didn't go there?" I asked, when I looked to my left and saw a fine high-yellow gentleman wearing tuxedo pants and matching vest with no shirt underneath standing behind the bar. Just for me, he turned around and flexed his well-oiled muscles.

"You ain't seen nothing yet." She pointed toward the far right corner where the DJ stood wearing tight blue jeans and no shirt. He leaned over like the incredible hulk and flexed his muscles, which glistened as well. "You know you're my girl. Tomorrow is one of the biggest days of your life, and I'm for damn sure gonna make certain this is the best night of your life."

"This is too much." I folded my arm around Anyah's as she led me to a chair that was beautifully decorated with satin material. One by one, the guests started to shower me with gifts. "Thank you so much," I said over and over again as they placed them around the chair.

"Let's see what you have, girlfriend," Anyah said, handing me Mother's gift first.

"Mother," I screeched when I opened the small box carefully wrapped in silver with a large black bow and pulled out a black leather thong, matching bra, and a whip.

"How do you think I kept your Daddy in line?" she said, then covered her mouth with both hands from laughter. "I'll give you lessons later." After the initial shock of Mother's gift, I continued to unwrap presents that ranged from intimate apparel to bath oils and gels.

"May I have your attention please?" Anyah said. Everyone started to sshh each other and then there was silence. "Tatiana and I have been girls for a long time. She's the sister I never had and tomorrow is the day her mother has been dreaming about." She pointed toward my mother.

"Maybe now I'll get some grandchildren," Mother shouted out.

"And I'll get to be an auntie, because I'm not having any children," Anyah said, laughing. "All jokes aside. I just wanted to take this opportunity to tell her how much we love her and to wish her the best. Everyone, please lift your glasses." She paused while everyone lifted her glass. "Tatiana, this is to the first day of the rest of your life."

"Cheers."

"Now, let's get this party started, DJ," she said, nodding her head and gesturing with her hands for me to stand. I watched as the DJ and the bartender started to walk toward me. "Good Lawd," Anyah said when the DJ stood in front of me, ripped his jeans apart and tossed them across the small dance floor. "It ought to be a law," she said when the bartender stood behind me and started to grind against my body. To stop me from moving, he removed his vest and wrapped it around my waist. "What the heck?" I asked Anyah, then lifted both arms in the air.

"Anyah, look at this," I said when she walked away. In front of me the DJ gyrated, using only his stomach muscles, then lowered himself onto the ground. In utter amazement, I watched as he made his body do things I thought were impossible. I looked down and visualized Courtney gyrating for me the same way.

"Enjoy, girlfriend. That's all I got to say," Anyah said, then waved for the other guests to join us on the dance floor.

"Relax, little mama." The DJ whispered into my ear as Anyah handed me a glass of champagne. "We got you tonight," he said, then turned me around to face him.

Chapter 16

Tatiana

"I wish your father were here to see you," Mother said, wiping a tear from the corner of her eye. "I know he's watching from Heaven because you look like an angel." She took a step back to look at my reflection in the mirror. My strapless cream silk chiffon wedding dress defined elegance at its simplest. My Grandmother Cora's pearl teardrop earrings hung delicately from each ear lobe and the matching necklace adorned my neck.

Eager to make a public confession of our love, Courtney and I had taken two months to plan our wedding day. We chose a wedding chapel downtown that suited all of our needs and decided to honeymoon at a nearby five-star hotel.

"I'm so nervous. Please don't make me cry," I said, batting my eyelashes to fight back tears. Of course I did want my father there, but, like Mother, I believed his spirit was there to guide me. Then I felt a warm tear roll down my cheek.

"I'm sure your Grandmother Cora would want

you to have this," she said, patting the corner of my eye with a white cotton handkerchief embroidered with red roses and delicately trimmed in red thread.

"Thank you, Mother. This means the world to me," I said when she neatly folded the handkerchief and placed it in my hand. Remembering stories of her mother, I wrapped my fingers around it and placed it next to my heart.

"It's only natural to get cold feet at the last minute," Mother said, rubbing my shoulders.

"Would the two of you like some time alone?" Anyah asked, then wiped a tear from the corner of her eye.

"No, I really need you guys here with me." I inhaled to compose myself.

"We're with you every step of the way," Mother said, then confirmed her words with a soft kiss on my cheek.

"I love the two of you so much," I said softly, fighting back another tear, then reaching for both of their hands.

"It's ten o'clock. Are you ready?" Anyah asked with a warm smile that eased the emotional tension in the room.

"Yes, I'm ready."

"Here's your bouquet," Anyah said, handing me five calla lilies that were held by a cream satin bow.

I took a final look at myself in the mirror as Tatiana Yvonne Anderson and blew a kiss. Anyah took a moment to check my makeup and then I stood so Mother could take another look at my dress.

Anyah opened the door and arm in arm Mother and I walked out of the dressing room and followed the short hallway to the chapel. I stood to one side while they entered the chapel and closed the door. At the cue of the prerecorded wedding march, an assistant opened the door and I looked down the short aisle. Mother, Anyah, and Courtney's friend Octavious were seated in the front row to my right. The minister stood beneath a brass arch decorated with artificial ivy and Courtney stood to his left. Two brass spiral candelabras intertwined with ivy, and holding twelve candles whose flames twinkled delicately, stood nobly on each side of the arch.

After a few steps Courtney and I stood side by side.

"I love you," Courtney whispered, reaching for my hand.

"I love you too." That very moment I felt his love and my tension was eased. Almost instantaneously, my mind reverted to the night we met. The way his stare captured me from the other side of the room was spiritual. The connection we had on the dance floor was metaphysical. With him I felt safe, even secure.

I'd met several guys in the past but they were never without flaws. Courtney had never been married, had no children, and had a career. At first it seemed too good to be true. Knowing at that moment that I was getting ready to marry my soul mate, I turned to face the minister. Individually, we professed our love before God and the witnesses who attended the ceremony.

"Mr. Courtney Wilkes, you may now kiss the bride," the minister said after a short but intimate prayer. Courtney rubbed the back of my neck as we leaned into each other for a passionate kiss.

"Congratulations, little sister. You did it," Anyah said after jumping up and hugging both of us. "Take good care of my girl."

"Congratulations, baby. Maybe tonight the two of

you can practice on my grandbabies." Mother stepped forward from her front row seat, hugged me, and kissed me on the cheek. "Welcome to the family, son," Mother said, then hugged Courtney as well. "Please take care of my baby," she said with a warm concern that could be felt from the intensity in her eyes.

"Mrs. Anderson, I promise she's in good hands."

"Man, I still don't know what she ever saw in you," his friend Octavious interjected, making us all bend over from laughter.

"Whatever, man." Courtney said, shaking Octavious's hand, then pulling him in for a hug.

"Enough. Enough," Anyah said, then approached me with a powder sponge and lipstick. "Let's get this face back together because it's picture time," she said, blotting my foundation and refreshing my lipstick.

"Can I get the new couple together first?" the minister turned photographer said as he adjusted the lighting and placed his camera strap around his neck. "Sir, if you would for our first pose, please face the beautiful bride," he said, motioning with his hand for Courtney to turn toward me.

"Wait a minute, let me get my camera," Mother said, opening her purse and pulling out a disposable camera. All I could do was smile as she started to crank the loud and annoying dial.

"Me too," Anyah and Octavious said together, opening their cell phones.

"I love you so much," Courtney said despite the sudden commotion, kissing me on the lips.

"I love you too, baby."

"Hey, lover boy, stop it. You two have the rest of your life to do that," Anyah said then popped him on the shoulder. "Now I've got to redo her lipstick," she said jokingly, then reapplied my lipstick.

"All right, let's show some love," the minister said as we moved for what seemed like forever from one pose to another.

"Love you guys and thanks for everything." Ready to consummate our vows, we bid everyone farewell and exited the chapel as Mr. and Mrs. Courtney Wilkes.

Courtney

I would have paid a million dollars to have captured the look on her face when I opened the chapel door and a black stretch limousine was parked outside. The driver was waiting beside the car and dressed to the nines in his black tuxedo.

"When did you do all of this?" she asked, looking around at the romantic layout after the driver assisted her into the car. On one silver platter I had a bottle of champagne and two glasses. On another platter I had fresh strawberries, grapes, whipped cream, and chocolate.

"For you, my love." I poured two glasses of champagne.

"Courtney, I'm speechless."

"My love, I promise this is only the beginning," I said, holding up my glass for a toast. "To the rest of our lives together as one." I stopped to stare at my bride. All of a sudden the reality of my situation hit me like a ton of bricks. I'd fallen in love and gotten married. Tatiana had my last name.

It didn't seem like it had been two months since I'd gotten down on my knees in the middle of the floor and asked her to marry me. I never knew what came over me. I'd met a lot of females and no one ever measured up to Tatiana. Yeah, some were freakier, but they couldn't pop popcorn. Then there was one chick who could lick me in all the right ways and make me forget my name. But she lived in the projects and had three children with three baby daddies. Tatiana was beautiful, never been married, had no children, and—best of all—had a career. Not a job, but a career. On top of that, she had dreams and goals. Now that was the type of woman I could work with. I had to give her my last name. If I didn't, someone else would come along, get to know her, and the rest would have been history.

"As one," Tatiana repeated as we allowed our glasses to touch. Like the bubbles that bounced off her glass, her eyes sparkled. In amazement I watched her drink.

"Open wide," I said, dipping one of the strawberries into chocolate.

"Mmm," she said after taking a huge bite.

"Take another one." I double dipped the strawberry in chocolate, then put it against her lips. Slowly she took a bite. Watching her chew and seeing the extra chocolate ooze onto her lips was so erotic.

"Mmm," she said again, leaning her head back and closing her eyes. I looked at the driver, then closed the partition for privacy. I didn't give a damn what he heard, as long as he couldn't see it.

"Courtney, that's cold." She squirmed when I dipped another strawberry into the whipped cream and rubbed it down the side of her neck. I let her bite the end and chew while I traced the trail of whipped cream with my tongue.

"Whew," I said, wanting to make love to her right

then and there. "We're here," I said with a smile once the driver drove underneath the exterior covering and stopped at the hotel's front entrance. Proud of my bride, I got out, then stood and waited with my hand extended. Arm in arm, we walked through the lobby and to the elevators. I pressed the button with the up arrow and waited impatiently until the bell dinged and the doors opened. We stepped inside, then fell into each other's embrace. I planted soft kisses on her face until the elevator stopped moving and the doors opened. Hand in hand, we walked to our room, which I had already reserved for the rest of the weekend.

"Ready?" I asked after sliding the magnetic door key into the card reader.

"Yes, baby, I'm ready," she said, giggling when I scooped her up in my arms and carried her over the threshold. Still holding her, I used my leg to shut the door.

"Two days of uninterrupted pure passion and pleasure," I said, then spun her around.

"You can't handle me," she said when I stopped and placed her on the edge of the deluxe king-sized bed.

"Oh, really?"

"Really." She leaned back on her arms and pulled her dress up around her waist.

"Let's see."

"I'm waiting," she sang.

To tease her, I took off my jacket and tossed it over a chair. I turned my back, unzipped my pants, then turned back around. Then I unbuttoned my shirt, snatched it off, and flexed my chest muscles.

"Come to mama," she said, obviously enjoying the foreplay and knowing what buttons to push for more.

"You want Big Daddy?" I asked after getting down on my knees in front of her.

"You know I do." She grabbed the top of my head and lowered it onto her lap.

With my teeth I gripped the lace garter belt and slid it down her leg to remove it. I slipped off one shoe at a time, then eased my hand underneath her dress to remove her pantyhose. Taking my time, I swirled my tongue up her bare leg, between her inner thighs and removed her panties with my teeth. Ready to satisfy my new bride, I kissed the tip of her big toe and didn't stop until my head disappeared between her thighs. I didn't give a damn about her wedding dress and stayed there until she yelled from pleasure. She was my wife, and I for damn sure wanted her to know it.

Chapter 17

Tatiana

"There it is," Cathy Sue said, pointing toward my hips when I strutted by her and waved. It was my first day back to work after becoming Mrs. Tatiana Wilkes.

"There what is?" I asked, stopping in front of her door and posing like a runway model with one foot turned at a forty-five-degree angle and placed slightly in front of the other.

"The newlywed walk," she said, rolled her neck, and put a hand on her hip.

"I'm afraid to ask." I shook my head from side to side before speaking again. "What is the newlywed walk?"

"You're limping from having sex all weekend," she said after leaning closer to my ear and laughing.

"I'm not limping." I laughed then stopped abruptly. "I'm not, am I?" I asked. Except to use the restroom and eat, we had made love all weekend long.

"You know what the old folks say. The truth will

always walk a lie down," she said with a smile, then pinched me on the hips. "No, girl, there's nothing wrong with your walk. As a matter of fact, I couldn't be happier for you. Since Christmas break you've had a natural glow. It's obvious that you and Courtney are meant for each other," she said, then hugged me.

"I have pictures from the wedding and the shower. You'll have to stop by my room during lunch and look at them," I said when the chattering students started to fill the hallway.

"See you later."

"Good morning, Mrs. Wilkes," the students sang in unison once they were settled into their seats.

"Good morning, class," I said with a smile, not yet used to my new title and last name. "Did you all behave for the substitute yesterday?" I asked, looking at Mitchell.

"Yes, ma'am, I was very good," he said, then looked over his shoulder at Joshua, totally giving his innocence away.

"Yes, Elaine," I said, acknowledging the hand that was raised in the back. She stood and walked to the front of the classroom wearing a huge grin.

"Yesterday when you were absent, we made you a wedding present." She turned an easel around.

"That is so thoughtful. Thank you so much," I said after looking at the drawing of a three-tier wedding cake with all of their signatures and personal notes inside.

"Mrs. Wilkes, we just wanted you to know that we are happy for you. You're our favorite teacher."

"You're my favorite students," I said, then started to read some of their comments. "I'm going to frame this and hang it in my studio at home."

"For real?" Mitchell shouted from the back.

"Yes, Mitchell, for real. Now let's get to work."

"Aww, man, thought you'd like the present and give us a free day today," Mitchell said.

"Not a chance." I moved the easel to one side, then clapped my hands to get their attention. I turned around when I heard my cell phone vibrate. Without disturbing the class, I walked behind my desk to open the drawer and peep inside. It was a text message from Courtney.

Courtney: Missing you already, Mrs. Wilkes. I love you.

Tatiana: Love you too, I responded. I smiled, put the phone back into my purse, and turned my attention back to the class.

One period after another, my students entered, then left. Wanting to work on lesson plans, I ate lunch in my room and was surprised when Cathy Sue didn't barge in to interrupt me with a million and one questions. Forty-five minutes later the routine continued as students hurried in and out of my classroom until the final bell rang for the day.

Making several attempts to unlock the door before the telephone stopped ringing, I struggled with my keys. *If it is important, they'll call back,* I thought to myself as I inserted the key into the lock, readjusted my purse and tote bag on my shoulder, then opened the door. "Hello," I answered, gasping for breath.

"You know I've been waiting on your phone call," Courtney said once I answered.

"Hey, babe. I had a few errands to run immediately after work. We were gone all weekend and I needed to get groceries and a few other household items. My cell phone was on. Why didn't you call it?" I said, relieving myself of the purse and tote bag by placing them on the couch.

"I did, and it went straight to your voice mail," he said, then took a deep breath.

"Hmm." I opened my purse to make sure it was on and checked the menu for any missed calls. Unless something was wrong with my cell phone, there were none. "I just checked and it was on." I closed my cell phone, then put it back inside my purse.

"Don't make me worry about you."

"Worry?" I asked, then smiled after thinking how lucky I was to have such a concerned husband. "Don't worry. I'm a big girl."

"Yeah, you may be, but now you're *my* big girl. So remember that the next time you have to run errands," he said sounding more authoritative than concerned. I'd heard that tone in his voice before but decided to ignore it. Then I wondered if my smile should become a frown.

"I don't think so," I said with an attitude, then rolled my eyes at the telephone. "I've only been Mrs. Wilkes three days."

"I was worried, that's all. I guess I'm taking my job too seriously."

"What job?" I asked unsure when being a husband had been classified as a job.

"Protecting you. See you when I get off."

"What time will you make it home?" I asked, wanting to make sure dinner was prepared on time.

"It should be no later than five. Remember who loves you."

"You do." I went back outside to get the groceries out of the car.

"Dang, Courtney," I said when I heard the telephone start to ring again. I hurried to reopen the door and almost dropped my groceries.

"Hey, Mrs. Wilkes. Whatcha doing?" Anyah asked when I answered the telephone gasping for breath. "Do ya'll ever get tired of having sex? You just finished your honeymoon."

"For your information, I wasn't having sex." I shut the door with my foot and tucked the telephone between my ear and shoulder. "I just made it home from the grocery store. I'm getting ready to cook dinner." I went into the kitchen, placed my bags on the counter, and started to unpack them.

"Cook dinner?" Anyah asked as though she were surprised. "Girl, when have I ever you heard you say 'cook dinner'? Blend a shake or heat up a meal—now I've heard that, but never 'cook dinner'."

"That's what I said. I like to have his dinner ready when he gets home. After his long day on the streets, that's the least I could do."

"I hear ya, Martha Stewart," she said ironically. "How was your weekend getaway?"

"Girlfriend, if I tell you the truth I would have to kill you." I picked up a manila envelope and started to fan myself.

"Did he put it on you?"

"Did he?" I asked, then had to lean against the counter. We'd made love in every position known to man, then invented some of our own. "Mmm," was all I could say after thinking about my multiple orgasms. "Everything from the time we left the chapel until the moment we checked out was perfect—almost fairy tale."

"I must admit I had my doubts, but I'm still happy for you."

"Thanks, girl."

"Let me let you go so you can be wifey," she said, laughing.

"Bye." I finished putting away the groceries, then

went into the bedroom to change into something more comfortable before starting dinner.

"Mmm, something smells good in here," Courtney said when he walked into the kitchen with his duffel bag thrown over his shoulder. His shirt was already pulled out of his pants and unbuttoned at the collar.

"Your timing is perfect." I removed, from the oven, the baked chicken seasoned with his favorite spices and smothered with onions and green bell peppers and allowed him to smell it. The standards my mother set as a wife and mother were high. Following them was my intention. Not only did she work every day; she also managed to cook healthy meals, kept the house immaculate, and supported my father.

"Let me kiss the chef." He leaned down and gave me a wet smack on the lips.

"Take a shower and get comfortable so that you can enjoy your meal."

"I'll be back before you realize I'm gone." He kissed me again, then went into the bedroom to shower and change clothes. When I heard the water from the shower stop running, I fixed our plates and set the table.

"How was work today?" I asked after sitting down at the table in front of him.

"An absolute trip." He shook his head from side to side, then used his knife to cut into his chicken.

"What was a trip about it?" I asked, then folded one leg underneath my body, ready to listen.

"I don't want to bore you with any details."

"They're never boring," I said, cutting into a piece of chicken and putting it into my mouth.

"It was the usual influx of domestic violence calls and a couple of car accidents. Baby, I'm home now and I'd rather not talk about it, if you don't mind. Home is my safe haven, and I'd prefer to keep it that way."

"You talked to me about it before Saturday," I said with a puzzled look on my face, thinking how graphic his descriptions could get. Why all of a sudden was there an attitude change?

"Things have changed. This is a new day. I want our house to be peaceful. When I drive off the precinct parking lot, that's where I want work to stay from now on. Can you respect that?" he asked with a stern look on his face.

"Sure," I said, more taken aback by his expression than his comment.

"Would you like to hear about my day?" I asked, forcing a smile, but wanting to share how my students had surprised me with an oversized wedding card.

"Maybe later," he said, never looking up and continuing to eat.

"Baby, may I have a second of your time?" Courtney asked after entering my studio wearing a huge smile, and holding a legal pad and ink pen in his hand. After his harsh comment, we'd finished dinner in silence. Then he'd gone into the bedroom and I cleaned off the table and washed dishes.

Instead of frustrating him with more questions, I thought it would be better to go into my studio. So I poured myself a glass of wine to unwind. Painting was always a good stress reliever, and most times it was when I was most creative. After seeing the smile on his face, it was obvious that both of us had needed the down time.

"Sure. If you don't mind, give me a few minutes to finish this piece," I said, doing a few more strokes and not stopping until I was pleased with my impromptu project. "Done." I put the paint brush down and wiped my hands on my smock.

"I didn't mention it to you, but I've been crunching some numbers at work for the past couple of weeks."

I took a sip of wine and turned to look at him.

"I've estimated that if we both contribute extra monthly to the household account, we should have our debts paid off in four months maximum."

"What debt?" I asked assertively. "I have one low-interest rate credit card for emergencies. The balance is less than four hundred dollars," I said, not quite comprehending his plan, then took another sip of wine. After our engagement, the two of us realized that splitting the household expenses fifty-fifty made more sense. That way the burden wouldn't be on one person. The household expenses included the rent, utilities, telephone, and cable—not personal bills, which we both agreed would remain separate.

"Baby, our marriage has a lot of financial potential. In order for it to work, we have to function as a team. You know what's mine is yours and what's yours is mine," he said, then placed his pad on my drafting table.

My eyes widened when I looked at his well-written, itemized list, which included every expense from our rent to his monthly credit card bills.

"Just think: one year from now, we could be like the Jeffersons, moving into your dream home."

"Oh really?" I asked then folded my arms in front

of me. After looking at his list, it seemed like more of his was getting ready to become mine.

"Let me show you," he said, turning the page on his legal pad. "If we stick to my plan, we'll qualify for a low-interest home loan in no time at all."

"OK, and how are we supposed to do this with no savings?" I asked, leaning my head to one side.

"Like I said, if we follow my plan, we'll be moving in a year. The way I see it, if we start with the lowest balance, we should have all the bills paid off in four months."

I squinted and leaned closer to look at the long list of balances underneath his name, then snapped my neck to look at him. From a quick glance, I counted four credit cards with a balance that totaled at least ten thousand dollars.

"Listen to me," he said, tapping the paper with his pencil to get my attention again. "Once we pay off all the bills, the money we used toward those can all go into our joint savings account."

"Joint savings account?"

"I'm off Friday. If you leave work a few minutes early, we can go to the bank and take care of it Friday afternoon."

"Really?" I asked, taking another sip of wine.

"Do you trust me?"

"Of course I do."

"Well, trust me with everything. I promise if you stick to the plan, it will work out beautifully." He stood behind me and eased his hands into my shirt, starting to rub my nipples between his thumb and index fingers. "You can thank me when we move into your dream home."

Thinking about his one-year plan made me tense. I had a million and one questions, so making love to him was the last thing I wanted to do at the time. My body didn't respond, so he leaned down and started to kiss the side of my neck.

"Just trust me. I promise it will work," he whispered softly into my ear.

"I don't know. What about—" I said, then stopped when I felt my nipples start to get hard. "How will we be—" I started to speak again, but he turned me around and lifted my shirt up to expose a breast.

"How will what be?" he asked, then put a breast into his mouth and started to tug on it gently.

"The only thing I know right now is how good your tongue feels," I said, closing my eyes.

Chapter 18

Tatiana

"I called your house and no one answered the telephone," Anyah said when I pressed the button on my earpiece to answer my cell phone. "Is everything OK?"

"Yes, everything is fine."

"Did you go clearance shopping without me?"

"Now you know I wouldn't do that. A local community center was having a health fair, so I signed up to paint faces for the children," I said, tilting the face of the six-year-old girl seated on a small stool in front of me.

"If I didn't know you already, I would say that you were a saint. Your unconditional love for children is so obvious. Girl, I don't have the patience."

"Turn your head and look into the mirror," I said, pointing toward the small mirror on the table beside me.

"Ahhh, it's a butterfly. Mommy, look what the nice lady painted on my face."

"It's lovely. How much is it?" her mother asked, opening her purse and removing a wallet.

"Donations only," I responded with a smile.

"Thank you," she said, dropping a five-dollar bill into my container.

"Sorry, girl. I'm back," I said, readjusting my ear piece.

"Interested in a shopping spree later this afternoon? That is, if you and hubby don't have plans."

"Sure," I said hesitantly, then leaned the bucket with loose change and a few dollar bills to one side.

"What time will you be done with your community service?"

"The carnival ends at two. So give me time to get home, shower, and change clothes."

"I'll pick you up at three o'clock. Wear some comfortable shoes."

"See you," I said, then focused my attention on three giggling girls looking through my sample book. For minimal donations, I continued to paint faces for two more hours.

"Let's go into Guess," she said, pointing toward the store and cutting through a crowd to the other side of the mall. "I see sale signs," she said, after I caught up.

"Fine," I said, following without as much enthusiasm.

"My purse." All I heard was a high-pitched squeal as she scurried to the back of the store. "I've been watching this baby all season. Now it's twenty-five percent off. Don't you love it?" she asked after putting it on her shoulder and modeling in the full-length mirror. "Look, they have another one," she said, grabbing an identical one off the shelf and handing it to me.

"What am I going to do with this?" I asked, ready to return it to the shelf.

"Are you ill or did you inhale too much of that paint today?" she asked, turning to look at the purse from another angle.

"I have enough purses," I said dryly, trying at least to convince myself.

"No woman alive has enough purses or shoes."

"Maybe next week." I took a final glance at the oversized emblem I loved so well, then tossed it back on the shelf.

"Oh my God," she said seriously, putting her hand on my forehead as though checking for a fever. "If you're not feeling well, let me take you home."

"I'm fine." I moved my head away from her hand. Having that purse on my shoulder was like kryptonite to Superman. Clearance shopping was an all-time favorite event for us and my biggest weakness.

"Are you pms'ing? When does your period start?"

"Anyah," I said slowly to get her attention. "I'm fine. I promise." Then I debated how badly spending eighty dollars on a purse I didn't need would really affect our new budget.

"If you don't buy this purse, I know something is wrong."

"I love the purse. Courtney has developed a one-year financial plan. Our first priority is to eliminate all credit-card debt by doubling monthly payments," I said, watching each corner of her lips curl.

"So, this one-year plan excludes an eighty-dollar purchase?" she asked, placing her index finger on her top lip.

"We both agreed to limit our spending. Initially I

didn't see how Courtney's plan would work. Then I realized he was right. We are a team and together we could be like the Jeffersons. Willing to give it a try, I set aside my fears and implemented the first step of his plan, opening joint accounts. The second step was to limit our spending and contribute more toward the household account," I said slowly, reminding myself of the commitment we'd made to make it work.

"Don't you work every day?" she asked, then started to look at other purses on the clearance shelf.

"Yes, and what's your point?"

"Here girl, look at this one," she said, turning around and placing an even prettier purse on my shoulder. I looked at it, then put it back on the shelf.

"Xavier and I practice the 80-10-10 plan."

"Yeah, I know all about your plan. Eighty percent of your income is used for household expenditures, ten percent for saving and the last ten percent to reward yourself."

"OK, now get your purse." She picked up the first one and handed it to me.

"It's OK. I don't need it."

"Well, I need mine." She snatched the purse out of my hand and strutted toward the sales counter.

"Happy Birthday," she said, handing me a huge red shopping bag.

"Hey babe," I said, walking over and kissing Courtney on the forehead. It was after ten o'clock and he was lying down on the couch watching television. Anyah and I hadn't been shopping in months and didn't leave the mall until they made the closing announcements.

"What's that in your hand?" he asked, pointing at my shopping bag.

"A new purse." I lifted the bag, proud of the gift Anyah had given me. Courtney wasn't at home after the fair so I'd called him on his cell phone, letting him know that dinner was in the fridge and Anyah and I were going to the mall. "I'm pulling some overtime. So have a good time," was all he'd said.

"What about our one-year plan?" he asked sternly, repositioning his body in an upright position.

"What about it?" I asked, shocked by his immediate response. I wasn't in the mood to have our first argument as husband and wife. My feet were hurting from hours of walking and my calf muscles were throbbing.

"We agreed to limit our spending. The plan will not work if you don't stop your impulsive shopping sprees," he said, pointing at my bag again. "Never mind what's in the bag. The question is how much did you spend?"

"Excuse me?" I asked after my head almost spun off my shoulders. I had agreed to his one-year plan but never agreed to be treated like a child.

"How much did you spend?"

"How much did I spend?" I repeated, placing a hand on my hip from disbelief. Out of anger, I looked down at my shopping bag, then looked at him. If my new Guess purse wasn't so pretty, I would have smacked him with it.

"How much did you spend?" he repeated slowly as though I were deaf and didn't hear him the first time.

"I'd been single longer than I've been married. Plus, the last time I checked, I was a working, taxpaying adult," I said sternly after he pushed me to verbalize my previous thought.

"Yes, Tatiana, I'm serious about our finances."

"You're no more serious than I am." I pointed at him, then pointed back at myself. "After you walked into my studio with your little memo pad and explained your plan, you asked me to trust you. As a matter of fact, you asked me to trust you with everything. Well, the trust goes both ways," I spouted. "For your information, I didn't spend anything. Anyah bought it for me after I told her about our ridiculous one-year plan," I said, regretting that I didn't spend the eighty dollars myself. Upset beyond words, I turned on one heel, went into our bedroom, and shut the door.

Courtney

"Damn," I said, wanting to kick myself in the ass after pissing Tatiana off. *Should I give her time to cool off or should I follow her into the bedroom?* I asked myself, putting my hand on my head and falling back onto the couch. It was the first time I'd ever seen her that mad at me. We'd had our disagreements, but that time I saw her bottom lip quiver. *I'll give her a few seconds to calm down. Maybe she'll come out first,* I thought, then sat there and watched the bedroom door like a dumb-ass.

She ain't coming out. To hell with it. She isn't going to bed mad at me tonight. I peeled my ass up off the couch and walked toward the bedroom. "Tatiana," I said after easing the door open, hoping she wasn't standing behind it ready to hit me across the head.

"Yes." She was sitting on the edge of the bed with her arms folded and her legs crossed.

Being a man of the law, I knew that wasn't a good

sign at all. She was pissed. Getting her to talk to me or scream at me was a better option than silence. "Look," I said, holding both hands up in front of me. "I want to apologize for overreacting when you walked through the door. I should have asked questions before making an assumption."

"You're damn right you should have," she said then rolled her eyes at me. It was the first time she'd ever cursed at me.

"We've talked about our dreams and goals. As your husband, I feel that making them happen is my responsibility," I said, hoping that anything I said was making sense to her because it for damn sure wasn't making sense to me. "Please accept my apology." I walked toward her slowly, making sure there was nothing within arm's reach for her to throw.

"Getting married was a huge step for me." She started to talk but her arms were still folded. "I've never had to discuss my finances with anyone. Let alone get anyone's approval before making a minor purchase," she said, uncrossing her legs. "As a child, I watched my mother and how she was toward my father. Everything he said was the truth and nothing but the truth. But he respected her and her opinions. That I did know for a fact. He wasn't a tyrant. As your wife, I want to give you that same support. But one thing for sure—treating me like a two-year-old isn't how you're ever going to get it," she said sternly, unfolded her arms, and stood up. "I'm an adult and expect that you treat me that way."

"Tatiana," I said, grabbing her by the arm as she tried to walk by me. She was mad as hell but seeing the fire in her eyes made me horny as hell. I wanted to rip off her clothes and make love to her in the middle of the bedroom floor. "I'm sorry. Will you forgive me?" I asked, hugging her against her will.

Chapter 19

Courtney

"Tatiana," I called from my computer desk in the great room. Proud of my accomplishment, I swiveled my leather chair from one side to the other, then leaned back. She had been in her studio painting all evening. Her seeing what I was about to do was imperative, so I interrupted.

"Yes, Courtney," she said after walking to the door.

"Baby, you have got to see this," I said, waving for her to come and look at the information displayed on my monitor. It had been four months since I presented my plan to her and, one bill at a time, we'd paid them off and increased our savings. I worked every hour of overtime I could, picked up some side cash, and Tatiana did extra projects and had sold a few paintings.

"OK. Look at what?" She looked at the monitor, then at me.

"Do you see this Web site?" I asked, pointing at the monitor.

"Yes, I see it," she said with a puzzled look on her face.

"It is the last creditor we owe." I wrapped my arms around her waist and leaned her against me. "Voilà. Let's make the balance of this last bill disappear." I hit enter on our keyboard to electronically pay off our last bill. "A few months. Just like I said. Now it's time for us to implement phase two of our master plan," I said, opening the drawer to get the memo pad I'd written my original notes on.

"Wow, I'm impressed." Tatiana said, staring at the monitor.

"My name is Courtney Wilkes. Didn't you know I was a bad man?" I asked, then pretended to pop my collar.

"I do now." She gave me a big hug and kissed me on the forehead.

"Go into the bedroom and put on something nice. We're going out to celebrate tonight." After accomplishing phase one, I wanted to celebrate our success. We'd managed to stick to our budget for four months and one night on the town wouldn't divert my plan any.

"What?" she asked, then put her hands on her hips. "Aren't we on a budget?"

"Tonight, baby, no rules apply. Now go and get dressed," I said, giving her a hard pat on the behind.

Tatiana

"I don't know how, but he did it. Well, I know how he did it. He did it with my support." I turned on the water, undressed, and stepped inside the shower. In four months, all of the bills were paid off. He asked me to trust him with the finances and that's what I did. Contributing to one account and allowing him to manage the bills was a stress reliever. I was productive at school and spent more time in the studio working on art projects.

"What do you think about me now?" He undressed, opened the shower door, and stepped inside. Like Superman, he put a hand on each hip and inhaled to expand his chest.

"I'm impressed." I filled the washcloth with shower gel and turned around to lather his body. Making large circles, I started at his neck area, massaged his chest, then moved downward to wash each leg.

"Now all we have to do is start phase two." He turned around so I could scrub his back. "I know you didn't think I could do it." We changed positions so he could stand beneath the shower head and rinse off. "Did you?" he asked, wanting an answer.

"Baby, I knew you could do it all along," I said with a smile, but remembering my initial doubts. We changed positions as I filled the washcloth with gel and lathered my body. He reached over my shoulder for the washcloth and washed my back.

"Yeah, baby, it's called teamwork. Two heads are always better than one." He handed me the washcloth, then turned my body around to rinse off my back.

"Now, let's get ready for a night on the town. What do you have in mind?" he asked, lifting my chin with his finger.

"I don't know," I said, suddenly excited that we weren't going to be bound by spending limitations.

"You can think about it while we get dressed." He grabbed a towel off the rack, then stepped out.

I thought of ten different things to do while finishing my shower, then turned off the water. "Let's go dancing, then out for breakfast afterwards." I reached for the other towel and patted myself dry before stepping out.

"Pretty lady, put on your dancing shoes," he said with a smile, doing a few dance steps in the middle of the floor.

Together we walked inside the closet to find something to wear.

"How long has it been since we've been out dancing?" I turned to ask Courtney once he paid our cover charge and we entered the well-known night club. It was dim, but variously colored fluorescent track lights rotated angles to create a spectacular light show. One level up, red vinyl booths with tables facing the large dance floor lined the walls. The enclosed DJ booth was to our left and the bar was close to the door. The bass beat was deafening and it was standing room only.

"I didn't think it had been that long." Courtney shouted into my ear, then looked around the room filled with twenty-something-year-olds. "I feel like somebody's granddaddy in here tonight," he said, rubbed his face, then laughed. "I thought this club catered to a more mature audience."

"The last time I was in here the crowd was mature," I said, then laughed when a group wearing baggy blue jeans and matching T-shirts started to do a routine in the middle of the dance floor.

"Is this the right club?" Courtney asked, looking around the room for any other significant changes.

"Excuse me, sir," a young lady wearing tight blue

jeans and a halter top said after bumping into
Courtney.

"'Sir,'" he said, then looked at me. "Do I look like
a 'sir' to you?"

"No, you do not look like a 'sir'," I said, then
kissed him on the lips. "We've paid to get in. Let's
at least go to the bar and have a drink." I held his
hand to weave through the energetic crowd and
was relieved to see a slightly different age group
around the bar. "I see two seats on the other side."

"Good, because a drink is exactly what I need
right now." With a look of disappointment, he
plopped down at the bar. I, on the other hand, was
just glad to get out and didn't care how old the
crowd was.

"What can I do for you?" asked the male bartender, who didn't look one day over twenty-one.
His brown skin was smooth and he only had a
shadow for a mustache.

"Rémy and coke for me and white Zinfandel for
the Mrs."

"Gotcha," the bartender said, fixed our drinks,
and placed them in front of us.

"To phase two." Courtney lifted his glass for a
toast.

"Phase two." We toasted to celebrate our accomplishment, then started to groove to the music.
Soon Courtney's frown disappeared, and his movements became more fluid, as though nothing really
mattered.

"Listen, baby that's our jam," I said when the DJ
played one of the slow songs we'd danced to the
night of the Christmas party. Suddenly the younger
crowd migrated off of the dance floor and stood
against the walls. "Baby, let's dance." Hand in hand,
we went to the dance floor, which soon filled with

three or four older couples. Like the night we met, I rested against his chest, closed my eyes, and started to groove to the music.

"Who is that?" Courtney asked, tapping me on the shoulder.

"Who is who?" I asked, never opening my eyes.

"That dude over there against the wall." He tapped me again, then pointed.

"What dude?" I asked after opening my eyes and looking in the direction of his finger. No one in the crowd looked familiar. "I don't see anyone," I said, then leaned back against his chest.

"If you don't know him, what in the hell is he looking at?" Courtney asked, then stopped dancing before the song ended.

"Baby, I don't know what he's looking at," I said calmly, still unsure why he'd become so uptight.

"He's looking at something," Courtney said with an attitude, leading me by the hand off the dance floor and back to the bar.

"Rémy and coke," Courtney said after tapping the bar to get the bartender's attention.

"Same thing for the lady?" the bartender asked Courtney, who didn't respond.

"Yes, that will be fine," I said, turning to look at Courtney. He'd already sat down and I was standing there waiting on him to assist me. He was staring at the stranger and never looked at me. "What is wrong with you?" I sat down and placed both arms on the bar.

"Nothing," he said, still staring across the room. Then he felt behind his waist where he usually kept his gun strapped off-hours.

"OK, nothing," I said when the bartender placed our drinks in front of us. Now that was a first. *Was he getting ready to create a scene?* I wondered, then leaned to one side to look at him. I took a sip of my drink and tried to ignore his behavior. It had been months since we'd been out, and I wasn't going to let a stranger ruin my evening. I rolled my eyes at Courtney, then started to groove to the music.

"Let's get out of here," Courtney snapped.

"We've only been here one hour," I said after looking at my watch.

"I'm ready to leave." Courtney turned up his glass to finish his drink, moved his chair back, and stood.

Not wanting to create a scene, I looked at the couple beside me and smiled. I finished my drink, then stood to leave. I reached for Courtney's hand, but he kept it to his side. "What was that all about?" I asked with an attitude once we exited the building.

"You tell me." He took long steps to the car, unlocked the doors from his side, then got inside.

What in the hell just happened? I thought to myself, opening my door after he made it obvious he wasn't going to, then got inside. Forgetting about anything we were supposed to celebrate, we rode home in silence.

Courtney

Who in the hell was that dude who kept staring at Tatiana? I thought to myself after we got into the car and drove out of the parking lot. When we moved in together I asked her if there were any acquaintances I should know about and she said no. I asked her if there were any boyfriends that could potentially be a problem and she said no. Christopher was the only person she mentioned. *Who in the hell was that?* I asked myself again, then looked over at her. Her arms were folded and she was staring out the window.

"What was up with that?" Tatiana asked me once we turned onto our street.

"All I wanted to know was who was the dude who kept staring at you."

"And I told you I didn't know who he was."

"That's what you said, but he looked at you like he knew you."

"How can someone look at you like they know you?" she asked, then turned to look at me.

"The way he did," I said, thinking back on the many nights I'd managed to send signals to married women from the other side of the room. With one look, I could have a female in the back of the club ready to pull her panties down. The look he had on his face was the look I was known for giving. "You know the look I'm talking about."

"You know what—this is ridiculous. I'm not going to argue with you tonight, Courtney Wilkes. We were supposed to celebrate our accomplishment and you managed to ruin a perfectly good evening," Tatiana shouted.

"Damn, Tatiana, what in the hell are you doing?" I asked when she started to open the car door as soon as I turned into the driveway. I panicked because the car was still moving. "Don't kill your damn self," I shouted, trying to reach over her body and shut the door.

"Stop the damn car," she said, gritting her teeth.

"Tatiana, please wait a minute," I said, grabbing the steering wheel with both hands and pressing on the brakes.

"No, you wait a minute," she said, opening the

door. I put my arms over her lap to stop her from getting out.

"You don't understand." She didn't understand that my demons were slowly coming back to haunt me. I thought I could erase my memory and forget about all of the low-down things I'd done to females in my past. *Some things weren't meant to be forgotten,* I thought after finally coming to my senses.

Tatiana was a beautiful woman and I couldn't overreact every time someone complimented her with a look. Being her husband should make me proud. "You're beautiful," I said, turning her head to look into her huge brown eyes. "I've never been the jealous type, but tonight the way that guy stared at you made me furious." Ashamed, I shook my head from side to side.

"Courtney, I've never seen that man before in my life," she said with sincerity in her eyes. All of a sudden I felt like a damn fool for ruining our evening, and I hoped she would forgive me.

"I have to remember you're my wife now. Look is all another man can do. Right?" I asked, looking at her for confirmation.

"My last name is Wilkes."

"Are you still hungry?" I asked, hoping she would accept that as an apology.

"Very."

I exhaled, then backed out of the driveway. Even though we rode to the waffle house in silence, we spent the rest of the evening discussing phase two of my plan.

Chapter 20

Tatiana

"Mrs. Wilkes, how does it feel?" he asked, unlocking the door of our new three-bedroom home with two and a half baths and a two-car garage. We'd spent hours on the Internet and scanned the newspaper weekly. Finally, a house within our price range seemed appealing. It was the perfect find, and we both fell in love after the first tour. The five-year-old colonial style home with all brick exterior was in the suburbs and less than thirty-five minutes from either of our jobs. The half-acre lot was professionally landscaped with shrubbery and the kitchen's eating area had a bay window that looked out into a floral garden.

"Like a dream come true." I was caught off guard when he turned around, placed one arm around my shoulder and the other one beneath my legs. I laughed when he lifted me and carried me across the threshold. I held onto his neck tightly as he walked through the two-story foyer into the middle of the great room, then spun me around. He stopped and stared into my eyes as he lowered me to the floor.

It had only been a few months since we implemented phase two of his plan, but things seemed to move at lightning speed. We worked extensive amounts of overtime, paid household expenses with one check, and put the rest into our savings account. With dreamy eyes, I stared at the antique gold light fixture that hung so gracefully, illuminating the foyer. "It will feel like our home in no time. All it needs is a little touch of color and my artwork. I can put my latest piece over the fireplace and put another piece on an easel in the corner." Excited, I pointed at each of the bare walls, then went into the master bedroom to look around. The large room with a sitting area, visually separated by two eight-foot columns, was painted a classic tan color. The master bathroom, with an arched doorway, featured the same wall color that perfectly coordinated with the neutral ceramic tile flooring. In one corner was a five-foot-long Jacuzzi tub surrounded by cream marble and next to it was a full-sized shower.

"I promise this is only the beginning. Make love to me," Courtney said after grabbing me by the waist and turning me to face him.

"What about the movers?"

"What about them? It will be at least an hour before they get here," he said, referring to the driving distance from our condo to the new home.

When I parted my lips to speak, he put his index finger over them. Courtney unbuttoned his pants, then unzipped them. His breathing became deep as he placed his hand over mine then stroked himself up and down. Suddenly the movements stopped. Following his lead, we took large steps backward until he was standing against the far wall. He stepped out of his pants, then slid along the wall onto the floor. I watched as he unzipped my pants and lowered them around my ankles. One leg at a time I stepped out of them. He spread my legs apart and lowered me onto his lap. He stared into my eyes and moaned as he gyrated beneath me. Aggressively, he pulled me closer and pulled my breasts out of my cotton T-shirt. He held one in each hand, pushed them together and put them both into his mouth. The sensation was unbelievable, as he sucked on my nipples until they were firm. I wrapped my arms around his neck and my legs around his waist as he stood, then leaned back against the wall. He entered me with such force that I didn't know whether to scream from pain or moan from pleasure. So I held my breath and dug into the hollow part of his back with my fingertips. I was shocked by his aggressiveness but dared not complain.

"Oh, baby, this feels so good," he said as his knees started to tremble.

"Please don't hold back." It was at that moment that I knew I had it all. What I thought was too good to be true had just become a reality. Together our bodies slid along the wall onto the floor.

"I'm ready to start a family," Courtney said when I picked up his paper plate and cup. The movers had been late and we'd spent all evening unpacking boxes and arranging furniture. We ordered take-out and decided to have a picnic in our new dining room since it was the only room without furniture.

"Start a family?" I asked, stepping over his legs, which were spread across the blanket we'd put in the middle of the dining room floor.

"I'm ready for you to quit your job and concentrate on having some little Courtneys." He looked at me, then leaned back on his elbows.

"Stop playing. You know we're not ready to start a family," I said, thinking about our new financial responsibilities.

"Tatiana, I'm serious. I hadn't said anything to you, but I've been thinking about this for a while. As a matter of fact, I've been crunching numbers and working on another plan."

"Plus, we just moved and need both incomes to support our new home."

"I've thought about that, too. Things seem to be looking better for the city and we can get unlimited overtime. I can pay all our bills on one income."

"You're serious," I said, suddenly excited that he wanted us to have a child together. I had doubts about starting a family so soon, but the smile on his face gave me butterflies.

"We have three bedrooms. One can be the nursery and the other can be used as your studio. I'm sure you could make more money selling paintings and be happier doing it from home."

"Painting full-time has always been my dream, but not until we're ready," I said, wanting to be sure he wasn't delirious before I got my hopes up.

"We're ready," he said, standing up. "I'm ready to practice." He reached up and rubbed my stomach.

"Courtney, I need to clean up our mess," I said, playfully pointing at the open food cartons placed around the blanket.

"Believe me, it can wait." With an intense look, he took what I was holding out of my hand and placed it on the floor. Then he reached for my hand and pulled me down on top of him.

Chapter 21

Tatiana

"Girlfriend, what's up?" Anyah asked when I answered my cell phone. Courtney had gone to work, and I was on my way to the store to pick up some groceries and cleaning supplies.

"Everything," I said, still excited about the conversation Courtney had had with me the previous night about starting a family.

"How did the move go?"

"Everything was fine once the movers arrived."

"Xavier and I can't wait to visit. What about this evening?" she asked with excitement in her voice.

"This weekend will be better. It will give me more time to unpack and clean up. I'd hate for you to see the house in such a mess," I said, looking at myself in the rearview mirror. The house wasn't the only thing that was a mess. I had a bandanna on my head and was wearing a pair of torn blue jeans and one of Courtney's T-shirts. *Humph, that's unusual,* I thought. Traveling two cars behind me was an old white van. I could have sworn one of the two gentlemen in it was looking into my car with a pair of binoculars. *Maybe I'm seeing things,* I thought, returning to our conversation.

"Girl, I'm not coming to look at your mess. I'm coming to look at that house of yours."

"Tell you what. I'll cook, and the two of you can have dinner with us."

"Sounds like a plan. What time do you want us to be there?"

"Six?"

"We'll be there."

"See you later." I turned into the parking lot, parked, then got out of my car.

"Girlfriend, I want to be like you when I grow up," Anyah said when I opened the front door. "We brought you a little housewarming present." She handed me a bottle of champagne with a red bow on top.

"Thanks, girl," I said, then hugged her and Xavier. "Welcome to our new home." I moved to one side so they could enter.

"Where's the man of the house?" Anyah said, looking into the great room.

"He's in the shower and should be out in a few minutes," I said, wondering how long he would stay in the shower. He'd had a long day and seemed uneasy when I told him about my decision to cook for Anyah and Xavier.

"Well, never mind him." She flicked her wrist toward the bedroom. "Give us the grand tour."

"Come on and let me show you around," I said proudly, leading them into our great room first. Showcasing one room at a time, I showed them the entire house.

"Dinner smells good. What did you cook?" Anyah asked when we finally ended the tour in the kitchen.

"Tonight I fixed your favorite meal—sautéed shrimp and pasta."

"Hello, Courtney," Anyah said when he finally showed up in the kitchen. He was frowning, making it obvious that he didn't want to entertain guests. "Courtney I'd like for you to meet my husband, Xavier."

"What's up, man?" Courtney said dryly, extending his hand.

"You have a wonderful home," Xavier said, shaking his hand.

"Thanks, man," he responded with no more enthusiasm.

"Courtney, Anyah and Xavier gave us a bottle of champagne. Let's open it," I said, handing the bottle to Courtney, hoping a drink would take the edge off of his dull mood. He popped the top while I got four glasses out of the cabinet and rinsed them off.

"Still enjoying married life?" Anyah asked Courtney while I filled the glasses with champagne.

"It's fine."

"With all of these new rooms to christen, it's going to be more than just fine," Anyah said, cutting her eyes toward me.

"Guys, dinner is ready," I said, ignoring her candid comment.

"Since you all don't want to talk about sex, setting the table is the least I can do," Anyah said, picking up the stack of plates with silverware on top and placing them on the table. I followed her with the food. Together we sat down and ate.

"Nice home you guys have," Xavier said to Courtney, trying to initiate guy talk during the meal.

"Thanks," Courtney said dryly, glancing at me as if to say he really wasn't in the mood to socialize.

"Your 'vette is gleaming," Xavier said. "What year is it?"

"2004."

"What do you have underneath the hood?"

"Man, just a few horses. I drove it off of the showroom floor and straight to the garage. A friend of mine races and helped me hook it all the way up," Courtney said, finally perking up once Xavier hit a topic he was interested in.

"Think we can catch the rest of the game?" Courtney asked Xavier. Then they both jumped up and went into the great room.

"Men," Anyah said as we got up and started to clean off the table. We both got an armful of dishes and went into the kitchen.

"What's new, girlfriend?" Anyah placed her dishes on the countertop while I opened the dishwasher.

"Courtney wants me to quit work to start a family," I said with a huge smile.

"He wants you to do *what*?" Anyah asked, folding her arms across her chest and leaning back against the counter.

"He's ready to start a family and wants me to quit work." To mute our conversation, I turned on the water.

"Kinda soon, don't you think?" she asked, peeping around the corner to make sure neither of the men was listening.

"In a way, but he deserves it," I said, looking around the kitchen with custom oak cabinets and stainless steel appliances, thinking about all we'd accomplished. "A child would be the perfect gift for everything he's done."

"Everything he's done?" she asked, putting a hand on her hip. "Don't you mean everything the two of you have done together?"

"You know what I mean," I said, then started to rinse the dishes and place them inside the dishwasher.

"I don't mean to rain on your parade, but children aren't gifts, they're responsibilities," she said with a stern look on her face.

"Anyah, can you ever be happy for me?" I asked, putting a hand on my hip and looking at her. "You always see the negative side of everything."

"No, I see the practical side, while you're looking through rose-colored glasses. All I'm saying is, slow your roll. You and lover boy got plenty of time to have children," she said sternly, then frowned. "Enjoy your marriage a little bit. Take a few vacations. Have sex in every room of your house. Hell, have sex in the backyard. Have a little fun first. That's all I'm saying."

"Baby, are you ready to go?" Xavier asked after walking into the kitchen and putting his arm around Anyah's waist. Courtney walked in behind him. "You know we've got to leave before it gets too dark outside. They don't have streetlights out here."

"We'll finish this conversation later," Anyah said underneath her breath. "Girlfriend, we would like to thank you for a delicious meal," she said pleasantly.

"Congratulations on your new home. The meal was fantastic," Xavier said, hugging me and shaking Courtney's hand.

"Thank you for the housewarming present. Let me walk the two of you to the front door." Together we walked to the door. "Be careful," I said as they followed the walkway to their car. I closed the door and went into the kitchen to finish cleaning it up. Courtney went into the other room.

I picked up a dish, thinking about my conversation with Anyah. Knowing how badly Mother wanted grandchildren, I thought she'd be happy about our decision to start a family. Disheartened by her initial response, I leaned against the counter and closed my eyes. To ease the tension in my neck, I moved it from side to side, then rolled my head around. After a few seconds, I opened my eyes. From where I stood, everything was perfect. I'd married the man of my dreams, moved into my dream home, and been given the opportunity to stop teaching and paint full-time. Why should I doubt Courtney now? Exhausted from another long day, I poured myself a glass of wine, and went into the bedroom to shower and get ready for bed.

Chapter 22

Tatiana

During my twenty-five-minute commute to work, I visualized the look on Courtney's face when he talked about starting a family. His eyes sparkled when he said "little Courtneys." I could see him nestling an infant in his massive arms and providing it comfort against his strong chest. Seeing him waiting on the other side of the room with outstretched arms as the baby took its first steps seemed natural. Watching the two of them, wearing matching football jerseys and playing catch in the backyard. Courtney coaching a little league football team. With a son, all those things would be possible.

I turned into the school's parking lot, turned off the engine, and sat a few minutes to observe a group of children at play. Their jovial spirits could only add joy to any parent's life. And yes, they were gifts—gifts from God. It was that moment that I decided to quit. In pursuit of happiness, I smiled, grabbed my purse and tote bag, then got out of the car. At a slow but steady pace I walked across the parking lot lined with big yellow buses and entered the building.

"Good morning, Mrs. Wilkes."

"Good morning, Cathy Sue." The morning was no different as I waved at Cathy Sue and stopped to exchange greetings. Because I know she would be disappointed after working together for so many years, I opted not to tell her about my resignation. Holding on to my decision, I greeted students in the hallway until the bell for homeroom rang, then went inside my classroom. With the passing of students in and out of my classroom, the day progressed, and I spent lunchtime alone drafting my letter.

On my computer I opened up a word document and started to type the heading. I knew ending my teaching career to start a family and become a full-time artist was the right decision, but I fought back tears as I brought the letter to a close. I proofread the two paragraphs, still searching my soul, then printed the document. I folded it, placed it in a white envelope, then addressed it to Mr. Henderson. Still giving myself an opportunity to change my mind, I placed it on the corner of my desk and ate my lunch. If I hadn't discarded the letter before the end of the day, I would take that as a sign and turn it in.

By the end of my last class, the white envelope hadn't moved. I got my purse, tote bag, and the white envelope and headed to the main office. Mr. Henderson's door was open, and he was sitting in his chair with his arms folded on top of his desk, counseling a student. He smiled at me, then held up one finger. I nodded, then had a seat in one of the burgundy leather chairs that sat against the wall outside his office. The secretary was bent over her desk shuffling loose papers.

"Mrs. Wilkes, come on in," called Mr. Henderson, the short, burly gentleman who was the principal when I started, as the student left his office.

I stood with a firm grip on the envelope, then walked inside.

"How is married life?" he asked casually, then gestured with his chubby fingers for me to have a seat.

"Great," I said, sitting down in a chair directly in front of him. A large executive mahogany desk whose aged wood was chipped and scratched separated the two of us.

"What can I do for you today?" he asked, leaning back in his large leather office chair and clasping his fingers across his stomach.

"Mr. Henderson, teaching at your school has been a pleasure," I started, then inhaled. "It is the only school I've taught at and I don't regret a single moment, but life has presented me with another opportunity," I said, handing him the white envelope.

"Tell me this isn't what I think it is," he said.

For a "yes," I nodded.

"You're one of my best," he said, then leaned forward to remove the letter from my hand. "Is there anything I can do to make you stay?" he asked, then tapped the envelope against his fingers. "If someone is offering you more money, I can call the board right now and negotiate a higher salary. The children love you."

"Mr. Henderson, I'm flattered, but my husband is ready to start a family. I'm going to pursue my art career full-time while doing so," I said with a smile.

"Well, Mrs. Wilkes, I hate to lose you, but congratulations. Remember, you still have two weeks to change your mind." He held up the letter, which he never opened, and placed it inside a desk drawer. "I'll keep it in here."

"Thank you, but my mind is made up. I appreciate your time." I rose, then waited as he stood to shake my hand. Knowing that my hard work hadn't been in vain, I exited the building with a sense of self-satisfaction.

I got into my car and drove in the direction of my doctor's office. It was time for my annual physical and Pap smear. I'd already decided to stop taking my birth control pills but wanted the doctor's approval before getting pregnant.

When I saw the large white numbers of the doctor's office, my stomach fluttered. The thought of starting a family suddenly gave me butterflies. With a sense of anticipation, I turned into the parking lot and found a spot near the front entrance.

I greeted the young receptionist sitting at the front desk, then signed my name on the clipboard. No sooner than I sat down and browsed through the unkempt stack of magazines, the nurse was calling my name. "Mrs. Wilkes," she called with a smile.

I put the magazine down and walked toward her.

"Mrs. Wilkes?" the nurse I'd seen on several occasions asked with the same smile.

"Yes, I've gotten married."

"Congratulations," she responded, rubbing me gently on the back. The routine hadn't changed, she checked my weight, blood pressure, and temperature. All my vitals were normal, so I followed her down the short hallway and into an examination room.

"Please remove all your clothing," she said, handing me the thin white paper gown. I took it and waited until the door was shut before removing my clothes.

There was a soft knock on the door.

"Yes, I'm ready."

"Mrs. Wilkes," Dr. Armstrong said as he eased the door open and stepped inside. As was required for my examination, his nurse followed. "Tatiana, how are you doing today?" he asked with a radiant smile. The first time—at least twelve years ago—his six-foot-four-inch frame entered my room I was intimidated. He looked like a center for the LA Lakers and wasn't at all how I visualized a gynecologist. Then I realized that he was a gentle giant.

"Great," I responded.

"You didn't get my permission to go and get married," he said playfully, then patted the side of my leg.

I laughed at his joke.

"Congratulations, he's a lucky young man."

"Thank you."

"Any changes since your last visit?" he asked, then opened my chart and reviewed the notes.

"I've been doing well. I do have one concern."

He looked up. "Yes, what is it?"

"I've stopped taking my birth control pills. My husband wants to start a family."

"The effects of the hormone therapy should wear off in a month or so. The time frame for conception after being on birth control does vary for different women. I'll examine you thoroughly and we should get your test results back in a week. Let's get started."

I leaned back on the table and slid my body forward. I took a few deep breaths and that part of the examination was over. He stood, changed gloves, then moved to my side. I turned my head when he did my breast examination.

"All done. You can sit up now."

I sat up.

"Everything looks good. Like I said, there's no reason why you can't start a family. You'll be hearing from the office when your results come back. Take care of yourself," he said, then exited the room. The nurse discarded the exam tray, then exited behind him.

I slid off the end of the table and rubbed my stomach before shedding the paper gown. I dressed, then said my good-byes as I left the office, trusting my long-time physician's word. I got into my car and drove away, ready to make Courtney's dream a reality.

"Hello," I said, happy to hear his voice after a long, mentally exhausting day. It was after six o'clock when I finally made it home.

"Hey, baby. Please accept my apology. My partner and I made an arrest at the end of the shift. You know the routine. We can't leave until all the paperwork has been completed. It will be another hour at least."

"Apology accepted. Dinner will be waiting when you get home." Unbeknownst to him, I'd gone to the mall looking for the perfect lingerie. The intent was to start a family, but that didn't mean it had to be boring, so I purchased a black lace baby doll top with a matching thong. To add more sex appeal, I didn't stop there and ended my spree with a pair of high-heeled open-toe satin slippers trimmed in faux fur. During my drive home, I put in my favorite jazz CD and thought of several ways to surprise him. "I'll be waiting when you get home," I said, then purred like a kitten. Instead of laboring for hours in the kitchen, I got out a frozen microwavable pasta meal.

* * *

"Wow, baby that was good. Where did that come from?" Courtney asked, out of breath, when I moved my legs and sat up.

He'd called me when he was on his way home. I'd jumped in the shower, sprayed on his favorite scent and put on my new outfit. When the locks tumbled, I met him at the door. As though I couldn't get enough of his affection, I showered him from head to toe with kisses. His clothes started to come off at the front door and we barely made it to the couch. I initiated the act and remained in control from beginning to end.

"Starting a family should be exciting. I went to my ob/gyn today for my annual physical, and he gave us the go-ahead."

"Whew," he said, sitting up on his elbows. "I don't know if I can take this every day." He looked at me, then fell backward onto the couch.

"I can't have a baby by myself." I leaned on top of him and started to roll my hips. Soon his manhood was throbbing against my thigh. Again, my body welcomed him inside with a new wetness. I gripped his body with my thighs, then rode until he moaned from pleasure. His next climax was followed by a soft snore.

"Hello Mother," I said softly when the telephone rang. Both of us had fallen asleep on the couch without eating dinner.

"Now that you all have moved into that big house, are you working on my grandchildren?"

"Mother?" I said, embarrassed that she would talk to me that way, then laughed after I rolled off Courtney.

"How do you like it out there?"

"It's different. I'm so used to hearing city noise and the only thing I hear out here is the crickets." Not wanting to disturb Courtney, I tiptoed into the bedroom, got a sheet out of the closet, and went back to cover him. He didn't move, so I kissed him on the forehead.

"I have to remember that no news is good news now that you're married."

"Please accept my apology. I've been so busy. As a matter of fact, I turned in my two weeks' notice today," I said, then turned to one side and visualized myself pregnant again.

"Has it been that long since we've talked?"

"No, it really hasn't been that long."

"Do you have a new job?"

"I applied for a housewife position." I laughed at my comment.

"Housewife?" Mother asked.

"Courtney asked me to quit teaching and focus on us starting a family. We're converting the extra bedroom into a studio."

"Amen, it's about time."

"So does that mean you're happy for me?" I asked, remembering Anyah's response.

"I'm elated. Well, honey, don't let me keep you on the telephone any longer. You've got to work on my grandbabies."

"Mother," I sang, embarrassed again. "I love you."

"Love you, too."

Chapter 23

Courtney

"What's up?"

"Hey man, let me hit you back." I'd avoided conversations with Octavious for the past month. It was near the end of my shift and I wasn't in the mood for his nonsense, but I answered anyway.

He was single and I'd gotten married. Out of respect for my new wife, I couldn't go to the gentlemen's club every week. When I needed a beer or two, I went to the sports bar where the atmosphere was more appropriate for a married man. Hell, if Tatiana continued to pull rabbits out of her hat like she did last night, all of my needs would be taken care of at the house.

"Before you start with your excuses, listen up," Octavious rattled off.

"Yeah." Octavious knew me too damn well. To end the conversation, I was getting ready to turn on the sirens and fake a call.

"Remember my boy Neal that moved to ATL about two years ago?"

"How could I forget him?" I asked, remembering a New Year's Eve party he threw at his condo a couple of years ago. Free food and booze. The exotic females, most of whom had flown in from Atlanta, outnumbered the males three to one. "He was a bigger freak than you."

"Humph. Well, that freak was in town for the weekend, and he's a millionaire. He pulled up at my apartment complex in a two-seater Benz. It wasn't a rental, either. You know I checked."

"So what's that to me?" I asked, not knowing why he thought I cared at all about his friend's financial status.

"Got a deal I wanna talk to you about off line."

"Man, get off yo' ass and get a job like everybody else," I spat into the phone.

"Where you at?"

"Cruising Watkins Avenue."

"I'll call you when I get to the community center."

"A'wight."

Fifteen minutes later, my cell started to vibrate. Not in the mood for his nonsense, I looked at my display but didn't answer. The vibrating stopped for a second then started again. "Yeah."

"I'm in the lot."

"See you in five." I ended the call, made a U-turn, and headed in his direction. When I pulled into the lot and backed in beside Octavious, he looked at me and smiled from ear to ear. Before getting out, he grabbed something off the passenger's seat. I watched as he walked around the front of the squad car and got in.

"Take a look at this," he said, handing me a small envelope. I snatched it out of his hand and opened it. I looked at him sideways when I removed an X-rated DVD.

"Is this what you interrupted my day for?"

"Look at the label."

"OK." Other than the naked models, nothing got my attention.

"Red Lace productions is Neal's."

"What the hell?" I asked, then looked at the cover again. Sure enough, it said Red Lace in all capital letters with flames around them. "How is he producing this?" I asked, holding up the DVD.

"Easy. Good video equipment, a few freaks, and the Internet. He done made a million. Said he could hook me up. Are you interested? Writing speeding tickets and arresting a crackhead every now and then got to be gettin' boring."

"Man, you know I'm trying to do the right thing." I slid the DVD back into the cover, thinking if I wasn't married I'd do it in a heartbeat. My occasional collection on the streets was nothing. But being in a room doing a sex shoot was unthinkable. The temptation to cheat would be too damn great.

"See there, that's what I'm talkin' about."

"Have you ever been married?" I asked, handing him the envelope.

"Hell, naw. Just hearing you say the 'm' word sounds boring as hell, and that got to get old. Man, are you interested?"

"Our past is the past. I'm a married man now."

"Just what I said. Boring as hell."

"Get the hell outta my car." He opened the door; I put the car into drive and allowed the wheels to start moving forward.

"Hurt if you wanna, and I'll sue yo' ass."

"You want to get a million." He shut the door; I turned on the siren and sped out of the parking lot. *Damn,* I thought to myself, then called Tatiana.

* * *

"Ready to work on little Courtney?" Tatiana asked after getting into bed wearing only her T-shirt and panties. She got underneath the covers, moved her body against mine, then eased her shirt up so I could feel nothing but skin.

When I got home she had the most perfect dinner prepared and the table was already set. I know she'd spent hours in the kitchen cooking the steak, mashed potatoes, and vegetable medley. Not to mention that she had a fresh set of clothes and clean towels waiting for me on the bed. I showered and joined her for dinner. I felt relaxed, but our conversations were limited. Blaming my lack of words on fatigue, I finished dinner and decided to watch television in bed.

With Tatiana not working, Octavious's proposition left me with a lot to think about. A millionaire? Who wouldn't turn down an opportunity to make that much cash? As an officer, including my street collections, I couldn't make that much during my entire career.

"Naw, baby, I had a hard day." I kissed her on the cheek, then turned onto my side. *I should have never met Octavious's ass,* I thought to myself, gripping the sheet in my hand. I wanted to get an erection but couldn't. It was the first time I didn't feel a thing.

"In the morning?" she asked, then rubbed my back and moved her hands around to my chest and down my stomach.

"In the morning," I said, closing my eyes.

"Good night," she said, moved her hand, and turned over.

"Good night." With my eyes closed, I waited until she was sound asleep. The night before our wedding, I'd thrown out all my pornography. Well, almost all of it. There was one movie that was a favorite and I decided to keep it for emergencies like the week of her period. I'd masturbated for years but hoped with a wife I would totally lose the urge.

Thinking Tatiana would eventually wake up, I didn't move and just grabbed myself. All I could think about was the sensation I got from masturbating. There was nothing wrong with Tatiana, but pornography used to place me in a fantasy and kept me there. What man alive wouldn't want two or three women pleasuring him at the same time? Trying to erase the memory, I closed my eyes tighter, but thoughts made my erection stronger. Tatiana was lying beside me and her body was warm, so I held myself with one hand and rubbed her bare hips with the other. Really wanting to make love, I allowed my hand to follow her curves until I felt hair, then bare skin. She twitched but not enough. I wanted an immediate response, and she didn't give it to me. Starting to get angry, I removed my hand and turned onto my side, never letting go of the big man. I stroked him up and down, but that wasn't good enough. Seeing Octavious's video made me think of times past. Something had to be done, so I eased out of the bed. She didn't move.

Remembering the image of the two women with the big boobs and perfectly rounded butts on the cover of the DVD Octavious had shown me, I tiptoed out of the bedroom. Like a maniac, I rushed upstairs to the extra bedroom. In the dark, I felt around the wall, opened the closet door, and felt across the top shelf with my hand until I found the video. My portable DVD player was still on the closet floor where I'd left it. I closed the bedroom door, locked it, then sat down on the floor. Like a crackhead, I fumbled in the dark to get the movie into the player and started. Only needing a few minutes, I stared at the tiny screen, then slipped into my fantasy world.

Like I thought, when I got back into bed beside her, she was sound asleep and never knew I'd left.

Chapter 24

Tatiana

"Surprise!" all my students shouted together as they jumped to their feet. The teachers followed their lead and joined in with applause.

"Cathy Sue. Were you in on this all along?" I asked, never thinking twice when she came to my classroom at the end of the last period and pulled me away to gossip. She smiled, then hunched her shoulders. I looked around the room and my eyes filled with tears. On the back wall was an enormous collage titled "You Made a Difference in Our Lives." I walked closer to it and covered my mouth with both hands when I saw that one of my underachievers had displayed the best piece.

"Are you sure about this?" Cathy Sue asked after handing me several tissues. With tear-filled eyes, I looked at her, parted my lips to speak, but couldn't respond. "Tatiana, it's not too late to change your mind. Remember how they make you feel," she said, rubbing my back for consolation. "You've told me a million times that seeing them come to life in your art classes validates your purpose in life."

"I'm sure." Really fast I wiped the tears with the back of my hands, then turned to face my students and the other teachers. I had to convince myself that not teaching any longer to start a family was the right decision.

"Speech! Speech!" my students cheered.

"Guys," I said, then spread my arms, wanting to hug them all at once. "I don't know where to start." Trying to prevent another tear from rolling down my cheek, I dabbed the corner of my eye. "My passion for art started at your age in a classroom just like this."

"Mrs. Wilkes, did you see my picture?" Alexander asked, pulling me by the hand.

"Yes, I did, and I'm so proud of you," I said, still unable to believe the quality of his work. "When did you take the time to paint it?"

"I worked on it every night at home before I went to bed. You know you always said we could be anything we want to be when we grow up."

"I tell you that every day."

"Well, guess what?"

"What, Alexander?"

"I want to be an artist and teach school just like you. Everybody else laughs at me when my words don't come out right. You never laughed. You told me to take my time and think before I speak."

"Alexander, this means so much to me."

"I did what you said. I took my time," he said, wrapping his arms around me.

"Can you keep a secret?" I asked, leaning closer to his ear.

"Yes, ma'am."

"Your picture is the best. I'm going to frame it

and hang it in my studio at home." I hugged him, then gestured for my students to come up individually for hugs and words of encouragement. I fought back tears long enough to eat refreshments and drink punch.

"You know I'm going to miss you the most." Cathy Sue said, once everyone left the room. There was silence as we both started to clean up.

"I didn't realize leaving would be this hard," I said after taking my gift off the easel. I sat down at my desk and looked around the room. Cathy Sue responded with a hug.

"You have all my contact information, so please use it."

"I will." I reached for a tissue and dried my eyes once again. I stood, then took a second to regroup. We each picked up a box and I took a final look around the classroom, then shut the door behind me. It was like the end of a chapter.

"How was it?" Anyah asked, timing my ride home perfectly.

"The hardest thing I've had to do in a while. I loved working with the children every day. I love painting, but they gave me purpose." Just then another tear fell from the corner of my eye. I wiped it with my fingertips. What should have been the happiest day of my life seemed like the saddest. How many mothers would love to walk a mile in my shoes? I had been given an opportunity to stay at home before the child was born.

"I hate to hear you sound so upset."

"I'll be OK. I know it's the right decision."

"Are you sure?"

"I'm sure."

"I know I was hard on you at your house, but it was all out of love. Give yourself time. Look at the bright side. You can always go back if you have to."

Courtney

"Honey, I'm home," I said, getting an ego boost when my voice echoed through the large kitchen. "Tatiana." She was usually in the kitchen cooking dinner, so I checked the next logical place, her studio. "Baby, what's the matter?" I asked when I saw her sitting in the middle of the floor sorting through two cardboard boxes.

"Hey, baby," she said, looking at me. Her eyes were bloodshot and swollen. "I was sorting through my things from the classroom. Look at the going away present the students made for me." She pointed at an oversized collage of some sort. "Isn't it wonderful?"

"Yeah, it's great." I squinted, trying to see what was so special about the huge board filled with amateur drawings.

"Alexander did the best piece." She leaned her head down and started to cry. Not really knowing how to respond, I walked over and rubbed her shoulder. I'd given her the opportunity of a lifetime and she was upset. Now that I couldn't relate to. "I'm sorry." She wiped her tears with the back of her hand. "This is supposed to be a good day and I'm sad."

"I'm sure you're going to miss your students." It was the first thing that came to mind. I really didn't know what to say.

"Yes, I'm going to miss them so much." She started to thumb through her boxes again. "Let me get up and fix dinner. I thought we could eat something light tonight."

"Never mind cooking dinner. It was your last day at work, and that's a cause to celebrate," I said, trying to add some excitement and help her see the good side of things.

"Are you sure?" She extended her hand so I could help her up off the floor.

"I'm positive," I said, hugging her. "Plus, you've got the rest of your life to cook for me," I said, then kissed her on the forehead. "Now go wipe off your face, put on some makeup, and get dressed."

Tatiana

Since neither of us was in the mood for a long wait, we decided to have dinner at a nearby sports bar. So Courtney could enjoy food, alcohol, and television, we sat at the bar.

"Tatiana?"

When I heard a familiar voice call my name, I turned to look over my shoulder. "Andre?" I asked, barely recognizing his face. I stood and responded to our unexpected reunion with a hug.

"I hadn't seen you since graduation night," he said, stepping back and holding on to both of my hands.

"I know. How have you been?" I asked, amazed to see how much he'd changed. In high school, Andre weighed one hundred forty pounds wet, played bass guitar for the jazz band, and hid a pair of hazel eyes behind wire-rimmed glasses.

"Hanging in there. You know the fight is tough for the black man."

"I can't tell it's tough." I pointed at his perfectly tailored two-piece suit and designer shoes. "Please forgive my rudeness." To get Courtney's attention, I touched him on the shoulder.

"Please introduce me to the lucky man," Andre said, extending his hand when Courtney turned his upper body to face him.

"Courtney, this is Andre. We've known each other since kindergarten."

"What's up?" Courtney responded rudely with a firm handshake.

"I was a softy in elementary school. Since I didn't have a big brother, Andre taught me how to fight." I tapped him playfully on the shoulder. Wanting to ease the tension, I let Courtney know in so many words that Andre was a fellow geek and not an ex-boyfriend.

"Yeah, you were a target for all the bullies with your long braids and little school teacher glasses," he laughed, obviously ignoring Courtney.

"Whatever. Anyway, Courtney has already seen all of my nerd photos." I looked at Courtney, who was staring into space.

"You haven't aged a day since high school."

"How are you going to follow an insult with a compliment? You haven't changed at all."

"I'm serious. So what did you do after high school?"

"Three months after graduation, I moved to New York and attended art school."

"What are you doing here?" he asked with a surprised expression.

"You can take the girl outta the country, but you can't take the country outta the girl."

"I hear you. Too many bright lights and big

dreams?" He looked at me, shook his head, then placed his hands inside his pockets.

"It was definitely different, but there were advantages and opportunities. Home is where the heart is. I want to diversify our students here."

"That's the Tatiana I remember."

"What did you do after graduation?"

"I majored in Political Science, then went to law school."

"Law school?" I asked, then put my hands on my hips.

"For someone that hid behind glasses and a bass guitar, I know that's hard to imagine." He followed his comment with a hearty laugh.

"A lawyer? You were so quiet and we never saw you without your guitar. Do you still play?"

"My girl still relaxes me after a long day at work," he smiled, then pretended to strum his guitar strings. "I see my colleague walking through the door. Courtney, it was nice meeting you. This is a good woman you have." Andre extended his hand for a handshake, but Courtney nodded his head instead. "Tatiana, it was good to see you." He looked at me, hunched his shoulders, then walked away.

"Are you ready to order?" I opened the menu and ran my finger down the page. I really didn't appreciate his attitude toward my classmate but refused to ruin another evening out. His random acts of jealousy were getting out of control.

"Let's get it to go."

"Get it to go?" I asked, then rolled my neck and turned my head toward him.

"Baby, we just got here. What's the rush? Neither of us has to work in the morning." He ignored my comment and waved for the bartender to take our orders. With a discontented look, I placed my finger underneath my chin and stared at him. As though I weren't there, he ordered a beer and stared at the television. *What the hell?* I thought to myself. *What in the world is going on? Is this what happens to Prince Charming when you marry him? He turns into a frog,* I thought, then started to swing my leg back and forth underneath the bar stool to stop a million thoughts. *I'd rather go to my grave than ever to admit Anyah was right. Maybe things had gone too fast and my head was stuck so far up his behind, I couldn't smell the smoke?* I asked, still continuing the conversation with myself. *It's still not too late for me to go back to work.* I looked at him, then rolled my eyes when the bartender placed our food on the counter.

"Let's go," Courtney said abruptly, finished his beer, then all but slammed the empty bottle on the counter. "I have a headache."

"I keep aspirin in my purse for emergencies. Let me give you two." Ready to call his bluff, I opened my purse and looked inside.

"I don't need any medicine. All I want to do is get out of here." He snatched two twenty-dollar bills out of his wallet and tossed them across the counter.

"No problem," I responded, now upset about his sudden headache, then grabbed our food. He stood, nudged his way through guests waiting to be seated, then took long strides across the parking lot to the car. From several feet away, he disabled the alarm, walked to the driver's side, then got inside without assisting me. Before I could close the door and fasten my seat belt, he'd started the ignition and put the car into reverse.

"What was that all about?" he blurted, after we'd ridden several blocks in silence.

"What was what all about?" Resenting his tone of his voice, I turned to make eye contact.

"Conversation with o'boy." His neck stiffened as he looked straight ahead.

"Excuse me?" I asked defensively. "Was there a problem?"

"Yeah, I didn't like how long he talked to you. He totally disrespected me."

"How did you feel disrespected?" I asked, replaying the encounter in my mind.

"If you don't know, you will never know. You are a grown woman. Some things a wife—especially my wife—just shouldn't do."

"Oh really?" I said, folding my arms across my chest and looking out of the window. All the way home he drove like a bat out of hell and I dared him with my menacing stares to have a car accident. Going what seemed like forty miles an hour, he swirled into the driveway and slammed on the brakes in front of the garage. The door lifted and we both got out of the car and stormed inside. He stopped into the kitchen, and I went into the bedroom and slammed the door shut.

Chapter 25

Tatiana

"So where's Mr. Wilkes?" Uncle Henry asked before pulling another piece of meat off his chicken bone. "I'm starting to believe you don't have a husband."

"Hello, everyone." Wearing a fake smile but not answering his question, I walked into the dining room and hugged everyone. Courtney and I hadn't talked in two days. Even though he wasn't working, I knew inviting him to dinner would have been a huge mistake. The tension between us would have been too obvious. Unlike experienced couples, we hadn't been married long enough to have an argument and hide our anger behind smiles.

"Well, where is he?" Uncle Henry asked again.

"Uncle Henry," I sang. "He's at work." I bit my tongue, because he was at home watching television.

"Pretty soon he's going to be more than a man," my mother said with a slight smile on her face.

"What's that supposed to mean?" he asked her,

stuffing a piece of chicken into his mouth and staring at me.

"It means Tatiana has stopped teaching to start a family."

"Well, it's about time. Girl, you know your clock is ticking."

"Henry, do you have any manners?" Aunt Helen asked, then hit him on his thigh. For speaking prematurely, I looked at my mother and rolled my eyes to the top of my head. At the rate my marriage with Courtney was going, getting pregnant was beginning to seem like a mistake.

"You better sit down and get you something to eat then," Uncle Henry said, pointing at an empty place setting at the table. "Let's talk some more about the soon-to-be father of my great-niece or great-nephew," he said, handing me the bowl with Aunt Helen's potato salad in it first.

"He's a nice, hardworking young man." Mother piped in before I could respond.

"What kinda work does he do?"

"He's a police officer," I said, scooped out a hunk of her potato salad, and plopped it onto my plate.

"So you done got you a law man. A man with benefits. Well, I guess you can have my approval. But if he gives you a minute of trouble, you know where to find me." With a mouth full of chicken, Uncle Henry laughed. I smiled, then continued fixing my plate. Mother had advised me that marriage came with many ups and downs, but jealousy was an emotion I hadn't figured into the equation. Everyone talked around me as I ate in silence.

"Baby, can we talk?" I heard Courtney's voice but couldn't see him. Except for the reflection from the television, the great room was dark. Pretending not to hear him, I walked toward the bedroom. "Tatiana," he said louder, then sat straight up on the couch.

"Yes." I stopped and turned to look at him. *No he didn't,* I thought to myself. He was wearing a tank top and boxers. Still upset, but unable to ignore how fine he looked, I turned my head in the opposite direction.

"Can we talk?" He lowered his legs onto the floor, then patted the couch for me to sit down.

"Talk about what?"

"The way I behaved the other night. I was a complete asshole and I know it. Look at me," he said, pointing at his face. "In two nights I haven't slept more than three hours."

"Humph," I said, not feeling the least bit of sympathy when I looked at his eyes, which were dark and swollen. For all I knew, he could have rubbed them hard while I was away to irritate them.

"If you don't want to sit down beside me, at least listen. I've been under a lot of stress lately. With your support, I can handle all of the overtime, but every now and then it gets to me."

"What does your overtime have to do with the way you acted at dinner?" I asked, then putting a hand on my hip.

"Tatiana, I was tired. I came home after a long day at work and you were stressed out. So I tried to put my feelings aside and think about you. I was exhausted but thought giving you a break from the kitchen would make you feel better."

"Giving me a break from the kitchen did make me feel better. You're avoiding the topic at hand. What did your overtime have to do with my old classmate?" I asked, starting to get frustrated all over again.

"Damn, Tatiana, I was jealous. Don't you get it? Do I have to spell everything out in black and white just for you to understand?"

"No, you don't have to spell out anything in that tone of voice," I said, walking toward the bedroom.

"Don't make me sleep on the couch another night." He jumped up and grabbed me by the arm. "I said I was an asshole. Can you please forgive me?"

"Courtney, why don't you trust me?" I asked, looking into his eyes, which were red from fatigue.

"Baby, I do trust you but—"

"But what?" I snapped.

"Nothing." He lowered his head onto my shoulder. "I'm so sorry. That is one flaw I have to work on."

"Yes, you do," I said softly after he started to nibble on my earlobe.

"I love you more than anything in the world." I watched as he got down on his knees, unfastened my pants and lowered them around my ankles. He gripped my hips firmly then pressed his head into the place where my thighs met. When my knees began to weaken I held on to his shoulders and allowed my head to fall backward. "Oh, Courtney, I love you, too," I screamed after an explosive release. His lips glistened as he stood and stared into my eyes.

"I love you, too." He led me into the bedroom to finish what he'd started.

Chapter 26

Courtney

"Watz up, dawg?" Octavious shouted into my ear when he answered his cell phone.

"Count me in," was all I said. After several hours of long personal debates, I'd decided *what the hell*. What was the worst thing that could happen? I was working from sun-up to sun-down at the station and my checks were being eaten up by Uncle Sam. Hell, it was my idea for Tatiana to stop working to start my family. I couldn't punk out of the deal with her. What would she think of me if she knew that all my planning on paper wasn't working out in real life? I took over the bills months ago, and she didn't know how much anything was or when it was due. So to her, everything looked perfect, even though the shit was about to hit the fan.

"What the hell did you just say?" Octavious repeated.

"I said count me in." Just to make ends meet and get ahead, I could do the gig with Octavious for a few months, then get out. If it was what he said, I should make enough to get ahead in less than six months.

"Are you at work?"

"Yeah."

"What time you gettin' off?"

"About three."

"Meet me at my crib."

"Later." I looked at my cell phone and debated whether or not to call him back. I'd worked so hard to get the house and would hate to risk losing it all. *Maybe I could get a part-time job until I get ahead,* I thought, then rubbed my temple when I felt a sudden tension headache. *What the hell. It will only be a few months.*

Tatiana

"Nothing," I said, then got butterflies in my stomach after pulling my panties down. "Maybe this is it." My cycle was like clockwork and I was three days late. Courtney had already left for work, so I had plenty of time to rush to the local pharmacy and get a home pregnancy test.

I took a quick shower, threw on a pair of jeans and T-shirt and grabbed my purse. I jumped into my car, turned the ignition, and put the car into reverse before the garage door had completely lifted. I backed out of the driveway and called Anyah as soon as I got a signal.

"Long time no hear, girlfriend," Anyah said when she answered the telephone.

"You know I've been busy." I felt bad because I hadn't talked to her since my last day of school. And that day she'd called to check on me.

"Yeah, busy trying to make babies," she said, laughing.

"I'm so nervous." I rubbed my stomach to calm the nervous jitters.

"Nervous about what?"

"I think I'm pregnant. My period is late. I called you because I'm on my way to the store now to get a home pregnancy test."

"For your sake, I will cross my fingers. You sound like you're about to jump out of your skin."

"I am," I said, becoming more anxious when I turned into the parking lot of a local convenience store.

"Calm down."

"OK, girl. I will." I pulled into a parking spot, turned off the ignition, and took a few deep breaths.

"Are you going to be OK?"

"Yes, girl, I'm so excited. This could really be it." With both hands, I grabbed the steering wheel.

"Call me and let me know how things turn out."

"OK." I got out of the car, took a few steps, then realized I'd left my purse on the seat. I laughed at myself and turned around to get it. I took a few deep breaths, slowing my heart rate as I waited for the automatic glass doors to separate, then entered the store. I looked at the aisle markers and went straight to the women's section. I read a few boxes and decided to get the one that would deliver the fastest and—preferably—most accurate results. I hurried to pay, then rushed home.

I opened the door, tossed my purse onto the kitchen counter, and tore the package open to read the directions. *I hope this is it,* I thought, going into the bathroom and shutting the door. I followed the directions to the letter, then set the test strip on the sink. Three minutes couldn't pass fast enough as I watched the urine migrate over the testing area. Hoping there was an error, I picked up the instructions and compared it to the strip. "Negative." I sat down on the toilet and lowered my head into my hands. "Negative."

Disappointed, I put the test strip into what was left of the box and decided to throw it away outside. I didn't want Courtney to see it and become excited when it was nothing but a false alarm. I looked at my reflection in the mirror, then walked into the kitchen. I grabbed the plastic bag off the counter and put the box inside it. Frustrated, I used both hands to crumble the package, then went outside to throw it away.

The telephone started to ring, so I went back inside to answer it. "You didn't call me back," Anyah said when I answered the telephone.

"Negative," I said, then opened the freezer, took out a package of chicken, and placed it in the sink to defrost.

"I know you don't feel like talking, but give it some time, little sister."

"I will talk to you later."

Courtney

"I'd been waiting on that call, man. I knew you wouldn't let me down. It was just a matter of time," Octavious said, then patted me on the back when I walked through the door of his apartment. "Remember Neal?" he asked, then pointed toward his partner, who was sitting on the couch with his legs crossed. He was wearing a tan, tailor-made suit, cream shirt with cuff links, and damn ostrich shoes that looked like they'd never been worn.

"What's up, partner?" Neal said, nodding his head.

"Man, he straight. He ain't no real cop," Octavious said, then laughed.

"I got my business on lock. I don't have time for any technicalities," he said, looking at me from head to toe.

"Man, look, this is my boy, and I promise you he's straight."

"If he isn't straight, the blood is on you," Neal said, pretending to point a gun at me and pull the trigger.

"You know what, man, I'm out," I said and turned to leave, already thinking of a million reasons why I shouldn't hook up with Octavious's friend.

"Man, wait, just give us thirty minutes to give you the lowdown on the project," Octavious said, putting his hand on my shoulder and pointing toward a laptop on his sofa table.

"Talk to me," I said, then looked at Neal, letting him know he was the one who needed to worry. I had more connections than the telephone company and could have him and his little hustle destroyed with one telephone call.

"The business is tight." Neal uncrossed his legs and leaned forward. "All you have to do is follow the model I've already set up, detail for detail. "Bamm," Neal said, smacking the table. I guarantee the two of you will be millionaires in less than a year. All the honeys you want will be at your beck and call."

"Dig that," Octavious said with a grin so wide, I could see his tonsils.

"How do we start?" I said, at least willing to give

his business a shot. I sat down in a chair opposite Neil. Two hours later, I was convinced and ready to set up our studio. If all went according to his plan it should go over without fail. He had every detail from production and marketing to distribution already set up. For using his plan, there was only a small fee, and the rest of the money was profit.

"What did I tell ya?" Octavious said. "It's tight."

"Yeah, it's tight," I said, looking at my cell phone to check the time. "I need to take it to the house." I stood, then gave Neil and Octavious some dap.

"We'll talk tomorrow," Octavious said after following me to the door.

"For sure." I got into my car and drove straight home. In order for anything to work, I couldn't make Tatiana feel uneasy. My schedule had to stay the same. Even when I worked overtime, it was no more than four hours at a time and I always made it home to eat dinner.

"Hello, baby," Tatiana purred like a kitten when I walked through the door. She had dinner already on the table and was wearing nothing but a T-shirt and panties. I looked at all I had waiting on me at the house and felt like shit. I'd just left Octavious's house after making a deal to start a porn business.

"You look so sexy," I said, wrapping my arms around her waist. I hugged her, then closed my eyes. "Damn," I said, then opened them when I visualized two strippers standing behind her.

"What's wrong with you?" she asked, looking over her shoulder. "You look like you just saw a ghost."

"Nothing, baby," I said, pulling her back against me.

"Go and take your shower. Dinner will still be hot when you finish."

"All right, babe." I took another look at my beautiful wife, then went to shower. When I returned, she was sitting at the table with her legs crossed, waiting on me. "How am I supposed to eat dinner with you sitting here like this?" I asked, pointing at her. Her breasts were tender and it took everything in me not to reach across the table and grab one.

"I don't know. How can you?" she asked, leaning forward so I could see her cleavage."

"Oh, so it's a setup?" I asked.

"You're a cop, so you tell me."

"Was that a challenge?" I took two bites of my food, got up from the table, and took her by the hand into the bedroom. She'd know to never tease me again.

Tatiana

No sooner than Courtney reached his climax, I pushed his body off mine and elevated my hips. It was a tried and true method an older teacher at my school swore by. Why wouldn't I believe the mother of five?

"What in the hell are you doing?"

"Trying to get pregnant," I said, placing my hands on my hips and using my legs to elevate my body. I didn't share my disappointing details with him and decided to seduce him instead. If I wasn't pregnant that month, there was always the next month.

"What is that supposed to do? I don't mean no harm, but you look crazy as hell."

"Increase the chances of conception," I responded, using my hands to support my back. Mrs.

Norell never gave me any other particulars, so I maintained the yogalike position until I collapsed.

"Good luck." He got out of bed and went into the bathroom to shower. Dinner was still on the table, but I had to give the method time to work.

Chapter 27

Tatiana

"Hello, Mother." Courtney was at work; I'd already made dinner plans and was using my spare time to paint. Knowing how anxious she was for me to start a family, I never shared my false alarm with her.

"Do you have me on speaker phone?"

"Yes I do, but can you hear me?" I asked, turning my body more to face the telephone base. Just when I turned, I noticed the rear end of a white van drive by the window. My blinds were only partially open because I didn't want full sunlight.

I hopped off my stool and hurried to the window to look out. By that time it was already turning the corner and was too far away for me to read the license plate. If I wasn't mistaken, it looked similar to the van I'd noticed in my rearview mirror some time ago. Thinking it was a work van of some sort, I got back on my stool and finished where I left off.

"You know I hate those things. Sounds like you're

in a tunnel ten miles long," she said, laughing. "You must be painting," Mother commented.

"In two weeks, my work will be displayed in a major show. I'm so nervous." I continued to make strokes on a piece I decided to call Tender Mercies. It was an oil of a pregnant woman in a rocking chair, rubbing her swollen belly while reading to her unborn infant.

"No need to be nervous. I have faith in your God-given talent and know you will sell every piece."

"Thanks, Mom." Her reassurance made me smile.

"Call me back when you take a break."

"I can talk."

"Just got off the phone with your Uncle Henry. Couldn't believe it, but he had a good idea."

"I'm afraid to ask." The thought of Uncle Henry having a good idea made me laugh aloud.

"No, really, he did and it made a lot of sense."

"I'm listening." Wondering if I should have ended the call, I put down my paint brush and took a sip of wine.

"Thanksgiving is in two weeks and everyone is dying to meet Courtney and see your new home. I keep the pictures in my purse and show them to anyone who will give me two minutes of their time."

"Mother, where are you going with this?"

"Thanksgiving dinner at your home," she said with excitement as though I'd won the lottery.

"I don't know. This is so last-minute," I said, thinking of how Courtney would respond. "Plus, our home isn't fully furnished yet." It was furnished, but that was the quickest excuse I could think of.

"Your Aunt Helen can get all the tables and

chairs we need from the community center. Uncle Henry wants to smoke a turkey. I volunteered to fix the dressing, sweet potatoes, and spaghetti. You know my specialty."

"Mama, pause," I blurted out when she finally took time to breathe.

"I'm sorry, baby, but you know how excited I get over family dinners."

"Basically, all the plans have been made?" I could feel my face turn red.

"Yeah, we wanted to take the stress off you and Courtney."

"Mother," I said slowly but in a higher pitch.

"Oh boy, you're talking like a white girl so that means I'm in trouble, right?"

"Mother," I said even slower than before. "I don't mind the family coming over, but we should have talked about it before you called everyone and made plans."

"I guess you're right. And your Aunt Rebecca said she would make your favorite chocolate cake from scratch." Ignoring anything I said, she continued with her plans.

"Mother, stop it. I'm married now and the family has to respect that. Do not call another person until I talk to Courtney."

"Everyone is so excited."

"Mother, do not make another telephone call," I said sternly. "I love you and I will talk to you later."

When I heard the garage door open, I lowered the heat underneath my saucepan and walked over to unlock the door. "How was your day?" I greeted him with a wet kiss on the lips, then took his duffel bag.

"Stressful, as usual."

"You can tell me about it after showering and changing into something more comfortable."

"You cooked my favorite. I'll take my shower after I eat." Courtney got a beer out of the refrigerator and used the end of his T-shirt to twist off the cap. "It smells good." He took a sip of beer, then leaned against the counter.

"Mother called me today," I said, fixing his plate and putting it on the table.

"She did?" He took another sip of beer and sat down at the kitchen table.

"Thanksgiving is only two weeks away. Had you made plans for us?"

"None other than resting. It's my only off day. I really hadn't put too much thought into it. That's two weeks away," he said, cutting into his steak with a knife.

"My family wants to celebrate the holiday here at our house."

"I have to be brutally honest." After his comment, he paused. "I don't want strange people invading my personal space."

"Excuse me, but we're talking about my family." Because I never considered my family as strange people, his response made me defensive.

"Family?" he asked, putting down his knife and fork. "Family?" he repeated, putting his hand on his chin looking toward the ceiling. "Where was this so-called family when you lived in your condo? No one ever wanted to eat turkey and dressing over there, did they?"

"You know that analogy isn't fair."

"Analogy? So now we're getting proper. Use the big words on your school teacher friends who are impressed. For me, keep it simple."

"I'm proud of our new home. What normal person wouldn't want to share it with their family?"

"You're not sharing this one."

"Really?" I asked, folding my arms across my chest. "My family is coming. If you don't like it, you can disappear." I left the kitchen just like it was, went into our bedroom, and slammed the door.

I heard the chair slam against the kitchen floor, the back door open and slam, then the garage door lift. Angered by his response, I kicked off my shoes, undressed, then got into bed. I no longer cared whether he ate dinner or not.

Courtney

"I'm on my way." I called Octavious from my cell phone. Since Tatiana had decided to get mad at me, there was no better time to go over to his place and work on our studio. I stopped by a local convenience store and bought a six-pack of beer. Before backing out of the parking lot, I popped the cap and turned up the can. Feeling no regrets, and ready to make a shitload of money, I drove in the direction of Octavious's apartment.

"Watz up, dawg," Octavious said with a huge grin when he opened the door. "While you were at work, I repainted the bedroom. Come and check it out." To limit the costs, we'd decided to use his extra bedroom. Everything else was simple. Between the two of us, we already owned three video cameras. We installed two in the bedroom and kept one for backup. With the rest of my beer in hand, I followed him down the hallway into the bedroom.

"What do you think?" he asked after turning on the lights.

"Damn," I said, looking at the walls he'd painted a really deep gold, making the room look like something from the seventies.

"I thought a little color would spice it up. Make it feel more like the playa's den it is going to be," he said, laughing like a hyena.

"Where is the rest of the wiring?" I asked, opening another beer and setting it on the floor by the door.

"It's in the closet." He opened the closet door and got out everything we needed to finish the do-it-yourself project. He grabbed a beer out of the case, popped the top, and took a few sips. For the next hour we worked nonstop, drilling holes and running wire.

"This is too damn sweeeet," I sang when we installed our hidden and not-so-hidden cameras in our private studio.

"Can't wait to test it all out," Octavious said, then fell back onto the bed we'd decorated in red satin sheets and a plush red velvet comforter with heavy gold stitching. "Dah honeys gonna love this," he said, looking up at the mirrors we'd placed on the ceiling. We wanted to see everything from every angle.

"Hell, man, I gotta get outta here," I said, after looking at my cell phone. Even though Tatiana and I had had another fight, I couldn't make her feel insecure.

"Overtime?"

"No, we had a fight. I needed some breathing room."

"That's my boy. Go and do yo thang with the wifey."

"Holla," I said, took another look at our sex den,

and shut the door, leaving Octavious to deal with his own imagination.

When I opened the door, Tatiana was in the kitchen cleaning up. *Damn,* I thought to myself. *When I left, she was in the bedroom.*

"Can we talk?" she asked sweetly. She was wearing a pair of Lycra leggings and a tank top. Every curve on her body was visible.

"Let's talk in the morning." I walked by her, went into the bedroom, and shut the door. I really didn't want to start another argument to get her off me, but I would if I had to. Not wanting to be bothered, I hurried to take a shower and got into bed. I listened and Tatiana was still rustling around in the kitchen, so I closed my eyes and felt for the big man. With enough visual images in my mind, I didn't need to watch the videos any more. I did it strictly from memory.

Tatiana was trying everything to get pregnant, but what she didn't know was that I was slowly losing my attraction to her. We weren't making love but having sex for her to get pregnant. Everything became rushed and the pleasure was leaving. I wanted things to be the way they used to be. "Umm," I said once I started to rub the big man. I visualized a female between my legs and could feel him getting harder by the second. Feeling her wet lips around me I began to squirm. Then another one appeared and leaned forward, allowing her breasts to dangle over my mouth. One at a time I savored them until I reached my full potential. Satisfied, I turned onto my stomach and fell asleep.

Chapter 28

Tatiana

"Mrs. Wilkes." A female nurse dressed in dark purple pants and matching floral print lab coat stood in the doorway that adjoined the waiting and patient care areas. I put the magazine for new mothers on the table and walked toward her. "How are you feeling today?" There had to be an explanation as to why, after three months, I wasn't pregnant.

"I'm fine," I said, doubting my very own existence as I followed her through the door.

"You've been here enough to know the routine." She smiled at me, then pointed at the chair with an arm rest on each side. I sat down and positioned my left arm for her to take my blood pressure.

"Hmm," she said, removing the cuff and making several keystrokes on the keyboard situated on a desktop to her left.

"Hmm?" I responded back, wanting to know what caused her reaction.

"Your blood pressure is a little high. I made a note

on your chart for Dr. Armstrong. Step on the scale for me."

I stepped out of my pumps and stepped on the scale.

"Are you dieting for a summer vacation?" the nurse asked jokingly, then made more keystrokes on the computer.

"You know me. I'm always on a diet," I said, trying to cover my concern with a lighthearted response.

"You've lost ten pounds since we last saw you three months ago."

"Really?" I asked, looking down at the digital display. And yes, I'd lost at least ten pounds, if not more.

"Follow me." I followed her down the hallway to a small examination room on the end.

"I apologize, but this was the only room available."

"No problem."

"Have a seat and Dr. Armstrong will be in shortly."

"Thank you," I said with a smile as she left the room and closed the door.

The examination room was painted light blue from floor to ceiling. Hand-painted clouds floated on the walls and the ceiling was covered in white fluffy clouds. In one corner was a large plastic bin filled with children's books and toys.

"Tatiana," Dr. Armstrong said, once he opened the door and saw me sitting on the table. "What can I do for you today?" he asked with a concerned expression.

"On my last visit you told me everything was OK and there should be no problem with me conceiving," I said, maintaining direct eye contact.

"That's correct," he said with a head nod. "Everything looked good."

"Well, it's been three months and I'm not pregnant," I said, then thought about Courtney's drastic mood changes. "What did you do to me when you operated? I thought you said I had endometriosis."

"Tatiana, please calm down. Your surgery was six years ago and I'm certain I consulted with you after the procedure."

"Dr. Armstrong, I'm sorry. I've been your patient for many years. Please accept my apology. It's just—"

"I know. More than anything, you want to have a child," he said, patting me on the shoulder.

"More than anything," I said, lowering my head.

"It's been three months since I saw you last. To cancel any doubts you may have, I will do a few routine tests."

"Thanks," I said with a half smile.

"I'm going to step out of the room and a nurse will be in shortly to draw your blood for lab work. There is no need for you to undress." Again, he patted me on the shoulder, made a few notes on my chart, then exited the room.

There was a soft tap on the door. "Come in," I said. A nurse carrying a small tray filled with different colored tubes and needles entered the room.

"Please roll up your sleeve," she said, then placed her small tray on the bed behind me. She got a tourniquet, tubes, and a needle. Not wanting to look, I turned my head. "I'm done. She labeled the tubes, then exited the room.

The next few hours seemed like an eternity. There I was waiting for the doctor. Then there was a knock on the door. "Come in."

With a chart in hand, Dr. Armstrong looked at me and smiled. "Tatiana, I'm glad but sorry to say there's still nothing wrong with you. Physically you're in great condition and there's no reason you shouldn't be able to conceive," he said, made a few notes on my chart, then patted me on the knee.

"Give it some more time. If you haven't conceived in three more months, maybe your husband should get tested. Does he have any children?" he asked with a concerned look on his face.

"No," I responded.

"It's only a suggestion. Good luck."

Having expected to hear a solution, I slid off of the table and left.

"Mother." Needing to hear a comforting voice I called her as soon as I got into my car.

"How are you?"

"Fine," I said really wanting to tell her what was bothering me.

"Have you been working on my grandchildren?" she asked, laughing.

I couldn't control the warm tears that flowed from the corner of my eyes. "Tatiana?"

"Yes, Mother?"

"Baby, what's the matter? Did I say something wrong?"

"No, you didn't. I'm sitting in Dr. Armstrong's parking lot right now."

"Is everything OK?"

"Yes, that's the problem. Everything is OK, but I'm still not pregnant. It has been three months and I should be pregnant by now."

"Well, baby, you really can't put a time limit on it. You've been taking birth control pills since you were seventeen years old. I'm sure you need to give it some time. Everything will happen when the good Lord is ready for it to happen."

"That's why I called you," I said, forcing a smile. "No matter what, you always find the good in every situation."

"Now wipe your tears." Her voice was so sweet and I did exactly what she said.

"I love you, Mom."

"I love you, too, baby."

Just that fast, I realized everything would happen when it was time to happen. All my missed periods and my weight loss were due to stress and that could be the reason I wasn't getting pregnant. In time I would conceive. Wanting to see the brighter side of my then gloomy situation, I drove out of the parking lot and headed home. Courtney's dinner still had to be prepared.

"What are you doing?" Anyah asked when I answered the telephone.

"I'm in the kitchen cooking Courtney's dinner," I said, then opened the oven to check the temperature of the meat. Because I'd spent most of my morning at the doctor's office, I fell asleep when I got home and was late starting his dinner.

"Damn, every time I call, you either in the kitchen cookin' or cleaning up that big-ass bathroom of yours. Do you ever take a break?"

"Yes, for your information, I get breaks." I closed the oven door, then stirred my oriental vegetables, which were steaming on top of the oven.

"When? As many hours of overtime as Courtney works, you should have a maid."

"Girl, he has a huge problem with other people being in his home."

"There you go again. His home. His car. His bathroom. I wish Xavier would come to me with some shit like that. I work too. I pay the bills just like he does. That makes everything right down to that brand new-ass Mercedes he drives ours."

"That's the difference. I don't work anymore."

"Yeah, that's what I called you to ask about. How did your appointment go?"

"It didn't go well at all. Dr. Armstrong told me everything was fine. There's no reason why I shouldn't be able to conceive."

"I have faith God will make a way," I said, thinking faith would be my last resort. Maybe it was time for me to meet Mother at Bible study.

"Girl, let me tell you about God. When he created you, he gave you five senses. Use the damn things and see your way out of that situation before it's too late."

"That would be against God's will for my life. If you went to church sometime, you would know that."

"Look, I had enough church between the ages of five and eighteen to last me a damn lifetime. If nobody else knows me, God knows me. He created me, remember?"

"I've got to pray for you," I said, then laughed at myself.

"Humph. While you're praying for me, send up a few for yourself."

"Look, I've got to go. Courtney just walked into the kitchen."

"See, that's the shit I'm talking about."

Courtney walked into the kitchen and stood at the end of the counter. "Who is that on the telephone?"

"This is Anyah. She called to see how my appointment went," I responded, shocked by his stance and the intense look in his eyes.

"Girl, let me call you back," I said cheerfully, hoping she hadn't heard him on the other end.

"Tell him you are talking to me," she shouted into the telephone.

"I'll talk to you later." I ended the call before she could say anything else.

"Is my dinner ready?"

"Almost. The fish will be done baking in five minutes."

"If you hadn't been on the telephone, my plate would have been fixed."

"Excuse me?" I asked, then put a hand on each hip.

"You heard what I said. I'm going into the bedroom to shower and change clothes. When I come out, I expect my food to be on the table."

He brushed against me and walked toward our bedroom. "Oh hell, no. There is only so much a black woman can take," I said, following behind him. "Is there something we need to talk about?" I asked, then jumped in front of him, standing my ground. As though I weren't there, he continued moving forward like a bulldozer. Knowing his physical strength, I held up my hand to stop him and forbade him to take another step without an explanation.

"Tatiana, move."

"No," I said sternly, then stood on my tiptoes in an effort to get closer to his face. "I can only imagine what you deal with on the streets. Plus, being exhausted from the additional overtime, but bringing it home isn't fair."

"Tell me this," he said harshly. "While I'm out there in the streets, what are you doing all day?" he asked, looking around the room. "How many paintings have you done? Better yet, how many have you sold?"

"Me staying at home to start a family was your damn idea, not mine," I said, becoming angrier by the minute.

"And what have you done?"

"What do you mean, what have I done? I cook

all your meals, clean your house, and wash your funky-ass clothes," I said, looking him square in the eyes.

"Let me ask you again. What have you done? In all this time you haven't given me the one thing that I wanted. A damn son. What is wrong with you?" he asked, looking at me from head to toe.

"Nothing is wrong with me," I said, distraught that he would blame me for not getting pregnant. "The doctor said there is nothing wrong with me. Maybe it's you with the damn problem."

"Maybe you need to check again. It seems like I'm killing myself working all of these damn hours for nothing." He went into the bedroom, slammed the door in my face, and locked it. I kicked the hell out of it, then sat down on the couch. Sooner or later he had to come out.

"I'm going out with Octavious."

My neck snapped when he walked by me wearing a pair of black dress slacks and a silk short-sleeved shirt that I'd bought him. "Going out? What about dinner?"

"Feed it to Anyah. She seems to be more important than me."

Courtney

"I'll be there in twenty." A man has to do what a man has to do. Starting an argument with Tatiana was the only way for me to get out of the house. Octavious called before the end of my shift to let me know he had three actresses ready to work.

Using the excuse of overtime wouldn't have

worked in this particular case because none of them were available during the earlier part of the day.

"Hurry up, dawg. We might have to start this production without you."

"I am on my way." Just in case someone didn't recognize my car as I weaved in and out of traffic, I opened my console and checked for my badge. I didn't have time to explain to anyone why I was driving twenty miles over the speed limit. In less than fifteen minutes, I was parking in front of Octavious's door.

"We're in the back," he said with a huge grin, shutting the door once I stepped inside. I didn't know what they had been doing, but he was already burning incense to cover the smell of wild sex.

"Hello, Courtney." Juanna waved from a corner. She was wearing a short red satin robe with nothing underneath. Two other females I'd never seen before were already naked and lying across the bed admiring themselves in the mirrors above it.

"What the hell is she doing here?"

"Man, it's cool. This is business."

"Yeah, Courtney, this is business, so loosen up," she said, strolling toward me and starting to unbutton my shirt.

"Here man, drink this. It will be a'ight." Octavious said, handing me a beer.

Chapter 29

Courtney

"What's up, Trey?" I'd gone to the house converted into a barbershop for years. It was in the hood, and Trey gave me a perfect cut and line every time. I was wearing a fresh pair of starched Enyce jeans, matching jacket, and of course the latest Jordans. With my new financial status, it was definitely time for a wardrobe upgrade.

"You got it."

"How many, man?" I asked, pointing at the customers seated in the row of mix and match chairs that lined the wall.

"Hmm . . . about five," he said after counting his clients with his index finger.

"Man, I got to roll today," I said, in a hurry to get to our next shoot. Octavious had four females lined up for us and they were scheduled to arrive at his place within the hour.

"My man Dante can hook you up."

"Dante?" I asked, looking toward the rookie barber seated in the last chair.

"Tell you what. How 'bout we do it VIP. Cut me now and I'll pay for every hair cut you got plus a tip."

"Shit, cool by me," said J.T., a middle-aged man wearing a pair of worn coveralls and a plaid shirt, taking off his dusty work cap and fanning himself. He went to the barbershop at the same time every Friday. He didn't have much hair, but what he had was short, and he kept a cap on his head to hide a bald spot.

"Me too," a teenager seated on the opposite side of the room piped in.

"Hell, if he got it like that, let him pay and buy lunch," J.T. said after putting his cap back on his shiny, bald head.

"Since the fellows don't mind, let me finish hooking up this young brotha's line."

I waited for him to finish his last customer, then walked by everyone and sat down in Trey's chair.

"What ya'll think about Shaq this year?" an older barber shouted from three chairs down.

"Shaq ain't nothing. His goofy ass weak as hell. He wouldn't be Shaq without the team," J.T. shouted across the room.

"J.T., shut the hell up. You just mad 'cause nobody recruited yo' big crusty ass outta junior college."

"Go to hell," J.T. stammered, taking all of three minutes to process his thought.

"Yeah, I know how to shut yo ass up." He stopped cutting his client's hair and waved his buzzing clippers in the air just to make a point.

"Yo' none ball playin' ass right where you need to be, cuttin' hair."

"Got yo' latest DVDs and CDs right here," announced the worn-out brother who came into his shop every week wearing the same torn Levis and frumpy white converse tennis shoes.

"What I tell you 'bout comin' in my shop hustlin'," Trey said.

"Man, give a brotha a chance. E'rbody ain't got it like you," he said, still walking around with his black gym bag full of bootleg CDs, DVDs, generic cologne, and throwback jerseys. "For the black man out on the streets it's all 'bout the struggle. You got yo' chance at the big life," he said, opening his bag for a new customer to look inside.

"Now I'm giving you yo' chance to get yo' ass outta here before you get us all arrested and sent to jail."

"Check this out," I said, showing Trey a video clip stored on my phone. "'Bout a month ago, I was surfin' the Web and found this hot-ass Web site," I said, knowing it was ours all along.

"Dang."

"The movies will be delivered to your front door."

"Just like that?"

"Hell yeah, just like that. No more trips to the treat shop. All your eye candy without leaving the comfort of your home. Everything—and I do mean everything—can be done from your personal computer," I said, leaning back in his chair.

"Everything?" Trey asked.

"Do you have the Internet?" I asked, putting my phone back into my pocket.

"Yeah, man," he said, then spun me around to face the mirror.

"You've got to check out that Web site. It's off the chain." I checked out my cut as he brushed the excess hair off my face and neckline. He removed the cape and gave it a hard shake. "Keep the change." I reached into my pocket, took out a one-hundred-dollar bill and handed it to him.

"Have a good day, fellows." Proud to be Courtney Wilkes, I left the shop.

Tatiana

"Oh my God!" I said sharply, startled by the warm liquid that splashed against my body. Concerned only with my sketch pad, I held it above my head and hopped from my seat.

"Ma'am, I'm sorry." The tall and lanky man wearing wire-rimmed glasses and an outdated plaid shirt stuttered, then scrambled to prevent an armload of books from falling.

"No problem. Accidents happen." I reached across the table for the napkin holder, then grabbed a handful.

"Please, ma'am, may I replace whatever you were drinking?"

"Don't worry about it," I replied, thumbing through my sketches before wiping the front of my shirt.

"Please allow me," the stranger said sternly, using a deeper voice without stuttering and firmly placing a hand on my shoulder.

"Pardon me, but I meant no thank you." With wide eyes I looked up and attempted to stand.

"Tatiana Wilkes, it would behoove you to stay seated and listen."

"Who in the hell are you and how did you know my name?" I commented loudly, making sure the couple seated behind me could hear the distress in my voice.

"Cooperate by sitting down without causing a

scene and I will tell you," he said, leaning down and speaking into my ear.

"I'll sit down when you tell me who you are and how you know my name," I said defensively, still not lowering my voice. Eyeing the exit door, I held my sketch pad against my chest and reached down to grab my purse.

"Before you gun out of here, I'd advise you to sit down."

"You're a wacko."

"Leave and you could be charged as an accessory to a serious federal offense," he whispered into my ear after grabbing me by the shoulder.

"Pardon me?" I asked, stunned by his remark.

"That could equate to some time behind bars, Missy," he said roughly.

"Now I'm certain there's a discrepancy." Even as a child, my biggest offense had been stealing a tube of lip gloss only because Mother wouldn't allow wearing makeup before sixteen.

"Are you so sure?" he asked, gesturing for me to sit down.

"I want your badge," I said, extending my hand. "My husband is Courtney Wilkes, and he is a police officer. When I'm done, you'll never harass another female." Blindly, I reached inside my purse to feel for my cell phone.

"Sit down this second or come with me downtown, Mrs. Courtney Wilkes."

Still holding my sketch pad against my chest, I eased down into my seat and sat motionless in front of him.

"My name is Agent Brownstone," he said, using a more mellow tone of voice. "You look stunned, but it would behoove you to discuss this meeting with no one as you could jeopardize the investigation."

"Your husband has been under investigation for the past year. He started out slow, but overnight his illegal activity skyrocketed. No doubt this is a lot to handle at once, but take a couple of days to think about it." He passed me a card along with a DVD underneath the table, stood, and left as if nothing had ever happened. I turned to look over my shoulder, but he was already gone. In a state of panic, I went to my car and drove home in silence.

I opened the door, tossed my purse on the counter, and went into our bedroom. I turned on my television and placed the DVD inside the player. What I saw made me fall limp to my knees. In a state of shock, I watched the home video, trying to convince myself it was all just a dirty joke. Then I heard a familiar voice in the background. On my knees, I reached up, pushed stop, then ejected the video. I was convinced.

I barely stood, making it into my bathroom soon enough to hang my head over the toilet and expel my guts. For comfort, I hugged the toilet seat, wiped my mouth with tissue, then tried to stand. My knees buckled beneath me. "Oh my God," I screamed as tears started to flow uncontrollably down the side of my face. All I could do was cry, so I gave myself that time as the cold tiles on the bathroom floor supported me.

Realizing the DVD was only the beginning of the end, I stood, and walked to the sink. I reached for a face towel and turned on the cold water. *How much more is there?* I wondered as I placed the cold towel over my face. *His damn desk,* I thought, suddenly angered by the deception. I threw the towel on the floor and stormed into the other room.

One drawer at a time, I yanked them open and

scanned the contents, only to reveal a piece of interesting-looking documentation. My hands shook uncontrollably as I read, then reread, the paperwork in my hands. Unable to believe my eyes, I paced in circles around his desk. *What else could he be hiding from me?* I asked myself as I looked at the many drawers of his desk. I stopped to yank open a top drawer, then looked around for anything else suspicious. One hour later, my impromptu search uncovered nothing more than a medical bill for a vasectomy I held in my hand. Bombarded with anger, pain, and resentment, I fell into his office chair, then inhaled and exhaled slowly. My first thought: call him and interrupt his day. *Oh hell no, this documentation is gasoline and he is the fire. If I play my cards right, before long he will crash and burn.*

I stormed out of the room, grabbed my purse from the kitchen counter, and slammed the kitchen door so hard the glass shattered. I jumped into my car and turned the ignition key. In a state of fury, I put the car into reverse, and the wheels started to move before the garage door had completely lifted. Looking for my cell phone, I dumped the contents of my purse out onto the seat. "Anyah, I'm on my way to your house. I'm backing out of the garage now," I said, pressing the gas.

"Tatiana, what's the matter?"

"Please, I'm too damn upset to talk right now. I'm on my way."

"OK, girl."

Twenty minutes later, I was turning into her driveway and she was already standing in the door. "What is it?" she asked. I handed her the sheet of paper, then took the business card the detective had given me out of my purse. My hands trembled as I dialed his number.

"This is Agent Brownstone."

"Agent Brownstone, this is Tatiana Wilkes. We need to talk," I said, then placed my head in the palm of my hand and cried uncontrollably.

Chapter 30

Tatiana

I'd spent the past two days on the couch in the great room bundled up in a wool blanket like a cocoon. On the end table closest to my head, I placed the telephone handset, a glass of water, and some cold and flu medicine. Using the restroom was the only reason I moved. My pores reeked from fever, but I didn't have the strength to stand long enough to shower.

The telephone started to ring. I reached over my head, picked up the handset, then looked at the caller ID display. For the eighth time in two days, it was Anyah. I made a decision to wallow in my own self-pity, turned off the ringer, and tossed the handset on the floor.

I heard someone banging on the door but knew they'd eventually go away. The noise got louder and the beats became more rapid. Slowly I lifted my head, sat up, and lowered my legs to the floor. Wanting the person at my front door to stop, I used my hands to push myself off the couch and held my head, as it ached with every step.

"Tatiana, unlock the door." It was Anyah. I knew then I'd better open the door before she got loud and started to curse.

"If you didn't open that door I was getting ready to dial 911," she said, holding up her cell phone for me to see. "You had me worried sick."

She reached out and wrapped both arms around me. I was too weak to embrace her back. My arms were limp beside me as I turned around and dragged myself back to the couch.

"Girlfriend, I don't mean no harm, but you look like shit. Oh, hell, no. And what is that you're wearing? A T-shirt with a hole in the shoulder, oversized jogging pants and those god-awful fuzzy-ass socks."

"Thanks a lot. I really needed that boost of confidence." I plopped down on the couch, covered myself, leaned my head slowly back against the oversized pillow.

"Go into your bedroom this second and put on some jeans. I'm taking you to the emergency room right now."

"Please calm down. It's only a sinus infection and I'm not going to the emergency room."

"Sinus infection, my ass. Girl, you got more than a sinus infection. Stand up and look at yourself in the mirror."

She put a hand on her hip and pointed toward the mirror that hung above the fireplace mantel.

"You know I love you, right?"

"Yeah," I mumbled.

"Look at yourself in the mirror."

"All I need is some rest." I didn't need to look at myself in the mirror. No one including my best friend had to tell me how I looked. Over the past six months, I'd lost at least twenty pounds, didn't care what I wore, and barely brushed my short-cropped hairstyle, which had thinned from stress.

"Tatiana, I'm not playing. You've got me really worried."

What she didn't know was that for the past two weeks I'd been taking Extra Strength Tylenol every four to six hours for a low-grade fever and flulike symptoms. It was the third week of spring, so heavy pollination and fluctuating temperatures made me susceptible to sinus infections.

"I'll be ringing your doorbell in twenty-four hours. If you look like this, I swear on your grandmother's grave, I'm hauling your ass on my back to the emergency room."

"Lock the door and close it on your way out," I mumbled.

"Hell, no," she said, stopping dead in her tracks. "I'm taking your ass to the emergency room right now." She disappeared into my bedroom and returned holding a pair of jeans and a sweatshirt. She sat down beside me, lifted my head, and helped me to undress. I found just enough strength to put on the clothes she had in her hand. I stood, put my arms around her shoulder and allowed my weight to fall on her. "Where is your purse?" I pointed toward the counter. We got my purse and left.

Like a bat out of hell, Anyah drove me to the nearest emergency room. She pulled up to the double glass doors, parked, then went in for assistance. The car door opened and a young man was standing beside it with a wheelchair. Anyah helped to turn my body, then he assisted me into the chair.

With the same sense of urgency, he wheeled me inside while she went to park her car.

"May I help you?" asked a pencil-thin female with a dark brown complexion seated in the reception area.

Holding my head—which seemed to weigh a ton—in the palm of my hand, I parted my lips to respond. "I need to see a doctor."

"Name, please," she asked, making rapid keystrokes on her computer.

"Tatiana Wilkes," I responded, then answered all necessary registration questions as her fingers continued to dance on the keyboard. Before her last question, Anyah had returned and was standing behind me.

"Ma'am, if you would please roll her into the waiting area. Someone will be calling her shortly."

"Thank you," Anyah said, moving me to another side of the room.

"Tatiana Wilkes . . . Tatiana Wilkes," a burly gentleman standing between two silver doors shouted across the waiting room.

"Over here," Anyah said, rolling me in his direction.

"Mrs. Wilkes, what seems to be the problem?" he asked as we followed him down the dreary hall reeking of disinfectant, into a small room.

"She looks like shit," Anyah blurted.

"For the past two weeks I've been weak, running a fever and experiencing flulike symptoms. I think it's only a sinus infection, but my best friend freaked out," I said, too ill to laugh at my own humor.

"Well, we're going to check you out and tell you exactly what's wrong before you leave here today."

"Thank you," I said as he pulled out a thermometer and started to check my vitals. "I think you'll be more comfortable on the examination table," he said, helping me me get out of the chair, step up on a silver stool, and onto the table. "We'll need you to undress and put on a gown. A doctor will be in to see you momentarily." He handed me a dingy gray cotton gown, made a few notes on my chart, then exited the room. Anyah helped me undress and slipped the gown over my shoulders. Feeling weaker than before, I leaned back onto the table and rested my head on the flat pillow.

"Mrs. Wilkes," a young female resident said after fanning the curtain open and stepping inside my room. "My name is Dr. Broderick and I will be taking care of you today. I've reviewed your chart, but I need you to tell me what's going on."

"For the past two weeks I've had flulike symptoms," I said, never lifting my head and tired of repeating myself.

"Flulike symptoms," she repeated. "Any fever, nausea, or diarrhea?"

"Yes, I've been nauseated for the past two days. It's only a sinus infection."

"Let me be the judge of that. After reviewing your chart, and based on your symptoms, I want to do a battery of tests—in particular, an HIV test."

"HIV test?" Anyah and I asked at the same time. "I came here because I have a sinus infection, not for a death sentence," I yelled, ready to sit up, dress, and get the hell out of there.

"Don't panic. Based on your symptoms, it's only protocol. We might as well do a thorough examination before releasing you. Our goal is to make you better. A phlebotomist will be in shortly to collect your blood," she said, looked at me, then left the room.

Anyah and I both sat speechless, as I hadn't told

her the entire truth about Courtney—only because I was too embarrassed. Suddenly, the past year of my life flashed before me. How long had Courtney been cheating on me? How many women other than his so-called business associates had he slept with? For that matter, how many of their actresses had he slept with? Whether it was one or one hundred and one, each time we made love, I slept with them all. Burdened with those possibilities, my body became numb. I turned my back to Anyah as tears started to well up in the corner of my eye and flow onto the sheets.

"Mrs. Wilkes," the resident called as she entered into my room over an hour later. "I've written you a prescription for a broad-spectrum antibiotic. Please take it as prescribed, get some rest, and drink plenty of fluids."

"Am I OK?" I asked with both arms folded beneath my head.

"Like you said, it is a horrible sinus infection." She patted me on my shoulder and exited the room. I sighed from relief.

Chapter 31

Tatiana

"Courtney," I sang, letting each syllable roll off the tip of my tongue like a sweet melody when his keys hit the kitchen countertop. "Why were you hiding all the movies from me? I found this really good one on top of the cable receiver in our bedroom." The lights in the great room were dim and I increased the volume, making sure he could hear the moaning and groaning from the hallway.

"Tatiana, what in the hell are you watching?"

"I'm so jealous," I said coolly, looking toward the entryway where he stood. "You've never touched me like that. Please have a seat," I said with a menacing smile and patted my hand on the couch. "I made enough popcorn for the both of us. Extra butter, just the way you like it." I filled my hand with popcorn and shook the kernels back and forth like lucky dice.

"Octavious, that low-down son of a bitch. I can't believe he'd go this far to break up my marriage."

"Octavious?" I asked, leaned my head back, and

tossed a kernel of popcorn into my mouth. "Are you telling me Octavious broke into our home and invaded our bedroom?"

"Please, Tatiana, turn it off and let me explain," he pleaded calmly, then walked toward the television to turn it off.

"Explain how it felt having sex with two women at the same time."

"It's not what you think. I swear Octavious set me up."

"Shh, wait a minute. Is that Octavious's voice I hear in the background? All of this time and I didn't know you were a freak. Didn't you feel funny letting all of your boys watch you?"

"If you give me time, I can explain."

"I've given you all of the time you need and then some." I stood, walked to the television, and ejected the DVD.

"You know what, Tatiana, believe what the hell you want. I have connections, and you don't wanna fuck with me. Think you got something with that little video? Hire the best lawyer, and you'll never get more than what I decide to give you."

"Is that a threat?" I asked, putting a hand on my hip.

"Try me. When we married, all you had was a two-bedroom condo and a played-out Maxima. Girl, I made you. Look around," he said, flailing his arms around. "You wouldn't have none of this without me."

"Oh really?"

"If it weren't for the money I'd stolen from drug busts or the hoes I had payin' me on the sly."

"Humph."

"Humph, my ass. So think twice before you run in there and call your little girlfriend."

What he didn't know was that my humph meant

Agent Brownstone had enough to arrest him. I had agreed to wear a wire. His confession had been recorded and his arrogance finally got him what he deserved.

Certain he could no longer hurt me, I arched my shoulders back and walked to the front door. Like a girl on *The Price Is Right,* I stood to one side and opened it.

"Courtney Wilkes you're under arrest for conspiracy to sell and distribute black-market pornography," the detective started and continued repeating a long list of charges as he handcuffed Courtney and escorted him through the front door.

"What in the hell is going on?" he asked with wide eyes, pointing at himself.

Slowly I lifted my oversized sweatshirt and revealed the device attached to my bra. I'd assured the detectives that hiding it anywhere on my body was safe. Courtney hadn't touched me in months.

"Tatiana, are you OK?" Anyah asked after breaking through the detectives and running toward me.

"I've never been better. Never been better," I said, grabbing her tightly around the neck. "Courtney's love for me was all an illusion. I've been through the fire but escaped without being burned."

About the Author

Recha G. Peay, who debuted with *Mystery of a Woman*, currently resides on the outskirts of Memphis, Tennessee. A graduate of the University of Tennessee in Memphis, she works as a medical technologist. When not dividing her time between her primary career and her family, she is fulfilling her lifelong passion of writing. Her support system consists of a loving daughter and son. Please visit her Web site: www.rechagpeay.com.